Otters In Space 3:

Octopus Ascending

By Mary E. Lowd

Otters In Space 3: Octopus Ascending

Production copyright FurPlanet Productions © 2017

Copyright © Mary E. Lowd 2017
www.marylowd.com

Cover Artwork © Idess

Published by FurPlanet Productions
Dallas, Texas
www.FurPlanet.com

ISBN 978-1-61450-377-4

Printed in the United States of America
Second Edition Trade Paperback 2017

Table of Contents

For my mother, husband, daughter, and son.

Chapter 1: Jenny

The pale glow of Jupiter lit the moon's watery surface. Europa's recently melted ocean reflected the gas giant's ruddy face back at itself, broken by ripples where *Brighton's Destiny* disturbed the water on takeoff.

The dark metal V-shape of the two-man spaceship skimmed over the ocean before veering upward in a sharp climb out of Europa's gravity well. Spacesuit clad paws eased off on the throttle, and *Brighton's Destiny* leveled off into a smooth arc toward Jupiter.

Jenny's otter heart ached to twirl the little ship in spins and loop de loops, but her octopus co-pilot insisted that she needed more practice with the basics of piloting a Whirligig Class vessel first. It hardly seemed fair. The ship, shaped like a two-winged maple seed, was clearly built for spinning. The very name *Whirligig* begged Jenny to lean on the left thruster and pirouette the ship until Ordol, perched on her shoulders, flailed his tentacles in dizziness. But Jenny restrained herself.

Tentacles sheathed by the clingy, clear fabric of a cephalopoidal spacesuit waved and writhed in Jenny's peripheral vision, working the controls that she couldn't reach. The ship had been designed for a biped and an octopod, working together symbiotically. In this case, the biped was an otter. Jenny was still getting used to the design.

Ordol lowered two of his tentacles into the center of her field of vision. He twisted the tendril tips of them, forming the Standard Swimmer's Signs to say, "Let's swing around Io. You need practice maneuvering at high speeds."

Jenny's whiskers lifted in a smile, brushing against her space helmet's faceplate. It wasn't loop de loops, but flying fast would do. She signed with her paws, "No argument here!" Then she pressed down on the throttle and felt the vibration of the thrusters roar in response. The whole ship moved around her, pressing against her back as it shoved her faster and faster toward Io, a small round shadow visible against Jupiter's ruddy face.

The two celestial bodies—gas giant and volcanic moon—were paintings from the same palette in different styles. Io's jagged surface roiled with molten lakes and sulfurous plumes as it grew in the viewscreen. Behind Io, Jupiter's creamsicle clouds slid and swirled past each other, smooth and serene. A timeless god, circled by a restless servant.

As they flew toward Io, Ordol's tentacles continued to work in Jenny's peripheral vision, running scans and taking readings. The ship's computer displayed the results in a language Jenny couldn't yet read. Sharp angular letters clustered erratically into words—or so Jenny assumed—and scrolled senselessly across the computer screens arranged beneath the central viewscreen.

The sight of the alien language made it impossible for Jenny to forget: this ship was stolen. They had disabled the homing signal to hide it from the original owners, but it was stolen nonetheless.

Ordol could read the writing, at least, a little of it. He'd been a slave to the aliens who'd built the ship, before it was renamed *Brighton's Destiny*; the aliens who wrote the inscrutable language that filled its screens and who still enslaved the rest of his people.

Jenny signed, "I'm going to practice veering to the left and right."

Ordol acknowledged her plan with a sign made by a single tentacle: "Okay."

Jenny fired the thrusters on the right, pushing *Brighton's Destiny* leftward and Io off-center on the viewscreen. The ship continued on its new arc until she cancelled the leftward momentum with a blast from the left thrusters. She overshot and repeated the process several times, causing the ship to swerve on a wiggling course—Io wobbling on the viewscreen—until she managed to straighten the ship's momentum out. Once again, *Brighton's Destiny* flew true, straight toward Io.

Jenny whooped at her success. She knew Ordol couldn't hear, so she repeated the sentiment with her fisted paw raised in a victorious gesture.

Ordol signed, "Now see if you can do it faster."

They were nearly halfway to Io. Jenny practiced three times before she could no longer resist: she leaned on the left thruster until *Brighton's Destiny* corkscrewed its entire way through a barrel roll.

Ordol's tentacles fluttered rapidly, too fast for Jenny to understand his signs, but she could read the anger in his movement.

The blood rushed to Jenny's rounded ears; she felt ashamed for upsetting her co-pilot. "I'm sorry," she signed, and then she did her best to straighten out their course as fast as possible. However, Ordol's continued signing flustered Jenny, and she felt herself losing control of the ship. *Brighton's Destiny* veered wildly away from Io, and then nosed back toward it, wibble-wobbling in an erratic course.

More and more frustrated, Jenny slammed her paws against the ship's control board. She raised them and signed, "Stop! Stop it! I can't understand you when you sign that fast, and I'm *trying* to fix it." As she signed, *Brighton's Destiny* barreled away from Io onto a course more directly toward Jupiter.

Creamsicle clouds filled the viewscreen. The soft shades of orange were marred by flecks of black. A fleet of enemy vessels had assembled between Jupiter and Io, and *Brighton's Destiny* was barreling right toward them.

Jenny realized that her octopus co-pilot wasn't angry with her; he was scared out of his mind by the sight of the ships of his former slavers. "I'm getting us out of here," Jenny signed. Then she leaned hard on the throttle, pushing *Brighton's Destiny* into the sharpest corner it could make. Jenny didn't worry about straightening their course out perfectly this time; she just aimed their little ship away from Io.

When Europa was securely in the center of the viewscreen and the fleet of enemy vessels was safely behind them, Jenny signed, "I don't think they saw us, and they can't possibly catch up to us before we get back to the base." The energy shield around Europa would protect them. "You're safe."

Ordol's tentacles calmed down, wrapped around Jenny's shoulders, and squeezed the otter in a hug.

But Jenny was still worried. There were plenty of other targets in the solar system less protected than the Europa base. After months of quiet, it was time to warn everyone: the raptors were on the move.

Chapter 2: Kipper

Paw prints marked the golden, glittering sand. Tiny, perfect kitten prints danced flirtatiously up and down the line of wet beach, slowly dissolving under the soggy, sloppy wavelets lapping at the land.

Larger canine paw prints marched straight into the oncoming waves, and the dog who made them—a wiry-furred, beard-faced terrier wearing blue and yellow swim trunks—splashed wildly in the surf. Sea foam clung to the fur on his ankles and his furiously wagging brush of a tail.

Up on the dry sand, safely stretched out on a beach towel with her littermates, Kipper the gray tabby, watched her brother-in-law Lucky play with his adopted children. Even further up the beach, a pair of secret service greyhounds in suits watched the family, keeping the stretch of beach clear to protect President Alistair Brighton and his loved ones.

"C'mon, kits!" Lucky barked. "The water won't hurt you!" He shook off his dripping head and droplets of water flew from his flopped ears and wiry beard. Three wide-eyed tabby kittens scrambled away from the flying drops, shrieking and mewing in terror and delight. Not one drop of water touched them.

Despite Lucky's urging, his adopted kittens were completely unwilling to wade in the toe-deep wavelets. Instead, they teased the waves, pouncing and prancing away before the water could touch them.

Kipper loved watching the kittens play with their adopted canine father. She'd grown up in a cattery, lucky to know her littermates at all. No one had taken them to play at the beach, certainly not a gregarious, affectionate father like Lucky. Times had changed. Cats and dogs married now; dogs adopted kittens; and her own brother had recently been elected President of the Uplifted States of Mericka. It was a far reach from the days when cats couldn't even vote.

As a kitten, Kipper had wanted nothing to do with life on Earth. She'd dreamed of dancing with the otters among the stars, and she'd realized that dream, becoming the only cat among a crew of space pirate otters. She'd even become a captain herself of a two-man ship, *Brighton's Destiny*, but she'd had to leave her ship behind and come home.

The raptors of Jupiter had forced the Persian cat colony on Europa to flee, all the cats scurrying home to Earth or Mars, but Kipper and her compatriots had foiled the raptor plans to retake Europa by discovering an ancient force field that protected the moon while melting its oceans.

Nonetheless, Kipper had known it was only a matter of time until the raptors attacked again, further afield from Jupiter. If Jenny's latest message was to be believed, then that time might be soon. Earth needed to defend herself.

"We need to ask the octopi for help." Petra, an orange tabby, always sounded like she was only a few steps away from angry, but her voice seemed particularly strident considering she was wearing sunglasses, lazing on a sunny beach, yellow sunlight glowing against her orange fur.

"Do we have to talk about this?" asked Alistair, another orange tabby, his ears flattening.

Petra's voice took a step closer to anger. "Is that how it's going to be? You're president now, so you always put everyone off? Never give anyone a straight answer?"

Kipper had spent her whole childhood listening to Petra and Alistair fight—or fighting with them. Somehow, she'd imagined that the fighting was caused by the cattery, or the bad jobs and tight money after they grew old enough that the cattery kicked them out. Once they were secure and safe in their lives, she'd always thought they'd stop fighting.

Maybe the fighting was inside them.

Or maybe it was the stress from the threat of the raptors.

"If you won't go to the octopus oligarchy yourself," Petra said, "you could send me as a delegate."

"Who would watch the kittens?" Kipper asked. It was a barbed question. Lucky and their friend Trudith, a black lab mutt who was ostensibly Alistair's body guard but had become more of a nanny, spent much more time watching the kittens than Petra did.

Petra glared at her sister. "Fine," she snapped. "Send Kipper."

Panic made Kipper's heart race. For all the time she spent with otters, she still hated water. She couldn't think of anything scarier than travelling deep under the ocean with thousands of meters of water above her head, crushing down on her. Even raptors. "Alistair can't send me," Kipper quipped. "I don't work for him."

"I'm not sending anyone," Alistair said. His voice got low and serious. "I'm not asking for help."

His sisters stared at him. Without help, the Uplifted States had literally no defenses against an attack from space.

Eventually, Kipper asked, "Do the Uplifted States have a space program I don't know about? A *secret* space program?" One of her otter friends was obsessed with spies and secrecy. Some of it had rubbed off on her.

Petra's ears skewed, and she looked pensive. "That would explain some of the inconsistencies I've been seeing in the budget..."

Kipper might not work for Alistair, but Petra was his right-hand cat. She'd been combing through all the government records and documents she could get her paws on since he'd taken office.

"No," Alistair said, looking frustrated. "There's no secret space program. We barely even have a military. We have a small number of nuclear missiles, but most were dismantled decades ago. It's not nearly enough to stop the raptors, but there are plenty of otters who have as much reason to defend the Earth as we have."

"Not *quite* as much," Petra muttered. Most otters lived in space these days.

"Regardless," Alistair brushed her off. "As I understand it, the octopi already have far more reason to fight the raptors—assuming they even have the necessary technology—than we do."

Petra stared at her brother levelly and saw right through him. "You don't want to look weak in front of the government dogs that you have to work with and all the cats who elected you."

"That's right," he said, unashamed. "I need to look strong."

Petra's voice twisted with mockery: "You plan to look strong by cowering and hoping someone else steps in to defend our planet from the raptors? You were elected as a *war* president."

Kipper stopped listening to her littermates argue and watched Lucky play with the kittens. He lifted one of the orange kittens onto his shoulders for a piggy-back ride. Another kitten grabbed his knee, trying to anchor him down, keep him from splashing back into the waves. The third kitten, a gray tabby like Kipper, settled farther up the beach with a yellow plastic shovel and pail. Sandcastles blossomed around her, beautiful and temporary.

The waves would knock down the sandcastles. And the raptors would come in their battleships—no matter what spiteful words Petra and Alistair said to each other. The question was: would Earth be ready? Or, better yet, was there any way to stop the raptors before they got here?

Kipper didn't think of herself as a brave cat, but she had done brave things as a member of the crew of the *Jolly Barracuda*. She wanted to be that cat.

Kipper closed her eyes and stood up. She took a deep breath of salty air. Then without stopping to think, she ran toward the waves, only opening her eyes when the lukewarm water splashed under her paws. Her tail lashed wildly, but she didn't stop. The waves crashed against her legs, and the current pulled at her. When it came all the way to her waist, Kipper closed her eyes and dove into it.

The ocean felt like the oxo-agua on the *Jolly Barracuda*. It echoed in her ears and lifted her fur. With her eyes closed and her paws off the ground, she could imagine she was in space, on her spaceship full of otters, orbiting Jupiter again.

She wasn't Alistair and Petra's quieter littermate; she was *Ship's Spy* and *Diplomatic Ambassador to Independent Cat Nations* and any other silly title that Captain Cod came up with for her. She was brave and heroic and did things that no other cat had ever done.

Or any otter either.

Only two people in the entire solar system had infiltrated one of the raptors' sail ships inside the upper atmosphere of Jupiter. And only one of them had seen the aquariums where the raptors kept octopi enslaved.

Kipper remembered the yellow eyes staring at her and pale tentacles. She remembered those tentacles writhing and struggling as raptors grabbed them, pulled them from the water, and forced them into electronic harnesses that overrode the octopi's own brains. Raptors hadn't merely enslaved octopi—they violated them, robbing the octopi of their own wills and bodies on a daily basis.

The octopi on Earth didn't know how much they had to fight for. They hadn't seen it. Space and Earth, sunny beaches and miles of deep dark water lay between the Earth octopi and the atrocities being visited on their Jovian siblings.

Floating in the shallowest edge of Earth's deep dark oceans, Kipper knew what she had to do. She had to go to those octopi and make them understand.

Kipper came out of the waves, dripping and shivering, to stand at the edge of Alistair and Petra's beach blanket. She interrupted their argument to say: "I'll go. I'll be an emissary to the octopi." She didn't want to, but it was what needed to be done.

Alistair's green eyes stared daggers at his dripping sister. He kept a laissez faire attitude through most of his fights with Petra, but now his orange stripes fluffed. "Like hell you will! I said I wouldn't ask for help. How do you think it would look if I sent my littermate to ask for me?"

17

"You can't send me," Kipper said. "And you can't stop me either."

Alistair didn't lose control often, and Kipper could tell it was rattling him even more that her fur hadn't fluffed out at all. That was one of the few advantages of wet fur.

"I'm the president," Alistair said.

"I'm not a member of the government, so I'm not in your chain-of-command. Captain Cod is my commanding officer. Not you."

"I'll tell him not to let you go. I don't think he'll defy the wishes of the president of the Uplifted States of Mericka."

Kipper didn't argue. She wasn't interested in building sandcastles. It was time to start making waves. Besides, she knew how to convince Captain Cod. She'd tell him that Alistair had to object officially, but *secretly* he wanted Captain Cod to send an envoy to the octopi to ask for help. That would tickle the otter captain's fancy, and he wouldn't think to question it. Captain Cod loved secrets.

Three kittens came running, skittering excitedly across the sand. "Auntie Kipper! You're all wet! What was the water like? Why did you dive in?" Childhood's eagerness and incessant questions obliterated all adult conversation until Lucky suggested it was time to pack up and find a suitable chowder house for lunch. Somewhere that Alistair's greyhound guards considered sufficiently safe for the president and his family.

While the others brushed sand out of their fur, shook out and folded up the beach towel, and readied themselves to go, Kipper borrowed Petra's cell phone. She didn't keep one of her own— it wouldn't work on the otter space stations and space ships. However, she was able to patch a voice call through from the cell phone, through *Deep Sky Anchor's* communications, to the *Jolly Barracuda*.

Boris, the sea otter pilot, answered. "What's up, Kipper?" He knew she'd be the only one calling from Earth right now.

"Can I talk to the captain?" Kipper walked a few paces down the beach to hear Boris better over the noise of the kittens.

"The captain and Trugger are playing poker on a ship docked a few berths down right now. Do you want me to get them? Or patch your call through to the other ship?"

"That's okay," Kipper said. She wished she could talk to Emily, the *Jolly Barracuda's* octopus chef, but Petra's phone wasn't equipped for vid-calls. "Can you have the captain call me when he gets back? I have a new mission for us that I think he'll be interested in." Kipper gave Boris the number for Petra's phone.

Then there was nothing to do but go eat clam chowder with her family, even though she was already steeling herself for the travails to come.

Chapter 3: Jenny

Safe inside the ancient octopus base on Europa, Jenny itched to be back in *Brighton's Destiny*, flying free, but the little Whirligig ship was parked, inert on the roof of the floating base. Jenny was stuck inside one the plethora of spherical rooms off of the main central chamber of the base. It was a reasonably sized room until someone had decided to shove a table into it. The curved walls and ceiling hadn't been designed to accommodate a rectangular table with four otters, two dogs, and a cat seated around it.

The spherical room had been designed for octopi, and the only octopus there was Ordol, clinging to the ceiling with his sucker disks, wearing a breathing apparatus that looked like inverse-SCUBA gear. He looked as uncomfortable as Jenny felt, and he was the only one who *should* have been comfortable in a room like that.

Instead, Ordol watched silently, reading the paws of the one otter from the Imperial Star-Ocean Navy who was taking the time to translate the arguments between his fellow officer-otters, the dachshund and Australian Cattle Dog from Howard Industries, and the yellow-furred former-empress of New Persia into sign language. The cats and dogs didn't know Standard Swimmer's Sign. Of course.

That didn't stop them from arguing over who should own a base designed by octopi, for octopi, and meant to float just under the surface of an ocean planet.

Jenny had always imagined that "fighting like cats and dogs" meant something exciting. She'd seen Earth sitcoms where cats sneered sarcastic barbs at dogs, and the dogs barked their heads off back at them—insults and obscenities flying both ways.

In reality, though, it was all skewed ears, raised hackles, carefully chosen words, and faked politeness. Jenny couldn't imagine anything more tedious, except, of course, for the way that the navy otters humored them, acting as though cats, dogs, otters, and octopi all had an equal claim on the Europa base.

"My colony has been reduced to a pile of floating wreckage," the former-empress said. Her pointed ears flattened against her head, nearly burying themselves in her fluffy yellow fur. "All of my people, except myself and my cabinet, were forced to evacuate back to Earth or the feline colony on Mars. I think we deserve some form of recompense."

"Obviously," the cattle dog said with a wide, infectious grin, "we all have a great deal of sympathy for the troubles that the cats of New Persia have undergone."

The dachshund chimed in with her down-home, folksy accent: "It's sure no fun having to pick up and move your whole life when you thought you were settled."

Jenny rolled her eyes at the way the Howard Industry dogs downplayed the destruction of an entire colony. She could see that the Persian cat was seething under her courteous facade.

"But the truth of the situation," the cattle dog intoned, the grin on his muzzle turning downward into a more serious expression. "The *real* truth is that you never had the proper government permits to settle a colony on Europa in the first place."

The senior navy otter, Admiral Mackerel, cut in to say, "The New Persians didn't need any permits. The land was unclaimed."

"With all due respect, Admiral," the dachshund said, "all of the cats of New Persia are citizens of Earth countries. Many of them—in fact, the majority—are citizens of the Uplifted States of Mericka, and citizens of the Uplifted States *do* need proper government-issued permits to settle on other worlds."

"That's why we're here," the cattle dog said. "Howard Industries is one of the Uplifted States' most trusted independent contractors. We have people on Earth right now working on getting those permits for you, *Empress*." The cattle dog kept a straight face, but his tail wagged under the table. "All you have to do to make your colony retroactively legal is sign on as an incorporated subsidy of Howard Industries."

"It's really their only option," the dachshund said to Admiral Mackerel, looking straight past the empress. "You may as well consider it already done."

"Which is why any reparations, in the form of a controlling interest in this base," the cattle dog said, "should be handed directly to Howard Industries."

"You mean to you?" said the otter who'd been translating the conversation into sign language.

The cattle dog and dachshund glanced at each other, looking mildly uncomfortable.

"To *Howard Industries*," the dachshund said.

"Of which I'm the senior local representative," added the cattle dog. "So, in a way, yes."

Jenny couldn't take it anymore. These negotiations had been going on for weeks, ever since the dogs from Howard Industries had arrived in their hired spaceship. Jenny didn't know why they'd bothered coming—this base clearly didn't belong to them—and she wished the former-empress and her cabinet had evacuated Europa with the other New Persians. *Why was Admiral Mackerel putting up with this?* It was a waste of time.

Jenny caught Ordol's eye and signed, subtly so the navy otters missed it, "Let's get out of here."

Ordol signed with the tip of a tentacle, "Please."

Jenny interrupted a painfully civil argument between Admiral Mackerel and the cattle dog about whether cats on Europa were still subject to laws on Earth to say and sign, "Ordol looks exhausted. I think he's getting dehydrated. We're going to go for a swim."

Ordol reached two of his tentacles toward Jenny, and she held out an arm for him to grab as he drifted lightly down from the ceiling in Europa's low gravity.

Ordol led the way out of the improvised meeting room into one of the winding, tubular corridors that characterized the Europa base. He pulled himself through the narrow corridor, grabbing the walls with his tentacles stretched out in every direction. The walls glowed wherever his sucker discs touched them. Tiny sparkles of light danced in the strange material of the walls.

The corridor was too narrow for an otter to stand upright, so Jenny crawled awkwardly after him, lighting up a denser trail of tiny sparkles in the material of the floor. She couldn't help thinking it would be much easier, much faster to swim. All the narrow corridors in the Europa base would be easier to navigate while swimming.

Come to think of it, Jenny realized that a lot of problems with the Europa base could be solved by flooding it. Cats and dogs were a lot less likely to fight over a base filled with water. The corridors would be easier to swim through. And besides, the base had clearly been designed to hold water; it would be much better for the long term structural integrity of the base.

In an underwater world, he who can breathe water is king. That meant Ordol. The base rightfully, in her mind, should belong to him anyway. At least, until some more octopi showed up. But the base was clearly designed for octopi. Let the octopus run it!

By the time that Ordol and Jenny reached the end of the corridor, her mind was made up.

The corridor opened out onto a yawning central chamber, several stories high and vaguely cylindrical. Its walls were riddled with the entrances to other narrow corridors, and the open space in the middle was crisscrossed by poles that stretched the entire height and width of the giant chamber.

Ordol swung gracefully from one pole to another, descending toward the workstations that honeycombed the floor. Jenny reached for the closest pole and slid down it like a firefighter. Going down was easy. Getting back up would be hard—but not after the base was flooded.

Jenny signed to Ordol, "Help me round up the other Barracu-ders. Try not to tip off the navy otters that we're up to something. Okay?"

"The navy ones wear the uniforms?" Ordol asked. He still had trouble telling otters apart from cats and dogs—let alone one otter from another. They were all fuzzy mammals, and he couldn't read the differences in their shapes any better than most otters could read the expression in an octopus's skin. Until a few months ago, Ordol had only ever seen other octopi and the raptors who had them enslaved.

"Right, the navy ones wear all the brass buttons and stiff collars and cuff-links," Jenny signed. "All that nonsense." The *Jolly Barracuda* idea of a uniform was much less formal—dark slacks, light vest, and a single golden pin shaped like an old Earth sailing ship.

Jenny and Ordol rounded up the half dozen members of the *Jolly Barracuda* crew who'd stayed behind on the Europa base when Captain Cod had flown back to Earth, ship filled to the gills with hissing and yowling Persian refugees.

Jenny explained her plan to the other otters, and they listened in silence. When she was done, Jenny said, "I know that Captain Cod left me in charge, but I'm not only asking you to follow my orders here; I'm asking you to go against the wishes of the ISON admiral."

Six otter faces stared at her, their whiskers downturned in serious expressions.

"Has the admiral expressly ordered you not to do this?" Destry asked.

"No," Jenny admitted. "But he won't like it."

"Tough jellyfish," Amoreena said. "If he hasn't forbidden it, then it's not against the rule of the Imperial Star-Ocean Navy. I'm in."

"He really should know better than to leave a big ol' gray-area loophole wide open around chaos-sowing pirates like us," Felix said.

"We're not pirates," Jenny corrected. "The situation with the Asteroid Artists' Alliance is a misunderstanding."

Amoreena rolled her eyes. Felix and Destry both chuckled. The other three chimed in to agree to Jenny's plan, pirates or not.

Like secret agents, they dispersed through the corridors of the Europa base. They went in pairs to the hatches around the outer edge of the base. Then like bank robbers, they turned the heavy metal wheels, unlocking the vault-like doors that held out the newly melted oceans of Europa. Water spat and gurgled around the edges as the doors started to open. Then it rushed in through the widening gap. They only opened the door a few inches, but that would be enough to flood the base soon enough. Jenny jammed the door open, smashing the wheel that controlled it with the broken length of one of the poles from the central chamber.

Jenny and Felix waltzed together in the sloshing, ankle-deep Europa ocean. It would be much deeper soon.

"Come on," Jenny said to her partner-in-crime, "let's get back to the others and start warning the cats and dogs to get out of here."

"We'll need to set up a camp on the surface," Felix said. "And rig up some breathing gear so that we can come back in here when it's done flooding."

"That's the idea!" Jenny grinned. Now things were happening! This should shake up those stuffy navy otters, entitled dogs, and the enigmatic empress.

Chapter 4: Petra

Petra hated waiting. The waiter was taking forever, and her three kittens were crawling all over her and Lucky, grabbing at the silverware and condiments on the table. The paper packets of sugar had already been counted, arranged in patterns, and finally scattered across the table top. Why did kittens have to make restaurants so hard? Why couldn't they sit still?

To make it worse, Petra could tell that Alistair and Kipper were still talking politics, but she couldn't follow their conversation at all. Every third word was covered by a kitten's mew. Her train of thought was constantly interrupted by inane, unanswerable questions: "Which sand castle am I thinking of?"; "Do you remember any fish?"; or "Can you make me a dog like Daddy?"

All Petra could say to her hassling but precious kittens, staring at her with wide, innocent, heart-tugging eyes, was, "What?" Over and over again, she answered their confusing, childish questions with "What?" while trying to hear past them to what her own littermates were discussing.

Then her phone rang.

Petra pulled the cell phone out of her pocket and held it out of reach of Robin's grasping claws. The number on the screen was international. No—it was from the space station. "Kipper!" Petra shouted past the baby orange tabby on her lap. "I think this call is for you."

Robin mewed a complaint when his aunt Kipper took the phone. Kipper put the phone up to her pointed ear and kept walking, away from the busy table, straight out of the restaurant. Petra hated her for being able to do that, for being freer than her.

"The space station?" Alistair asked, speaking up so that Petra could hear. "I thought we agreed that she was staying here."

"*You* agreed," Petra said, sarcasm dripping. "*She* borrowed my phone and called her otter friends."

Alistair looked like he was going to disagree or argue with her, but the waiter—a Norwegian Forest cat—finally showed up to take their order. The big cat's fluffy fur overflowed his apron. His ears flattened as Petra and Lucky's three kittens shouted their orders at him in piercing tones, but he took diligent notes. Petra could find no fault with him.

After the kittens ordered their kid's meals, Lucky ordered tuna toast, shrimp bowls, and a family style tureen of chowder for the table.

"Would the kittens like balloons?" the waiter asked, nearly cringing. Clearly, it was a question he was required to ask—not one that he wanted to ask.

Petra cringed and closed her eyes in frustration as Robin, Allison, and Pete exclaimed their delighted joy at the mere idea of balloons. When the bright red balloons actually arrived, the kittens were pushed over into frenzies of ecstasy. The joy soon died. Calamitously. The loud bang of a popping balloon was followed by the heartbroken, disappointed wails of a kitten. Then again. And again. Each kitten had to be given at least two balloons before learning not to bat at the delightful object with unsheathed claws.

By the time the balloon ordeal was over—each kitten quietly coloring the pictures on their kid's menus with balloons tied to their wrists, floating unmolested in the air above them—any semblance of adult conversation had been obliterated.

The waiter brought over the platter of tuna toast to get them started. Kipper came back with Petra's cell phone. She handed the phone back, and Petra slipped it quickly into her pocket before Robin noticed it. Fortunately, he was busy scribbling with a blue crayon all over the outlined picture of a dancing seagull.

Kipper looked smug.

Petra hated it when someone other than her was smug.

Petra started to snap something sarcastic at Kipper, but Lucky put a paw on her shoulder. He dug his rough paw pads and dull claws into her fur just enough to steady her. She hated it when he did that. But she also loved it.

"I have to leave right after lunch," Kipper said. "Captain Cod is booking a series of flights for me down to Ecuador. The first one leaves in three hours." She picked up a piece of tuna toast.

Petra wanted to dash the toast out of her sister's gray-striped paw.

But Lucky's paw was still on her shoulder, steadying her.

She shouldn't pick fights with Kipper, especially when Kipper was doing what Petra wanted her to do. It just made her crazy that Kipper got to do it instead of her.

Not so long ago, Petra was the cat with dreams, and her littermates were following on her coat tails. Now her brother was president, and her sister was a space pirate.

Petra had three kittens.

What did that count for?

Anyone could adopt a few kittens. Hell, most people gave their own kittens away to catteries. That's why there were so bloody many of them to adopt.

Petra flattened her ears and tried to stop this line of thinking in its tracks. It went nowhere good. She had wanted to adopt Robin, Allison, and Pete. Most of the time, she didn't regret it. She loved them.

The Norwegian Forest cat waiter brought over the family style tureen of chowder and bowls of shrimp. Lucky served up chowder for everyone, valiantly ignoring the sulky tone between Petra and her littermates. Or, possibly, he was actually unaware that all three of the adult cats were mad at each other.

"Aunt Kipper, why do you have to leave?" Allison asked. The little gray tabby climbed from her own chair and onto the larger gray tabby's lap.

"I have a very important, very secret mission," Kipper said, wrapping her arms around the gray kitten and hugging her.

"Will you be gone long?" Robin asked from his perch on Petra's lap. His wiggling made it impossible for Petra to eat her clam chowder without spilling it on her fur.

"I don't know," Kipper said, carefully. The adults hadn't discussed the raptor situation around the kittens. Petra didn't want to scare them. Neither did Kipper. "It depends on how the mission goes, I guess." Kipper hugged Allison tighter.

Then Kipper reached over and ruffled Pete's ears. He ducked his head, focused on his coloring, and whined, "Aunt Kipper!"

"I'll miss you," Kipper said, looking at Robin on Petra's lap. Or maybe she was looking at Petra. Either way, it mollified Petra a little.

She couldn't be Kipper and save the world. But she could protect and cherish the kittens who would inherit the world Kipper was saving. "We'll miss you, too," Petra said, speaking for her kittens. But also herself.

Chapter 5: Kipper

Kipper packed a few clothes and pictures of her littermates, nephews, and niece inside plastic sleeves to protect them. It wasn't much, but it was more than she'd taken with her the last time she went away. She was in more of a hurry this time, but it was less hectic. More purposeful. More planned.

Trudith drove her to the airport. It had been hard saying goodbye to her family. It was awful saying goodbye to Trudith, her best friend on Earth. There's nothing like a sad black lab mutt with melting brown eyes to crumble your heart to pieces. Even three cute kittens couldn't compare.

"Let me come with you," Trudith said, holding Kipper's purple duffel bag of stuff. She'd insisted on walking Kipper to the gate and waiting with her for the plane. "I could go buy myself a ticket."

Even the kittens hadn't suggested that.

"I need you here," Kipper said. "I need you to take care of Petra and the kittens. I'll be fine."

"You'd be better with a bodyguard," Trudith said.

"I'm meeting Captain Cod, Trugger, and Emily in Ecuador. You met Trugger. He won't let anything happen to me."

Trudith looked skeptical.

Trugger may have been big compared to Kipper, but he was substantially smaller than Trudith. Kipper didn't dare suggest that he was as loyal as Trudith. That would only insult her.

"Look, I'm only going down to the Galapagos to talk to the octopi. I'm not going to Jupiter to fight raptors or anything."

Trudith gave Kipper a pained look. She may not have been the smartest dog, but she was was bright enough to see through that: just because Kipper was going to the Galapagos first didn't mean she wouldn't take off and fight raptors before she came back. Before she saw Trudith again. Or her littermates. Or the kittens.

Kipper's head felt light. Trudith must have seen her distress, because she suddenly found herself in the middle of a giant bear hug. Dog hug. Warm black furred arms held her.

"I'll be fine," Kipper said, voice shaking.

Trudith pulled away, looked at Kipper, and finally nodded, flopping her ears. "You'll be fine," she said. It was what Kipper needed her to say. So she said it.

The plane boarded on time, and Kipper left behind a strangely still Trudith—no wagging tail, just set jowls. The image of her black lab mutt friend standing there, watching her leave, stayed with Kipper as she boarded the plane, stowed her duffel bag below her seat, and finally settled into the stiff, uncomfortable airplane seat.

She couldn't shake the sensation of loss, a growing void that was usually filled by everything in her life on Earth. But she was leaving it all behind. That space inside her felt empty.

Kipper pulled her hind feet up onto the airplane seat and curled her tail around her haunches. The seat was uncomfortable, but she was glad that it wasn't too small. A particularly large St. Bernard woman on the other side of the aisle had to struggle to fit into her seat at all. Her head kept hitting the ceiling and bumping the little buttons to turn on the light or air conditioning, and no matter how she folded her long, thick legs, they looked horribly cramped.

That was one advantage of being a cat. Airplane seats were never too small.

Kipper had a window seat, and she watched the city below shrink down to a toy model as the plane rose into the sky, flying south. She kept watching the Earth slide by outside her window, rich green mottled with the geometrical tan shapes of farms and cities, until they reached the ocean. Kipper couldn't handle looking at that much water, so she drew the shade on her window and fell asleep.

Kipper slept through dinner. She didn't miss much. Crunchy breaded chicken on an airplane couldn't compare to fresh seafood in a chowder house at the beach. It was night when she awoke. She lifted the shade on her window and saw only black outside. The ocean was down there, but she didn't have to see it anymore.

As the plane approached South America, Kipper started to feel excited about her journey. It was a small feeling at first—mild anticipation at the idea of seeing her otter friends again. Kipper found herself wondering what kind of vessel Captain Cod had chartered to take them down to octopus city in the Galapagos. Would it be an octopus vessel filled with water? Would she have to wear SCUBA gear for days without break? Would she be able to sleep like that if she had to?

What she was feeling was fear. But fear is a lot like excitement. They feel the same sometimes. Two sides of the same anxiety.

The flat black darkness outside Kipper's window split in half as the growing glow of the approaching sun defined an edge. Gray ocean, so large that Kipper thought she could see it curve, hid the sun. But the sky hollowed out in the sun's light, pale and white fading all the way to blue as deep as black. The sky was open. The ocean was shut. But Kipper was going to break into it.

She felt like a different cat than the one who had boarded the plane. She still missed her family, but it was a feeling contained, as if it had been put into a locket, close to her heart but locked away. It didn't consume her. There was room inside her for other things.

Captain Cod met Kipper at the airport. He was a big otter with a broad chest and whiskery face. He wore his linen vest open, showing his coarse brown fur, and turquoise bangles on his short arms.

He bounced on his webbed toes, and his face lit up in a wide smile when he saw Kipper. "Leapin' lamprey, Kipper! I've never been happier to lose a bet." He took her purple duffel bag and led her out of the airport to a taxi. They got in, and Captain Cod instructed the squirrel driver to take them to the docks.

Once the car started moving, Kipper said, "What bet?"

Captain Cod chewed on his whiskers like he didn't want to answer Kipper. "Oh, I just bet that you'd stay in the Uplifted States with your family. It didn't seem like you'd be coming back to us. I owe Trugger a pound of candied clams."

In honesty, Kipper hadn't been sure whether she would come back to the *Jolly Barracuda* either. She'd meant to—but then she'd gotten caught up in Alistair's new position and Petra's kittens. It was easier on Earth where the air was *air* instead of highly oxygenated liquid.

In fact, she still wasn't sure that she was going back to the *Jolly Barracuda*. She had an important mission—only she could tell the octopi how much they had to fight for. But that didn't mean she had to go back to the *Jolly Barracuda* and space adventures when her oceanic mission was over.

Yet, she felt hurt that Captain Cod had doubted her. It didn't matter that he was right to. It still hurt.

"I guess Trugger knows you better than I do," Captain Cod said.

Kipper muttered something non-committal.

"You're probably really tired?" Captain Cod said, suddenly looking her over much too carefully. "You can sleep on the submarine."

"Will it have air?" Kipper asked.

Captain Cod laughed and shook his head. Kipper couldn't tell if he was shaking his head in amusement or saying that the submarine wouldn't have air. She couldn't bring herself to press the point.

Kipper watched the shining city of Guayaquil slide by outside the taxi's window. It was a beautiful city, and she never had time to really explore it. She was always on her way elsewhere, in a hurry, when she came through. "Are we taking off right away?" she asked.

"Do pigeons wish they were penguins?" Captain Cod looked as if he thought his riddle answered everything.

Kipper flattened her ears. "What?" She was out of practice with Captain Cod's metaphors.

33

"Of course they do! Wouldn't you rather swim than fly?"

"No...?"

Captain Cod shook his head again. This time in bemusement. "Silly cat. Swimming's always best."

Kipper sighed. She could see the docks already out the car window. "Look, can we... I mean, I've never seen anything of Guayaquil. Could we go somewhere? Get breakfast at a restaurant or see some sort of tourist sight before we go under the ocean?"

The cab pulled over, and the squirrel driver looked into the backseat. She looked Kipper up and down with her dark, sparkling eyes. Her red-furred face was tiny and pointed. She was smaller than any cat or dog Kipper had ever known.

"You're that hero cat, aren't you? The savior of Europa?" the squirrel said in a surprisingly deep, mellifluous voice. From such a tiny person, Kipper expected a high, squeaky voice, but Captain Cod's voice was actually much squeakier.

Kipper nodded.

"We don't see a lot of cats around here. I bet you don't see a lot of squirrels where you come from?"

Kipper had never spoken to a squirrel in person, but she said, "I went to a squirrel restaurant on *Deep Sky Anchor* once. I ate nut-mash."

Captain Cod groaned. "Trugger didn't drag you to that dive, did he?"

The red squirrel rolled her eyes—Kipper wasn't sure if it was at her or the captain. "Let me drive you through Cedar Heights."

"Tree Town?" Captain Cod complained.

The squirrel grimaced at him and said, "*Cedar Heights*. It'll take half an hour." She turned her gaze back to Kipper. "If you're interested in eating real sciuridae cuisine—not the stuff made to appeal to the otters on the space station—I can point you toward a good restaurant there."

Kipper hadn't been crazy about the nut-mash, and she suspected that otter food, in general, appealed to her more than squirrel food would. While squirrels weren't actually herbivores, they kept mostly to plant matter and insects.

Still, Kipper liked the idea of seeing more of Guayaquil. She turned to Captain Cod and said, "Half an hour. The submarine can wait half an hour. Can't it?"

Captain Cod pointed out the cab's window at the docks. "See the one with the orange stripe?"

There were boats lined up with sails and rigging, but Captain Cod's claw pointed at the smooth metal hull of a submarine bobbing at the surface of the water at the far end of the dock. A simple steel gray fin with a single orange stripe poked out of the smooth metal. It was the only submarine at the dock, orange stripe or not.

"Sure," Kipper said.

"I'll start getting the submarine prepped. You go have fun." He handed a wad of cash to the squirrel driver. "Have her back at the docks in an hour."

The squirrel picked through the cash, flattening the bills out. She found several clam chews in plastic wrappers mixed in with the cash and handed those back to Captain Cod.

"You're not coming?" Kipper asked.

"I've seen Tree Town," he said. "But our driver here—"

He looked at the squirrel and waited until she offered her name: "Tamantha."

"Tamantha will take good care of you. Won't she?"

The squirrel finished flattening out the cash with her tiny paws and looked satisfied. She stuffed the money in her pocket. "Sure will," she said. After Captain Cod got out, she said to Kipper, "Why don't you come sit up front with me?"

As Kipper strapped herself into the front seat, she noticed that Tamantha had her seat adjusted all the way forward. Even so, it still looked like she had to stretch to reach the gas and brake pedals. Kipper wasn't used to feeling big, but next to Tamantha, she did.

"I've seen you on the news," Tamantha said, driving the taxi away from the dock again. "You're the cat who saved Europa."

Kipper's ears flattened in embarrassed modesty, and she looked out the window, away from Tamantha. "I guess so."

"And now you're planning to board a submarine? You're quite the adventurer."

Kipper didn't bite. She didn't feel like talking about herself. Instead she asked, "What can you do in Cedar Heights in less than an hour?"

Tamantha laughed sharply. "What can you do in any city in less than an hour? Not a lot. I'll give you a driving tour and take you to one or two of the best shops. Sound good?"

The buildings outside grew taller and narrower as Tamantha drove farther inland.

"It's better than getting straight into a submarine," Kipper said. "How will I know when we get to Cedar Heights?"

"You mean, will there be gleaming silver arches like intertwining tree limbs that rise over the street? Something like that?"

Kipper felt silly. "I'm sorry. I didn't mean to..." She didn't even know what she'd accidentally implied, but Tamantha's tone had been sarcastic. Then she saw the exact arches that Tamantha had described. The sun really did gleam in their twisting metal branches. "That's beautiful." She craned her neck to keep looking at the silver arches as they drove under them.

"The otters may call it Tree Town," Tamantha said. "But Cedar Heights isn't a ghetto. It's a really nice part of Guayaquil."

Beyond the silver arches, the buildings were narrow enough that four of them fit in the space a single building usually filled. They stretched upward so high that Kipper couldn't see their tops from inside the car. All the buildings had stairs on the outside, lacing back and forth like fire escapes. Except these stairs were unusually steep, almost ladders, and they were clearly meant for every day use. Squirrels raced up and down them as quickly as the otters in space swam through the rivers on *Deep Sky Anchor*.

"I think I like Tree Town," Kipper said. She hated swimming, but she loved climbing.

Tamantha didn't say anything, but she made a dismissive chirruping sound.

"I mean, Cedar Heights," Kipper corrected herself. "Sorry."

Was Cedar Heights the place Kipper should have been looking for when she went on her search for Cat Havana? Why in the hell was she about to let a bunch of otters drag her down to the octopus oligarchy when there was a whole squirrel culture here for her to explore?

Never mind the raptors flying in from Jupiter. Kipper sighed.

Tamantha told Kipper about the buildings that they passed—apartment complexes, business centers, banks, and restaurants. All the normal sorts of buildings that any city has. Then Tamantha pulled the taxi over to the curb, parked, and said, "We're getting out here."

Chapter 6: Kipper

Kipper followed Tamantha down a path between two of the towering buildings. Red and gray-furred squirrels passed by, their movements sudden and jerky. The way they moved—stopping and starting—made Kipper feel twitchy. Yet, their tails flowed smooth as rivers.

Behind the row of buildings that faced the street, there was a pedestrian square, surrounded by cafe awnings and outdoor seating. Squirrels in wicker chairs chattered and dined on crunchy-looking pastries. Ladders and open-air skywalks laced through the space above them.

In the center of the square stood a gray rock statue. It took Kipper a moment to recognize the central figure—it was taller than a Great Dane and had a knobbly face, no muzzle, and head-fur piled high in complicated braids. *A human woman*, Kipper realized, *wrought from stone*. The woman was wearing simple clothes, and her arms were outstretched. Stone animals clustered around her.

A hulking bear stood behind the human. A mouse perched on her left shoulder, and a rat on her right. A bunny, fox, and badger stood like stair steps to the woman's right—knee high, Kipper-sized, and waist-high. Each of them stared adoringly up at the human.

A stone otter with a wide grin stood to the woman's left, and in front of them all, a life-sized squirrel stood proudly with its tail wide and bushy behind it.

Kipper walked up to the statue and read the bronze plaque at the squirrel statue's feet: *"To strive for betterment in all ways, for everyone, for all time—uplift is but another step in the string of small and great steps of our kind—all our kinds," Breanna Schweitzer, Bio-Ethics Blog, 2031.*

"Who is Breanna Schweitzer?" Kipper asked. "Is it this human?"

Tamantha came up beside her, nose twitching. "You don't know her?" The squirrel cab driver's sparkling eyes showed shock. "Haven't you studied *any* history?"

Kipper's ears flattened as she thought back to the history classes she'd taken during her kittenhood in the cattery. They'd studied humans, but she didn't remember much. At least, nothing specific. She'd always pictured humans as a force of history, faceless and many, much like a force of nature. They'd fought wars, invented things, travelled to the moon, uplifted cats, dogs, otters, and squirrels. And, according to so many believing dogs, they would be back someday.

Humans were a massive *they.*

This was a singular *she.* An individual person.

"I never learned about a Breanna Schweitzer," Kipper admitted. "Was she important?"

The red squirrel stared slack-jawed at Kipper for a moment before pulling herself together and fixing her expression. "I'm sorry; I can't imagine never having heard of Breanna Schweitzer. She..." Tamantha paused, as if looking for the right words. Or perhaps because the right words were so fundamental to her worldview it felt ridiculous to have to say them. "She invented uplift."

Kipper looked back at the statue and stared into the stone woman's unblinking eyes.

As a cattery kitten, Kipper had never known her parents, but she felt like she'd just been handed an old, ragged photograph and told, "Here, this is your mother." *What could she learn about herself by searching this stone woman's face?* There must be something.

But the eyes were blank, gray, static. The face was *human*— even if it was the face of a woman who'd manipulated genes passed down through the generations to Kipper, there could be no physical trace of their connection in the granite cut of this woman's cheekbones or the slope of her nose.

Kipper looked at the animals around the woman more carefully. She understood the presence of the grinning otter and proud squirrel. But why the mouse, rat, bunny, fox, badger, and bear? And, more importantly, Kipper wondered why wasn't there a cat? Or a dog?

"She has an unusual collection of animals with her," Kipper commented drily, trying not to feel offended by the lack of a cat. "I notice they're all standing upright."

"These are the species Breanna Schweitzer uplifted." Tamantha spoke so matter-of-factly that Kipper felt a fool for bringing the subject up. "I mean, I know that badgers, foxes, and rabbits died off after the first generation... And there was only ever one uplifted bear. But Teddy Bearclaw *was* an uplifted bear, even if he was the only one."

Kipper's ears skewed, and her understanding of history morphed and telescoped confusingly. She'd never heard of uplifted badgers, foxes, or rabbits. Or a bear named Teddy Bearclaw—that name sounded more like a joke, cloyingly sweet, than an historical figure. Was this squirrel playing a practical joke on her? Telling her tall tales? "What are you talking about?!" Kipper spat.

Tamantha's red brush of a tail twitched wildly behind her, curling and uncurling. She took a step backward, away from the angry-looking cat. Kipper looked around the square and realized Tamantha wasn't the only squirrel watching her. Pointed red and gray muzzles faced her, glittery eyes watching with horror, from several of the cafes. A few squirrels even stared downward from the skywalks above.

Kipper had never been the largest animal in a crowd before. She wasn't much bigger than the squirrels—maybe a head taller—but from hanging out around terriers, spaniels, and all sorts of medium-sized dogs, Kipper knew that it didn't take *much* bigger to be a lot. "I'm sorry," Kipper said. "I didn't mean to raise my voice."

"That's okay," Tamantha chirruped, stepping closer to Kipper again. "I guess they don't teach much about the pre-plague times in a religious country like the Uplifted States."

Kipper started to object that the Uplifted States wasn't a religious country, but then her mind tripped over the word 'pre-plague.' Suddenly, her head hurt something fierce. Everything this squirrel said led her deeper down a rabbit-hole that she hadn't even known existed until she fell backwards into it. With great trepidation, Kipper asked simply, "Pre-plague?"

"Oh dear..." Tamantha stepped away again. "Look, honey, you need to get yourself a history text that wasn't written by First Race Believers. But right now, let's just get you some fresh almond buns and maple mead from Pine Nut Patisserie to take on your submarine. Then we can see about picking up a data-chip with some actual information on it."

The Pine Nut Patisserie was crowded. Shoulder-high squirrels skittered around Kipper, their ears twitching and tails waving like streamers in many different winds. They pointed at cakes and pastries in cubbyholes that covered the walls, and squirrels wearing aprons scurried about collecting the desired delectables, passing them to patrons, and counting out change. It was dizzying. Everyone twitching, everyone moving. Somehow they didn't bump into each other, but their constant motion made Kipper nervous and jumpy.

She was grateful when Tamantha finally handed her a paper bag of almond buns and sunflower crisps along with a box of various nut teas and a bottle of maple mead. Her paws filled with squirrel delicacies, Kipper wanted nothing more than to get back to her submarine full of otters, but Tamantha insisted on stopping at a data-exchange and buying her a data-chip with several history texts burned onto it.

Kipper promised she would read it. But she wasn't sure that she wanted to.

Chapter 7: Jenny

Jenny wanted to push all the buttons. So far, her science officers—Felix and Amoreena—had only let her press one. After a lengthy discussion where Ordol helped translate the language on all the newly-flooded Europa base vid-screens, Amoreena had figured out how to turn the base's heaters on. And only just in time. Europa's oceans were no longer covered in ice, but they were frigidly cold. Much longer and they'd have had to improvise space heaters or begun wearing their spacesuits which would have been ungainly and clumsy underwater.

With the base's heaters on, the water inside the base was a lovely temperature, and Jenny had loved pushing that button. She was very proud of her work.

But now she was taking turns with the other otters sipping air from a face mask affixed to a cylindrical oxygen tank, merely watching Amoreena and Felix discuss the base's controls with Ordol in Swimmer's Sign. They didn't need her. When Captain Cod had put Jenny in charge of the Jolly Barracuders who stayed behind to hold the Europa base, he had cast her into the role of a supervisor instead of a scientist. She didn't have time for both.

Jenny wanted to push buttons and find out what this amazing piece of octopus technology could do—*it had already melted a planet-wide ocean!*—but she needed to swim back up to the top of the submerged base and deal with the furious Admiral Mackerel, Howard Industry dogs, and Persian ex-empress on the surface.

"Report to me immediately if you learn anything exciting," Jenny signed to her officers. Then she took a long sip from the oxygen tank, kicked off from the floor with a flippered paw, and swam in a spiral upward through the main chamber of the base. The single breath of oxygen could sustain her otter lungs for nearly ten minutes. One of the perks of being an aquatic mammal.

Jenny allowed herself a few curlicues around some of the poles that ran vertically through the giant chamber as she swam, but she kept her rudder tail pumping vigorously, guiding her remorselessly up to the honeycomb of passages ending at an elevator that would take her to the surface.

The honeycomb passages of the base were a breeze to swim through. So much better than it had been awkwardly crawling through them with her long spine hunched.

Jenny emerged from the honeycomb passages into the bottom of the elevator chamber—a deep well that had been open to the Europa sky above until Admiral Mackerel ordered a portable atmo-dome inflated over it.

Water sloshed on the floor of the elevator as Jenny entered it, but the chamber was otherwise dry. Jenny pressed her paws into a hemispherical bump in the middle of the elevator floor, and the floor began to rise.

Jenny shook herself, spattering drops of water from the soaked fur on her head, arms, and tail. Then she squeezed as much water as she could out of her slacks and vest. They were both made out of quick-drying fabric. All otter clothes were. By the time the elevator pulled up level with the surface of the floating base, Jenny was only damp, no longer soaked.

The large red face of Jupiter, distorted and blurry, shone through the cloudy plastic ceiling of the atmo-dome. Jenny felt cold looking at it. Raptors continued to assemble under those ruddy clouds. The instruments on Europa detected some of them, but Jenny feared there were many more deeper inside Jupiter's protective cloud cover.

Dinosaurs had hidden in those clouds throughout the entire history of Jenny's race—since before the beginning of the race who'd uplifted otters. Their society could be massive.

Jenny shuddered.

Then she faced the spectacle before her: Admiral Mackerel glaring at her.

"You and your gang of miscreants caused a lot of trouble with that stunt." Admiral Mackerel looked more serious than an otter oughter be able to. Behind him, the Howard dogs and the Persian empress were yelling at each other, looking much closer to coming to the stereotypical cat-and-dog fight than before. The surface of the base was nearly a mile wide, but it still felt too small for the cats and dogs to share.

"It was the right choice," Jenny said coolly. "All sorts of systems turned on once the base finished flooding that we hadn't been able to make work before. This base was designed to operate under water. We were never going to get it fully operational while it was still dry and floating."

"Gutsy," Admiral Mackerel afforded. He eyed Jenny appraisingly, and his stance relaxed. "Well, you wanted to be in charge—you're in charge. Go tell those landlubbers what you expect of them while they're on *your* base."

Jenny choked on the words she wanted to say—*I didn't want to be in charge!* Instead, she squeaked out the words, "*My* base?"

"Under Naval law, I'm placing you in charge of this base."

Jenny's eyes widened, and she again felt the urge to shout, "*I don't want to be in charge!*"

Amusement twisted Admiral Mackerel's whiskers, and he seemed to infer her feelings. "You took charge when you flooded the base. I'm just making it official. Deal with it." He had clearly appraised her and found her worthy of taking an unwanted responsibility off of his paws.

Jenny nodded solemnly. Admiral Mackerel was right. She'd already been in charge—she'd felt the responsibility in her heart, and that's why she'd flooded the base. It was what had needed to be done, even if it came with complicated consequences. That was the act of a leader.

If Jenny was stuck in charge, she might as well have the official authority that went with it. "Does my new position come with a rank?" Jenny asked. Jolly Barracuders liked their ranks. "Perhaps, Grand High Poobah of Europa?" And the more elaborate, the better.

Admiral Mackerel rolled his eyes. He really was a strangely serious otter. "How about *Base Commander?*"

"I'll take it."

Admiral Mackerel almost looked amused. But not quite. "Good, then get those landlubbers out of the way, and we can have a *serious* conversation about the relationship between the Imperial Star-Ocean Navy and this base of yours."

What was it with this admiral and seriousness? It's almost like he wasn't an otter at all.

Jenny looked at the Persian cat in her ridiculous imperial robes hissing and spitting through her whiskers at the casually dressed dachshund and cattle dog. Admiral Mackerel was right—they were in the way, distracting all of the navy otters. The situation was dire enough without them adding to it.

Jenny hesitated though, unsure of how to get them out of the way. She couldn't order them to fly back to Earth. Leaving the shield surrounding Europa could be very dangerous. They wouldn't be any help inside the base now, since they couldn't hold their breath like otters. They needed a task to keep them busy.

Admiral Mackerel placed a webbed paw on Jenny's shoulder and shoved her towards them. "Go on. Show me what you've got."

What was with this admiral? Jenny kept herself from shooting him a glare. Even if he was a much more annoying superior than Captain Cod, he was her direct superior right now. She was better off not fighting with him. But he *seriously* needed to lighten up.

That gave her an idea.

Jenny strode over to the Persian empress and said, "When your colonists evacuated, did they take everything with them? Food? Furnishings? Other stuff?"

The empress's ears were already skewed from her argument with the Howard dogs, so Jenny couldn't tell if the cat was skewing her ears at the question. If anything, they seemed to straighten a little, and the fire in her eyes died down as she looked at the otter. "No, of course not," the empress said. "There wasn't time or space on the rescue ships. My people had to leave most of their possessions behind."

"Good," Jenny said without thinking it through too clearly.

The fire returned to the empress's eyes.

"I mean, not good. But we could use those supplies." Jenny turned to the Howard dogs, including them in the conversation and said, "I know you only arrived here recently, but my crew has been stuck on this moon working with this base for months."

The empress muttered bitterly under her whiskers, "My cabinet and I have been here just as long."

"We need a break." Jenny locked eyes with the empress in spite of the cat's fiery glare. "All of us do."

The empress looked a little mollified by Jenny pointedly including her. Her triangular ears raised to half mast in their sea of fluff. The empress was a very fluffy cat.

"What are you suggesting?" the cattle dog asked in his down-home accent.

"All of us otters are really busy trying to figure out the capabilities of this base—"

The cattle dog cut Jenny off to say, "Well, my fine aquatic friend, we can't really help you with that anymore since you went and sank the place."

Jenny bristled at the way the cattle dog talked to her. She wasn't at all sure that she liked him. He'd been talking down to the admiral and the empress too. While Jenny didn't know much about cat and dog politics, it seemed unwise to talk down to an empress. Even a former one. On general principle.

"We don't want your help inside the base," Jenny said. She managed to swallow the words, "*We want you out of our fur*," and jump straight to, "I'd like you to throw a party."

"A *what?*" The cattle dog sounded incredulous.

The empress looked surprised. But possibly intrigued.

The dachshund said, "That's not a bad idea."

The cattle dog looked at his colleague skeptically, one large triangular ear skewed to the side. Jenny was familiar with the skewed-ear look on cats—it looked completely different on this cattle dog. More bewildered, less supercilious.

"How do you figure?" the cattle dog asked the dachshund, having seemingly completely forgotten Jenny who'd brought up the idea of a party in the first place.

The dachshund shrugged. "Everyone's on edge." She anxiously tugged one of her floppy ears. "There's no telling when the situation will get better—we're out here all alone on this inhospitable planet worrying that, *humans help us*, dinosaurs will attack Earth, and for all we know, the information on this base could be our only real line of defense. I, for one, would like to see the otters working here functioning at maximum capacity."

"Rest and recuperation," the cattle dog said. "Relax and refresh."

"Exactly," the dachshund agreed.

The cattle dog slapped his paws together. "Good idea! Let's get on it."

Jenny refrained from rolling her eyes at the way the two dogs had cut her and the empress entirely out of the conversation. She was really seeing why Kipper had had trouble with dogs back on Earth.

"I'm glad we're in agreement then," Jenny said through gritted teeth. "In order to throw a good party, you're going to need supplies that we don't have on any of our ships." Jenny gave the empress a meaningful look.

The cat frowned and said through downturned whiskers, "You want us to salvage the wreckage of New Persia."

"I'd planned on avoiding the word *wreckage*," Jenny said. Then she felt like slapping herself on the head. The empress' burning eyes told her quite clearly that just because the empress had said it, didn't mean Jenny had been welcome to. "But, yes. And since you're most familiar with the layout of... uh... your *previous colony*, I think it would be best if you were in charge."

That smoothed the empress's fur.

"Well, hey, now," the cattle dog said. "There's knowledge, and then there's know-how. And while I may not be familiar with the local layout, I know how to make use of resources. Like the locals' knowledge. See, I have a lot of experience with leadership."

"More experience than being an *empress?*" If the sharp edge of a hissed word could draw blood, the empress's pronunciation of her own title would have left the cattle dog's face dripping red.

The cattle dog probably shouldn't have smirked as he said, "Seems to me, we can all probably agree that hasn't worked out too well for you."

"Are you *insinuating*—" Every *s* the empress hissed was another sharp dagger. "—that it's my fault prehistoric monsters from the depths of Jupiter attacked my colony and ancient technology melted its foundation?"

"You did choose to build on ice." The dachshund looked like she legitimately thought her comment was helpful.

Jenny had been curious about seeing a real cat and dog fight. But now she'd had her fill. "I am the commander of this base," she snapped. "And my position is backed by the Imperial Star-Ocean Navy. If you want to be welcome here, then you'll make yourselves useful. For the empress, that means throwing a party. For the two of you—" Jenny stared levelly at the Howard dogs. "It means *assisting* the empress."

The cattle dog looked like he was about to object when they were interrupted.

"Jenny?" It was Felix's voice.

Jenny turned around to face her fellow otter and said in a low voice, "New rank—*base commander.*" Fortunately, Barracuders were used to changing ranks often.

"Oh, uh, Base Commander Jenny, we've discovered something."

For a moment, Jenny was relieved to be offered an excuse to escape from the Howard dogs and empress. Then she noticed the quiver in Felix's whiskers. "What's wrong?" she asked.

"We can track the raptor ships now."

This should have been good news. On the scale of the solar system, a fleet of enemy warships was extremely small. Almost impossible to track, unless they wanted to be found. But Felix's tone wasn't happy.

"Go on," Jenny said, dread curdling her stomach.

"They're moving much faster than expected."

"As fast as the *Jolly Barracuda*?" Jenny asked. The *Jolly Barracuda* was an experimental ship that Captain Cod claimed to have won in a poker game. It was the fastest ship ever built by otters.

Felix's whiskers drooped even farther, and his narrow shoulders slumped. "Depending on their acceleration, they'll be to Earth in a month and a half—maybe two months."

"Holy First Race!" the cattle dog exclaimed.

"But we can track them," Jenny said.

"Yes."

The empress stepped forward and asked, "And they are heading to Earth? Not Mars?"

Both dogs gave the empress dirty looks. The dachshund said, "My family is on Earth." As the short-legged dog said it, the reality seemed to strike her. In a broken tone, she added, "I promised my mom I'd be back for the big family reunion next year. What if..." She couldn't finish the thought, but all of them were picturing raptor vessels wreaking destruction on their home world.

Admiral Mackerel had been listening, and he stepped forward to say, "We're not going to let that happen."

"No, we're not," Jenny agreed. *Base Commander Jenny*, she reminded herself and stood a little taller. "Which is why we need to get back to work, figuring out what we can do to stop the raptors from here. And I need you—" Jenny looked pointedly at each Howard dog and then the empress. "—to get to work on your project. I think we're really going to need it before this is all over."

The cattle dog's demeanor had changed completely—he was no longer a bullying braggart; he looked like a big scared puppy. He tucked his tail between his his legs and said, "Yes, ma'am." Turning to the empress, he added, "How can my team assist you?"

To her credit, the empress took the change in the power dynamic between her and the Howard dogs without any comment. Not the slightest sign of gloating. Mostly, she looked tired, like everyone else on Europa. "Let's put a plan together," the empress said. "Do you have any space on your ship where we could talk? Or..." She hesitated. "Well, do you have a place where my cabinet and I could stay?" They had been staying inside the Europa base. When the Jolly Barracuders had flooded it, the Persian cats had found themselves forced to evacuate suddenly, yet again.

The Howard dogs had come in a hired otter vessel, a merchant ship called *Riptide*. It was floating alongside the recently submerged base. To his credit, the cattle dog looked genuinely sympathetic as he said, "I'm sure we can clear out a few cabins for you."

Once the dogs and cat were gone, Admiral Mackerel reappeared to say, "Well done. I couldn't get a word in edgewise with them. Now what's this about tracking the raptor ships?"

Felix gave Jenny an uncertain look, as if to ask whether he should be sharing information with the admiral. After all, the Jolly Barracuders had all just committed some sort of treason against the Imperial Star-Ocean Navy. But Jenny nodded to let him know it was okay, and Felix said, "There's an energy beam from Jupiter—actually several—they point right to the raptor fleet."

"They're using beam-powered propulsion?" Jenny said wonderingly. She'd read about otter experiments with beam-powered propulsion. It had the potential to be very powerful, but it required a centralized infrastructure that was not well suited to the chaotic nature of otter politics. The Imperial Star-Ocean Navy comprised a very small part of the overall fleet of otter vessels. Most otter ships were owned and operated by independent merchants and adventurers, like Captain Cod and his Jolly Barracuders.

"If they're using beam-propulsion," Admiral Mackerel said. "Then there's a source of their energy. Here. In Jupiter."

"Knock out the source, knock out the fleet," Jenny said. "Can we pinpoint the location of the source?"

Felix nodded, but he looked scared. "We don't have a lot of ships here."

Admiral Mackerel pondered. "I have five ISON ships in low orbit. We have the Whirligig vessel that Base Commander Jenny has been training on, and there's the *Riptide* that the Howard dogs came on. Does the cat empress have any vessels hidden away?"

Jenny knew the answer to that. "None. All the cats came here on hired otter ships."

"That's not much to work with..." Admiral Mackerel's dark eyes lifted to look at the marbled orange face of Jupiter through the plastic ceiling of the atmo-dome. "It would need to be a tight mission. A strike force."

Jenny looked at Jupiter too. There could be anything beneath those swirling, ruddy clouds. Jupiter had more than 120-times the surface area of Earth, and if the Jovian raptors had come from Earth, their civilization was more than 70 million years older than otter civilization. Raptors could have technology otters hadn't yet dreamed of. There could be multiple dinosaur societies; splinter groups; they could be at war amongst themselves.

Admiral Mackerel seemed to be thinking along the same lines. "We could use better intelligence," he said, looking at Jenny pointedly. He didn't need to actually say that she had far more access to raptor intelligence than anyone else. They all knew it. Ordol would barely talk to anyone other than Jenny, Amoreena, and Felix.

Yet, while Ordol had lived in raptor society his entire life, he'd been a slave—confined to a small tank, except for when one of the raptors used him, usurping his own control of his nervous system, to gain the use of all those extra arms.

"Ordol doesn't know much," Jenny said. "We're going to have to do this blind."

Admiral Mackerel frowned.

"But it's better than doing nothing," Jenny added, determinedly. "If there's any way we can stop those ships before they get to Earth, we have to try."

Admiral Mackerel nodded. "I agree. The five vessels of the International Star-Ocean Navy are at your disposal."

Chapter 8: Petra

Petra had lots of plans. None of them were working out the way she wanted them to. No one would cooperate with her. She'd been sent from one end to the other of the beautiful but archaic, ancient human building that was the seat of the Uplifted States' government—the White House.

Sure, it had been renovated to suit the needs of dogs and cats who were on average much smaller than humans, but if you asked Petra they'd be much better off with an entirely new building with fewer beautiful columns and more properly proportioned rooms.

Partitions had been built into many of the previously cavernous rooms, but the ceilings still loomed far above; the original stair-cases made Petra feel awkward and silly as she uncomfortably clambered up or down their too high and wide steps; and the partitions had turned the whole place into a maze. Though Petra wouldn't be getting lost in it anymore. She'd drawn herself a map and tucked it into her vest pocket.

Not that the map helped. Knowing where she was didn't get her the financial files she needed. Petra could swear that all the other cats in the building were hiding things from her. In fact, she wanted to swear *at* each of them. The cat in the policy office had told her that the records she wanted would be in finances. The cat in finances had sent her to general records. The cat in general records sent her back to policy—*of course*—where she was told that only authorized personnel could search the files directly.

How much more authorized could you get than the president's sister and main advisor? And why were the files all kept on actual paper in metal filing cabinets anyway? Hadn't the government heard of computers before she and Alistair had shown up?

None of them understood how important it was either. Even Alistair and Kipper had seemed skeptical of her plans: the world needed saving from the raptors—how would paperwork help? But Petra knew there must be something Alistair had missed. The Uplifted States of Mericka was the strongest nation on Earth, but Alistair seemed to have almost no power at all. The power must be hidden, and Petra would find it.

Petra snarled to herself and sat down on one of the broad steps of the Grand Staircase—a ridiculous structure only suited to greyhounds, Great Danes, St. Bernards, and Mastiffs. None of whom were in evidence. No, it was all cats—Siamese, Birman, Himalayan, and Tonkinese—officiously guarding office doors for the dogs.

It made Petra just that extra bit more furious thinking about how all the cats in the building seemed to have some variation on that fancy regal coloring—black masked faces and paws over a coat of snowy white. It made her fiery orange tabby markings feel like a brand burning into her, marking her: *not purebred, doesn't belong, get out tabby!*

And yet all the fancy-schmancy cats who'd been working here for years were basically secretaries and lackeys. She and Alistair had fought their way into the tip-top tier of authority. Those fancy-schmancy secretaries should show her more respect.

Petra heard paw steps and rustling paper on the stairs above her, and then a canine voice said, "Well, well, pretty pussycat. Is the harsh reality of government finally getting the little tabby down? All those big numbers in the budget too much for you?" The fluffy sable-furred Sheltie was one of Vice President Morrison's cabinet. He was holding a sheaf of papers that looked like a stack of freshly signed executive orders. His long-muzzled grin made Petra's claws itch.

In an even tone, Petra said, "Don't get cocky, Jazon. Your alpha dog isn't here to protect you." Usually dogs like Jazon wouldn't acknowledge Petra at all, so she knew something was up. She didn't intend to give him the satisfaction of asking what he wanted.

"Poor pretty tabby," Jazon cooed, sitting down on the step beside her and resting his sheaf of papers on his knee. "You look so tired. Maybe you should take a break from working on the budget and go home to play with your kittens."

The fur on the back of Petra's neck ruffled. This *was* her break. At home, the kittens were probably climbing all over Trudith, pulling her floppy ears, scratching drawings on the walls with their claws, inventing new forms of havoc to wreak every hour. "Raising a litter isn't play." Petra spoke through clenched fangs. "It's hard work. Even harder than dealing with condescending mangy flea-balls like you."

Jazon laughed. "Well, now. You sound like you're halfway to becoming a statistic—yet another deadbeat mama cat who drops her kittens off on a cattery doorstep, 'cause she's too lazy to do a little work."

Petra spent her nights doting on crying kittens and spent her days, exhausted, trying to fix a country that was filled with preju-diced dogs like Jazon and catty cats who fed his prejudices. Right now, she wasn't sure why she bothered. It was more than she could take.

"If you're really worried about the budget—" Jazon's voice fell to a whisper. "Don't leave your worthless kittens at a cattery and cost the government more dollars. *Drown them.*"

Petra's claws took on a life of their own. Her paw swung. She wanted to swing at Jazon's black nose and see his brown muzzle grow wet with blood, but she took control of her paw and aimed lower. Before Petra fully knew what she was doing, long claw marks shredded Jazon's sheaf of executive orders.

They'd all have to be printed out and signed by Alistair and Vice President Morrison again.

Jazon grinned wolfishly.

With horror, Petra realized that she'd played right into his paws. This was what he'd wanted—he wanted to rile her up, push her past the limit, and get her to do something stupid he could use against her.

And she'd let him.

She hated herself for that.

But she hated him more.

Still, she'd gotten herself in enough trouble for the day, so she bit her tongue, sheathed her claws, and stuffed her paws deep into her vest pockets. She stayed that way—sulky and sullen—all the way through Alistair's aggrieved, shocked lecturing; Vice President Morrison's gleeful insistence that she be banned from the White House until further notice; and even through Jazon's triumphant snickering.

She was lucky she had controlled her paw at the last second. If she'd actually clawed Jazon's brown-furred muzzle, Vice President Morrison would never have settled for banning her from the White House premises. He would have pressed charges and turned the incident into a full-blown scandal.

Petra didn't think she could have pulled off claiming that she'd thought Jazon was *actually* threatening to drown her kittens. He hadn't been holding a wash basin, and her kittens had been nowhere near him. And no one would care that she'd had terrified nightmares three times in the last month about them drowning in the ocean—that was normal right? All parents were plagued by violent terrors in their dreams of what might happen to their precious but provoking kittens.

Petra wished Jazon and Vice President Morrison and all those stupid, superior cats who wouldn't let her at their records would drown.

It was exactly that kind of thought which turned into extended claws slashing an important sheaf of documents and getting her kicked out of the White House. She needed to control her thoughts better.

Petra growled, but she wasn't sure if it was at herself or everyone else in the world. They were all against her.

Tail swishing, Petra was escorted to her small office next to Alistair's by Keith, one of Alistair's greyhound guards. The gangly greyhound watched while she stuffed all the records she had managed to gather into the outer pocket of her briefcase, shut down her laptop computer, and stuffed it into the briefcase as well.

"Are you allowed to take that?" Keith asked.

Petra figured that if he didn't know the answer to that question, the answer might as well be yes. "Yes," she said. She left all the drawings her kittens had made of her and Aunt Kipper taped to the walls. She'd be back.

Keith gave her a sympathetic smile. His angled ears and dopey brown eyes made his long face well-suited to sympathetic smiles. "I've given Trudith a call. She's bringing the kittens over to meet you for a picnic on the South Lawn. That'll be nice, won't it?"

Petra looked up at Keith—the greyhound was nearly three times her height. It was hard not to think he was being condescending when he was *literally* speaking down to her.

Petra needed to simmer down. Keith was a good guy. He was one of Trudith's best friends. There was no reason for her to be mad at him, other than that she was generally mad. And that wasn't a good reason.

"Yeah, a picnic could be nice," Petra admitted, shouldering the strap on her laptop briefcase. The kittens would probably enjoy seeing the roses. As Petra understood it, some of the rose bushes dated back all the way to the time of humans. They were hardy little plants. Beautiful but also scrappy. Petra had to respect that.

And she could learn from it. *Roses kept their thorns to themselves.*

Keith led Petra through the labyrinthine warren of small rooms that filled the White House as if he'd been there for years. Though Petra knew he'd spent no more time there than she had, since he was also part of Alistair's team. She wondered if Keith navigated by an uncanny canine sense of smell. Or maybe he was just better at learning his way around than she was.

Probably because he wasn't thinking about anything else. Petra scolded herself for the uncharitable thought as soon as it crossed her mind.

Keith walked Petra all the way out of the building, past the Doberman and Rottweiler standing guard at the back door. She wouldn't be sneaking past them ever. It would take a brain-damaged fool to try. Now that Petra was securely out of the actual White House, Keith turned to her and said, "I'd love to stay for the picnic, but Alistair needs me back inside. Say 'hi' to Trudith for me!" So casual. As if he hadn't just dumped her on the other side of a door guarded by the scariest looking dogs in the world.

"Hey Keith!" the Rottweiler said as Keith passed by. "Are we still on for the marathon of *Small Dog, Big Heart* this weekend?"

The Doberman broke into a goofy grin and said, "I can't wait to re-watch the episode where Vanessa kisses the cat!"

The two guards broke out laughing at the memory of the famous episode of *Small Dog, Big Heart* where the heroine, a shaggy Maltese dog, was dared to kiss a scrawny tabby tomcat. It had been the first interspecies kiss ever to air on television, and it had been so controversial that it had been banned in half the country.

Interspecies relationships had come a long way since then—now the episode was merely a joke.

Keith shot Petra an apologetic look, embarrassed by his friends, but said, "Yeah, I'll be there."

Petra thought of several biting things to say to the guards but took a lesson from the rose bushes and kept her sharp tongue to herself. It wasn't easy when it felt like everyone was always making fun of her, taunting her, and disrespecting her. *She'd married a dog; she was a common tabby from a cattery; she was a mother and a cat, the worst combination of demographics.* She was the ideal target for ridicule, and the jibes came continuously from every direction.

But instead of picking a fight with dogs five times her weight, Petra strolled the South Lawn grumbling to herself until Trudith and the kittens arrived—a big black dog wearing a backpack, three little kittens trailing behind her like a row of ducklings.

They picked a nice, sunny stretch of lawn and while Trudith spread a picnic blanket and unloaded food from her backpack, the kittens pranced and swarmed around Petra, telling her all about their exciting day.

"Trudith took us to a thrift shop!" The tiny gray tabby, Allison, gave her mother a coy look from under a wide brimmed black hat and over a ridiculously large pair of sunglasses. "And she gave us each five dollars to spend!"

"Then I can guess where those came from," Petra said.

"I'm a private detective," Allison said smugly, raising the sunglasses to cover her green eyes again. "With my gray stripes, and this hat, I'll blend right into the shadows." She spread her paws wide and stepped nimbly backward, as if she were melting into a shadow. Except there was bright sunlight and green grass all around.

"What about you two?" Petra asked, turning to her orange-furred sons.

Pete had a long, blue, silky scarf tied around his neck. He grabbed the ends of it and fluttered them, exclaiming, "I'm an uplifted butterfly!"

That was a new one. "Oh?" Petra asked, sitting down on a corner of Trudith's picnic blanket.

Pete grabbed the plush cat doll that was always tucked under his arm and held it forward, "Mr. Pickles is a human scientist who discovered how to uplift EVERYTHING. And I'm a butterfly that was flying past his lab when *suddenly ZAP*. And now I'm uplifted."

Petra nodded solemnly. She could think of no other way to react to her son's delightfully absurd new game. Her other son, Robin, crawled onto her lap.

Trudith finished setting out the tuna fish sandwiches and settled onto the other corner of the blanket. It took awhile for Trudith to cajole the three kittens into settling down to eat their sandwiches—Allison had to be called back several times from trying to hide in a bush, and Pete kept insisting that he was too busy flying to eat. Petra felt guilty that she was simply watching Trudith do all the hard work, but she could hardly chase after Allison and Pete with Robin curled up on her lap.

Once the kittens were all under control, Trudith breathed a deep sigh of relief and picked up her own sandwich—chipped beef instead of tuna. Before taking a bite, she said, "You should ask Robin what he did with his money."

Petra waited, giving Robin a chance to speak, expecting him to eagerly volunteer his answer like the others. She couldn't see his face with him curled into her lap; only his ears and the back of his orange-striped head were visible to her.

"What did you do with your money?" Petra finally asked.

After a long while—long enough that Petra wasn't sure he intended to answer at all—Robin put a paw into one of his pockets and pulled out a wadded up five dollar bill.

"You saved it?" Petra asked.

Robin nodded. Then he took his mother's paw and gave the bill to her. Turning to look into her eyes, he said, "You said you were worried about money missing from the government's budget." His green eyes were so clear and innocent. "I wanted to help."

Petra squeezed him tight. "Thank you, Robin." She'd have to put the money aside, save it for him. Maybe not everyone was against her. Maybe there were still things worth fighting for.

Only now, she couldn't get back inside the White House to fight for them. Petra sighed. She would need help. She hated asking for help. So she waited, watching the kittens eat their tuna fish and then fight over the sweet cream cheese buns for dessert. Trudith talked meaninglessly at her about scramball games and sports scores. Couldn't Trudith tell that Petra didn't care? Wasn't listening? That there were more important things to talk about? Nonetheless, Petra didn't want to cut Trudith off.

Once the kittens were done eating, everything devolved into wild scampering—Allison chased Robin around the lawn, insisting that she had a lot of questions for him about a case she was trying to solve; Pete burrowed under the picnic blanket, knocking around the paper plates on top, claiming that it was his chrysalis, and he needed to hibernate now.

"Hmm," Petra mused. "You could use a book about butterflies if you think that's what a chrysalis is for."

The bump under the blanket showed no signs of hearing her. It was too busy hibernating.

"We could take them to the library," Trudith offered.

They were interrupted by Robin and Allison prancing their way across the middle of the picnic blanket. Pete shouted from underneath, "You're squishing me!" Much noise and crying ensued. The kittens were falling apart. That meant it was time to take them home.

Trudith helped Petra stuff all the picnic supplies into the backpack. Then her black-muzzled face split into a nervous grin. "Keith says they could use another pair of paws here. Now that you've got the kittens..." Trudith trailed off, but she didn't have to finish her thought. Petra knew what she was getting at.

"Yeah, that's fine. I've got the kittens." Petra gave the fuzzy little demons an appraising look—Pete had tied his blue scarf around Mr. Pickles; Allison was throwing her new hat like a frisbee; and Robin seemed to be practicing somersaults. "Everything's under control."

"Great!" Trudith's nervous grin morphed into a joyous one. "Here are the car keys. I parked by that coffee shop—" She gestured vaguely, but Petra knew the place she was talking about.

"I took the bus this morning," Petra said.

"I figured."

Taking the bus was much easier without the kittens. The kittens required greater containment than was offered by a bus full of other travelers to bug.

"Look—" Petra started to say. She hated admitting weakness, and she didn't want to ask for help. But Trudith had proved herself surprisingly competent in the past, and Petra didn't have a lot of options now that she was banned from the building that held all the records she needed. "I—"

"You'd like help getting those financial records."

"Yes," Petra said, dumbstruck.

"Don't worry," Trudith said. "I'm on it."

Petra was still worried. She watched the big black dog walk up to the White House, laugh with the Doberman and Rottweiler guards, and then go right in. She hoped Trudith wasn't planning to steal the records. Petra was already in enough trouble without Trudith doing something stupid on her behalf.

For better or worse, Petra couldn't worry about Trudith for long. She had three wild and busy kittens to herd back home.

Chapter 9: Kipper

Kipper hadn't expected the submarine to feel so cramped. There was plenty of space on the *Jolly Barracuda*—why should a submarine be any more cramped than a spaceship? They're both airtight vehicles, and if anything, space seemed like a more foreign and dangerous landscape than the ocean. The ocean is at least on Earth.

Well, a spaceship has to hold an atmosphere for its occupants to breathe. Whereas, a submarine has to be built to withstand the extreme water pressure created by the weight of miles upon miles of ocean water pressing downward on it.

At least, that's how Trugger explained the cramped quarters onboard the *Diving Canary* to Kipper.

Kipper didn't really mind the low ceilings, narrow corridors, and weird machinery jutting out from every angle. She was simply grateful that she got to keep on breathing good old gaseous air. True, she did have to slosh her way through waist deep water on the main level, but when she climbed up from the control deck to the sleeping quarters on the upper level, she could curl up on a trundle bed and dry off completely.

Kipper spent most of the two day trip from the coast of Ecuador to the Galapagos Islands reading the data-chip she'd picked up in Cedar Heights, munching on sunflower crisps, and sipping maple mead. At first, Kipper was nervous whenever an otter came splashing up to the sleeping quarters, dripping everywhere, but Trugger assured her that the tablet computer he'd loaned her for reading the data-chip was water proof. Apparently, pretty much all otter technology was water proof. Even computers.

The sunflower crisps, on the other paw, lost a lot of their crispness when they got soggy. Unfortunately, the almond buns hadn't lasted an hour onboard the *Diving Canary*—Kipper had had to fight Trugger off to eat even one of them before he gobbled the rest up. Their almond filling had been sweet and meaty, less sugary than actual marzipan.

Unlike the almond buns and maple mead, the information on the data-chip didn't go down so easy. The more Kipper read of the squirrel history books on the data-chip, the more confused she felt. It was like reading science-fiction. Or an alternate history.

Breanna Schweitzer had been an expert on gene therapy and a radical wildlife conservationist in Ancient England. She'd believed that the only way to truly protect an animal species was to uplift it to the point where it would indisputably deserve and share in the same rights as humans. Thus, she'd designed the techniques for using gene therapy to uplift various local species—basically, all those woodland animals Kipper had seen in the statue with her. Schweitzer had devoted most of her time to otters, developing an array of breeds based on the different species of otter all around the world.

However, Breanna Schweitzer had had difficulty funding her lab. So, she'd sold her techniques to anyone willing to pay, figuring that regardless of the purchasers' plans, once they'd fully uplifted an animal that animal would be able to turn around and sue for full *human* rights.

The main purchasers had been the American Canine Club, the Cat Enthusiast Society, and various independent dog and cat breeders around the United States of America—which, of course, was now the Uplifted States of Mericka.

Before reading these histories, Kipper had known that, back before uplift, humans had bred dogs and cats for particular characteristics. Some dogs were bred for hunting, some for herding, and some to be companions. Many dogs and cats were bred for aesthetic reasons—somehow, although Kipper had never really thought about it, that's all she'd thought cats had ever been bred for. Beautiful but useless; that was the message First Race culture spread regarding cats.

At any rate, the way uplift was presented to her growing up, Kipper had believed all the different breeds of cat and dog had somehow been frozen in place right before uplift began. However, these squirrel books suggested that the very process of feline and canine uplift in the United States had been a continuation of that long history of selective breeding. Rather than simply preserving the *supposedly* sacred breeds that had been designed before uplift, humans had *kept* selectively breeding dogs and cats for various purposes after uplift.

Why had Kipper never heard of German Baker Dogs, Butler Terriers, or Rescue Retrievers? What about Florida Hospice Cats and Domestic Shorthair Valets? Shouldn't she have heard of them if they were real? If they had ever really existed?

Yet according to these books, there really was no such thing as an uplifted common tabby. Uplifted breeds in Mericka—America—had all been by definition purebred, carefully controlled to meet standards set by the American Canine Club and the Cat Enthusiast Society, and most of them had been bred for specific purposes. Kipper's ancestors most likely *were* Domestic Shorthair Valets.

Kipper wasn't sure she liked that.

Though, she took a strange glee in reading that the fancier breeds of cats—Siamese, Persian, what-have-you—largely had been bred to meet standards set for beauty rather than brains. They had been bred to be show cats, unlike the Domestic Shorthair Valets who'd been bred to work as personal assistants.

All of this made Kipper's head spin, but the part she found truly unbelievable was the mice.

Yes, the mice.

See, there had only ever been one uplifted bear—Teddy Bearclaw. The rats, rabbits, foxes, and badgers had only been small populations, not enough to remain sustainable after the Great Anarchy struck—the time when the uplifted animals found themselves alone, not yet able to master the First Race's abandoned technology, not ready to fend for themselves. It had been a time of darkness, a black spot poorly recorded in the annals of history. And, apparently, a time when the rats, rabbits, foxes, and badgers—who Kipper had never heard of before—had all died out.

But not the mice.

Head spinning, Kipper put down the tablet computer. She couldn't read any more right now. Laying flat on the thin mattress, she stared blankly at the dull metal twisting pipes that made up the ceiling of the sleeping quarters—barely an arm's length above her. She tried to process how she felt, to understand how she could have spent her whole life so totally ignorant that she hadn't even known there were uplifted mice.

According to the squirrel book, the mice lived in a tiny city all their own, nestled inside the heart of New London. They called it Mousfordshire. And unless Kipper had horribly misunderstood—which actually seemed like the more likely, less fantastical option—the uplifted mice were still living there.

Trugger pulled himself up the little ladder from the main deck to the sleeping quarters and burst into Kipper's sanctuary like a torpedo. A very wet torpedo.

Kipper raised herself up on one elbow to look at him. His fur was dyed in red stripes now, like he was trying to be a tiger. "Mousfordshire," she said, the word somewhere between a question and an accusation.

"The mouse city?" Trugger asked, as if it were nothing. "What about it?"

"I used to watch *Deep Sky Anchor News at Eleven*!" Kipper exclaimed in defensive exasperation. "Why didn't they ever mention that there's a whole uplifted mouse civilization?!"

Trugger gave Kipper a funny look. She had no idea how to interpret it. Then he said, "Well, they're not very interesting." Trugger flopped down on the opposite trundle bed and put his paws behind his head. "Besides, *News at Eleven* isn't the real news.

That's the Uplifted States version of the news—trimmed to remove anything that the Church of the First Race finds offensive."

"But..." Kipper couldn't find anything to say. She'd known the Church of the First Race had a lot of power, but... They edited the news? Had she been living in a religious hegemony? Without knowing it?

"The real news is *Orbital Hour*. Or *Geosynchronous Now*."

"I've never even heard of those," Kipper said, feeling like she'd thought those words far too many times during the last two days. At least, it wasn't so bad to have not heard of a TV show. It wasn't like being unaware of an entire sentient species sharing your home planet.

"Yeah, they don't rate well with most canine audiences, so I'd be surprised if very many stations in the Uplifted States carried them."

He said it like the fact that her country was censoring out whole sections of ancient and current history was nothing. Just what you'd expect of a backwards religious country like the Uplifted States.

It was all extremely frustrating. It made her feel stupid and angry—stupid for not having seen through it all, and angry—well, angry at a lot of things. But mostly herself for being so stupid.

In a small voice, Kipper admitted, "I didn't know any of this stuff—Breanna Schweitzer, Teddy Bearclaw, Mousfordshire... And I didn't even know that I didn't know it."

Trugger turned his head to look at her. His expression was sympathetic. At least, it wasn't pitying. "That's the thing about not knowing stuff." He reached over to help himself to a pawful of her sunflower crisps. After several less-than-crunchy bites, he said, "But, hey, you know it now. Want to visit Mousfordshire with me some time? It's like a whole little city of doll houses all around the base of that ancient human relic, the clock building—you know, Big Ben. That's their city center."

Kipper hadn't known about Big Ben, but she liked the image of tiny mouse houses built all around a giant clock. "Yeah," she said.

"I'd like to go to New London sometime." She'd already seen so much of space—much more than she'd ever dreamed she'd get to see—but there were whole continents on Earth she'd never visited. "Maybe after we defeat this raptor army."

If we defeat this raptor army, Kipper thought. Otherwise there wouldn't be a Mousfordshire, nor any cats or otters to visit it.

Trugger casually grabbed the almost empty bag of sunflower crisps and leaned back on the trundle bed. "Oh, about that. We're almost to Choir's Deep." He poured the final soggy crumbs into his mouth; then he eyed Kipper to see if the tabby was upset about him finishing off the bag of crisps.

Kipper didn't care. She'd had enough sunflower crisps. Besides, if Emily's cooking was any indication, there could be some amazing cuisine waiting for them in Choir's Deep. "Can we see it?" Kipper asked. It might be worth sloshing down to the main deck where there were portholes to get a look at the octopus city.

Trugger shook his head, still staring at the twisting pipes of the ceiling. "Nah, it's nothing but a dull green glow from here."

The portholes had been nothing but murky midnight blue any time Kipper had gone down to check them. There was very little light this deep in the ocean. A dull green glow might not be much—but it would be a change. She weighed the relative merits of getting her first glimpse of Choir's Deep versus getting wet to her waist...

It was a close call, but she swung herself off the trundle bed and slid down the ladder to the main deck. "Don't finish off my maple mead," she shouted up to Trugger as she splashed into the tepid water. Thank goodness she was wearing quick-dry clothing made from otter fabrics.

"No promises!" he shouted back, but Kipper was already sloshing her way toward the front of the submarine.

The first porthole she passed was the same dark shade it had been for the last two days. So was the next. And the next. But when she rounded the bend to the nose of the submarine where Captain Cod was busy at the wheel—literally, piloting the submarine with a spoked wheel as wide as Kipper was tall—she saw the dull green glow of Choir's Deep on the viewscreen. It wasn't the same as seeing it with her bare eyes through a porthole, but the video image relayed to the viewscreen was probably higher resolution than her bare eyes could have made out anyway.

Kipper squeezed into the space between Pearl and Chauncey, two other otters from the *Jolly Barracuda*, who were busy working buttons and dials related to various radar screens and computer readouts.

"Come to watch the approach of the city?" Pearl asked.

Kipper spared enough attention to say, "Yeah," but the rest of her focus was entirely on the main viewscreen. She even forgot the lukewarm water sloshing at her waist as she peered into the dark image, trying to find patterns in the shades of dull green. She may have hated discomfort, but she loved exploring.

The variegated green image on the viewscreen grew sharper slowly, but Kipper knew how to be a patient cat. She had watched Mars—a single diamond speck—grow imperceptibly brighter for weeks as the *Jolly Barracuda* flew toward it. Waiting for the green glow on the viewscreen to resolve into the crenulated folds of the trained coral reefs that built the outer walls of Choir's Deep was nothing.

Choir's Deep was a city carved into the ocean floor between the Galapagos Islands. It was powered by geothermal energy pouring out of the Galapagos Rift—a hydrothermal vent a little to the east. The Galapagos Rift might be a volatile, volcanic region filled with underwater geysers that could power an entire civilization in lieu of sunlight and photosynthesis, but here the water was calm.

"It looks like a brain, doesn't it?" Pearl asked, breaking Kipper's trance.

Kipper skewed one ear, slightly annoyed by the interruption of her reverie, but she had to admit it was true. Choir's Deep looked like a giant green brain nestled into the crevice between two underwater cliffs.

As they got closer, the front lights on the submarine began to illuminate the scene. The colors grew clearer and more complicated—patches of peach and orange anemones grew on the coral like blushes of rust; darting schools of copper fish sparkled like pennies sprinkled down a wishing well; and strange plant-like growths in brilliant red and cobalt blue clawed upward like grasping hands.

In many ways, it was a more alien world than Mars or Europa.

"Do otters visit Choir's Deep often?" Kipper asked.

"Does an egret whistle?" Chauncey asked, his cheerful sea otter face providing no clue as to the answer.

"Does it?" Kipper asked. She'd learned long ago to just cut to the chase with Jolly Barracuder bird sayings.

"No." Chauncey looked pensive for a moment. His mouth narrowed until it nearly disappeared into the brown fuzz of his chin. "Actually, egrets sound kind of like frogs." His face widened into a grin again. "We'll be the first to visit Choir's Deep in nearly a hundred years!"

Kipper blinked. "That's because most otter-octopus interactions happen at a different octopus city?" she asked hopefully.

Captain Cod turned from his wheel to stare levelly at Kipper. He didn't usually do anything levelly, so it was quite disturbing. "That's because the only octopi that have been in communication with otters—or anyone—for the last century are refugees and exiles."

Kipper gulped. Suddenly, her little diplomatic visit to the nearest octopus city felt like a much weightier event than she'd realized. "You mean... I'm broaching communication with octopus civilization for the first time in a century?"

"You'll do great!" Captain Cod's confidence in her would have been inspiring if Kipper didn't think he halfway believed his own made-up tales about how she'd single-handedly commandeered the *Jolly Barracuda* to prove herself to him and earn the rank of Ship's Spy—or whatever he was calling her these days. "So... What do you want us to say to them?"

Kipper wished she had a hat so she could swallow it. That would have been the best way to communicate her feelings to an otter like Captain Cod. Instead, she had to settle for saying, "*Me?* You want *me* to choose what to say to them?"

"You're the Diplomatic Ambassador to Independent Cat and Octopus Nations," Captain Cod said cheerfully.

Kipper saw that her title had grown. "I see. Well... Is there a standard procedure for situations like this?"

"No." Captain Cod still looked cheerful.

Kipper wished that Captain Cod would stop looking cheerful. But that wasn't going to happen. He was going to keep grinning at her through his whiskers until she told him what to tell the octopuses.

Kipper wrung her paws, looked down at the water lapping at her waist, and considered her options. She couldn't claim that she was here on behalf of the Uplifted States of Mericka. Alistair had ordered her explicitly not to come, and she wouldn't lie. She couldn't claim to be here on behalf of any otters other than the single rag-tag semi-pirate ship she belonged to. That wasn't impressive. New Persia was destroyed, and Siamhalla would never accept a common tabby as their spokesperson—even if she had thought to ask them in advance. Which she hadn't.

Really, the only person she could speak for was herself.

And her first-hand observations of the raptor vessel inside the clouds of Jupiter.

"Tell them, *We're here on behalf of the enslaved octopus population of Jupiter. Please let us dock and enter your city.*"

"Perfect," Captain Cod said. "You have a beautiful way with words."

Kipper thought to herself, "*Sure, I avoid metaphors and references to birds... It's not that hard.*" But outwardly, she accepted the compliment with an embarrassed dip of her ears and a nod.

At the captain's order, Chauncey typed Kipper's message into the *Diving Canary's* computer and broadcast it to Choir's Deep in every written language the computer knew.

"Now we wait for a response!" Captain Cod didn't look at all nervous. He could have been confidence incarnate—the living embodiment of the emotion. "It shouldn't take long."

Kipper wasn't convinced that the captain's confidence was justified. After five minutes of waiting, she was even less convinced. In fact, she was starting to wonder if there were any octopi home—perhaps, they'd all moved to a different city?

After ten minutes of nervously dipping her paws into the water that lapped at her waist and then watching the water drip, drip, drip off her paw pads to pass the time, Kipper stopped worrying that the octopi would never respond and started to worry that they'd called an immediate, emergency war council in response to her message. Perhaps, they were in Choir's Deep right now deciding whether it was better to take the *Diving Canary* captive or simply shoot her out of the water.

What if their response wasn't a pleasantly worded invitation but instead a volley of underwater missiles?

Kipper wondered if that would count as a hero's death—they were on a mission intended to help save the world. Surely, that was heroic. Yet, it would be so meaningless to be shot down by xenophobic octopi before they'd made any difference.

Then Kipper realized that she didn't care—dead was dead, heroic or not.

Thank the First Race, Chauncy finally broke Kipper's painful reverie to say, "They've sent back two words in a pictographic language very similar to the written version of Swimmer's Sign."

Kipper's voice caught in her throat. So it was Trugger—who had waded up behind her—who asked, "What does it say?"

"*Please wait.*"

Chapter 10: Jenny

Jenny and Ordol were suited up and ready in *Brighton's Destiny*, but the two-man Whirligig vessel was still parked on the floating roof of the Europa base. The Imperial Star-Ocean Navy otters and their five ships were already in low-orbit, but Ordol hadn't even powered the Whirligig's engine up yet.

Jenny couldn't start the vessel without him. Too many of the controls were designed to be used by an octopus on the shoulders of a biped. Jenny couldn't see Ordol's eyes with him perched on her shoulders—but she could see the color of his tentacles through his translucent spacesuit. His flesh was bone white. He was terrified.

"What are we waiting for down there?" Admiral Mackerel's voice came over Jenny's suit radio. His words were echoed visually on one of the spaceship's readouts, translated from voice to text—a nice feature Amoreena had rigged up for them.

Jenny translated the words into Swimmer's Sign with her paws as well, "Hey, buddy, what're we waiting for?"

Shivers of blue passed over Ordol's tentacles. When the blue waves settled down, leaving his flesh white again, he signed, "I don't want to go back."

"You're not going back," Jenny signed. "You're never going back. Not really. We're just swooping past, lasers flaring. No stops. Then straight back here."

Ordol's tentacles hung limply, draped over Jenny's shoulders. Their color didn't even change. He was clearly unconvinced.

Jenny couldn't imagine what he was feeling; what demons he was struggling with. She'd been a free otter her whole life, and *she* was afraid of flying into the raptors' den. What if they were shot down? Left spiraling into the crushing depths of Jupiter to die? Or they could be captured... Jenny had no idea what the raptors would do with a captured otter.

She had a pretty good idea of what they'd do with Ordol—return him to their aquariums of captive octopi who lived in a cage until their very physical autonomy was robbed of them by a neural interface.

Was that worse than death? Ordol's terror suggested it might be.

"I won't let them capture us," Jenny signed. "We'll kamikaze rather than be taken captive."

Jenny thought she saw a slight orange tint flush Ordol's tentacles.

"Okay?" she signed.

The orange shade of Ordol's tentacles grew stronger but blotchy. And he still looked very pale. "Okay." He reached out with his two foremost tentacles and powered up the Whirligig's engine.

"No more waiting, Admiral," Jenny said into her suit radio. "We're on our way." The ground fell away in the windows as *Brighton's Destiny* soared upward.

"Glad to hear it," Admiral Mackerel replied. "Since you have the tracker set up on your computer, you take the lead."

"Aye, aye, Admiral."

Usually, Jenny loved take-off; she loved any part of flying where they went really, *really* fast. She looked forward to it like a home-cooked fillet of fresh caught salmon glittering with lemon-butter sauce. But now the rush of speed felt like a long anticipated feast turned to ashes in her mouth. She took no joy from flying toward Jupiter this time.

At *Brighton's Destiny's* top speed, it was a three hour flight from Europa to the outer atmosphere of Jupiter—a length which felt better suited to a road trip filled with rambling conversations and silly games than a stealth mission filled with tense silence.

The energy beams powering the raptor fleet originated in Jupiter's Great Red Spot, but they were passed around the massive girth of the planet by a series of orbital relay stations so that they never lost contact with the departing fleet despite Jupiter's rotation. Admiral Mackerel and Jenny had agreed that it was too ambitious to attack the primary source.

They intended to knock out as many relay stations as they could before the raptors caught up with them, starting with one that was about a third of the way around Jupiter from Europa right now. By skipping past the closest relay stations—the ones on the side currently facing Europa—Jenny hoped to increase the chances that their attacks would be mistaken for natural disasters. That might buy them time.

On *Brighton's Destiny's* tracking display, the relay stations were simple red dots placed at regular intervals over the blue surface of Jupiter, connected by red lines representing the energy beams being routed from the Great Red Spot. Although the relay stations were distributed all around Jupiter, they were far too small to see until *Brighton's Destiny* had nearly arrived at the first target.

By the time they were close enough to see the first relay station directly, Jupiter's face filled the viewscreen behind it. The small satellite was no larger than *Brighton's Destiny*, just large enough to capture and reroute the energy beam from the Great Red Spot. Jenny thought it looked like a dead spider, lying on its back with its long legs folded over it, floating on a puddle of melted creamsicle.

"Visual confirmation of target acquired," said one of the navy otters over the radio. The voice was so sudden, so surprising, in Jenny's ears after the hours of silently watching Jupiter grow on the viewscreen that she startled and jumped in her seat. Her motion bumped Ordol, but his tentacles kept deftly working the controls. Only a brief flush of yellow over his skin showed that he'd noticed her movement at all.

Officers from the other four ISON ships chimed in to agree that they could see the target relay station now. Then the captain of the *Riptide*, a civilian otter named Krysantha, said, "Are we gonna shoot it down or what? We've come an awfully long way, and I'm not hearing any orders to fire."

As far as Jenny knew, her Whirligig Class vessel had no weapons. It seemed to be some sort of scout ship. Its tracking systems, however, were perfect for leading the strike team directly to the relay stations and warning them if there were any other raptor vessels nearby. All they'd had to do was break *Brighton's Destiny's* homing signal, so it could fly silently.

Basically, Jenny and Ordol were only along on this mission to be guides and stool pigeons, spying on the raptors. So for this part, Jenny sat back and watched.

After another few moments, during which the dead spider of a satellite grew larger on the viewscreen, Admiral Mackerel's voice came over the radio: "Fire at will."

The *Riptide* fired guided missiles at the relay station, but the dead spider glowed red and exploded before they even hit.

"Woah," Jenny said. "Was that the new ISON proton beam?"

"Five of them," Admiral Mackerel answered. "Invisible but deadly."

"I guess I should have saved my asteroid-smashers," said Captain Krysantha. "Remind me never to go up against the navy."

"Remind yourself," Admiral Mackerel said. "On to the next one?"

"Leading the way," Jenny said, cooperating with Ordol to adjust the course of *Brighton's Destiny*. As per their plan, she didn't lead the strike force to the next closest relay station. They skipped past several. By randomly skipping relay stations—instead of attacking them in order—they hoped to keep their presence secret from the raptor forces for even longer.

The otter strike force knocked out a dozen more relay stations easily. It was slow work—twenty minutes of flying for every fifty seconds of proton beam explosions. They'd already done a full day's work. They'd have to disable at least forty, maybe fifty, relay stations to effectively diminish the power beam zinging the raptor fleet toward Earth. Still, Jenny could have kept it up all night, knowing that they were doing something to make Earth safer. If only *Brighton's Destiny's* computer screens hadn't lit up with ominous chatter on the raptor wavelengths...

"Can you read what those messages say?" Jenny signed to Ordol. She had a suspicion before he even began signing from the way his tentacles drained of color.

"The raptors have figured out that the explosions aren't natural," he signed. "Thirteen is too many to be a coincidence. They're looking for us."

Jenny said into her suit radio: "They're on to us." She also signed a translation with her paws for Ordol. "We're harder to predict if we keep up our random pattern. Harder to predict is harder to find."

Captain Krysantha snorted. "Unless they post guard ships at every relay station."

"With three hundred relay stations?" Admiral Mackeral sounded skeptical. "I don't think so. We still have time. Keep leading the way, Base Commander."

"Aye, aye," Jenny said, but she was worried about Ordol. His tentacles had turned a bluish-gray. To him, she signed, "We'll be okay. I promise."

Brighton's Destiny led the ISON ships and the *Riptide* to five more relay stations, but with each exploding spider of a satellite, Jenny worried more about the cryptic raptor messages streaming across her ship's computer screens and the darkening blue of Ordol's tentacles. There had to be a better way. They would never knock out all three hundred of the relay stations this way—they might not even knock out enough to make a difference. The raptor vessels were sure to find them soon, and sure enough, as they approached their next target, a cluster of red dots converged around it on the tracking screen. *Raptor vessels*—a dozen of them.

Jenny and Ordol rerouted their strike team towards a different relay station, but they had to fly past three more potential targets before they found one that was undefended by ominous red dots.

All the while, Jenny wracked her brain for a better plan. Splitting up was a bad idea; none of the otter ships could track the raptor vessels like *Brighton's Destiny* could. Attacking the original source of the energy beams in the Great Red Spot was a suicide mission.

Wasn't it? They didn't have blueprints for it, and even if they did, it was too much to hope that it had a single central weakness that could be exploited by a ragtag strike team of six otter ships and a stolen Whirligig scout. Definitely too much to hope.

Jenny wasn't any good at *not* hoping. "Ordol," she signed, "do you know anything about the source of the energy beams? Is it a mothership of some sort? Can we access blueprints for it on this ship's computer banks?"

"You want to attack the source?" Ordol signed, his tentacles moving slowly.

"I want to take everything out in one blow. BAM. We're done. Know what I'm saying?"

The blue-gray of Ordol's tentacles flushed turquoise. "If there are blueprints for anything on these computers, I don't know how to find them." He kept signing, telling Jenny about the ship's computer, and the color in his tentacles drained back to a pale version of his more usual orange tone. Telling her about the computer seemed to soothe him, but Jenny had stopped processing what he was telling her.

If she wanted to knock the whole system out in one blow, maybe it didn't have to be done from the source. She signed with her paws and said over the radio, "Could we overload one of these relay stations instead of destroying it? Some sort of feedback loop?"

Captain Krysantha said over the radio, "Setting off a domino effect that knocks out all the other relay stations without *us* having to fly to them? I like it."

"So we can do it?" Jenny said excitedly.

"No idea," Captain Kyrsantha said. "But I do like it."

Admiral Mackerel and the commanders of the other ISON ships argued for a while about whether it could be done, until Jenny was ready to give up hope. They clearly had no ability to overload a relay station—only desire to do so.

But then Ordol signed, "We'll need to get very close to the relay station." His signs were small, tentative. But his color was still good.

"Very close?" Jenny signed. "To do what?"

"To transmit the code I've written." His signs were larger, more confident. "It will spread from relay station to relay station, and then it will cause them to target all the energy they're rerouting to the same relay station. One after another. Until they're all destroyed."

Jenny's heart beat fast. That was more like it! "How close?" she asked, saying the words before she remembered to sign them.

"How close for what?" At least five different otters asked the question at once, but Jenny wasn't listening with her ears, only her eyes.

Ordol signed, "Ten meters."

She signed, "For how long?"

"Not long." His tentacles had flushed pink with excitement Or at least, adrenaline. "A fly-by is fine."

"Will it blow up right away?" Jenny signed, afraid that Ordol might really be planning a suicide run.

She was infinitely relieved when he signed, "I've written a delay into the program. That will give us time to fly away."

She breathed the words, "Thank goodness," and signed the words, "You're my hero. Let's do this." Then she spoke up, loud enough to break through the clamoring voices on the radio of all the other otters, desperate to know what was going on, and said, "At the next clear target, *Brighton's Destiny* will do a close fly-by and transmit a... *special package* to the relay station. Hold your fire, but cover us. If our plan works, we'll be done here and everyone can head home. Got it?"

Silence replaced the clamor. It lasted long enough to make Jenny nervous. Then Admiral Mackerel said, "We've got your back. Let's smash this clam."

Jenny grinned to hear Admiral Mackerel sound like more than a humorless navy officer.

The otter vessels flew in formation—the five ISON vessels, flat and round like sand dollars, fanned out behind the wide-winged *Brighton's Destiny*. The conical *Riptide*, like a steampunk conch shell flying through space, brought up the rear. But when they got to the relay station, *Brighton's Destiny* peeled away from the others.

Up close the relay station's mechanical legs looked less creepy than a dead spider's. They looked cold and soulless. It was a simple machine designed to redirect an energy beam. Nothing more. Void of malice. Yet terribly dangerous. Jenny shivered. "Are you ready to upload?" she signed.

"Uploading now," Ordol answered. His color still looked good and orange. "And... done."

"Let's get out of here," Jenny said and signed. "I'm waaaay ready to get back to Europa." The relay station passed by on the viewscreen, too close for comfort, and began to recede behind *Brighton's Destiny*.

"No," Admiral Mackerel said. "We need to see if it worked."

He was right. And yet Jenny knew they were on borrowed time. The raptors were going to catch up with them. "Okay," she said. "But let's not stay next to *this* relay station. Let's fly on to the next one—if our plan works, they'll all blow up. And if we keep moving, it gives us a better chance of staying hidden."

Admiral Mackerel agreed to her plan. The next relay station was hard to spot—it still appeared on *Brighton's Destiny's* tracking screen as a bright red dot, but the leggy dead spider had been replaced with a loose cloud of rubble.

The navy otters whooped over the radio, but Jenny saw what they couldn't.

A cloud of red dots on the tracking screen, coming from every direction, coming closer. They'd been found.

Chapter 11: Petra

The *pew-pew* sound of laser weapons blared from the television—the kind of sound that's always accompanied by a rain of colorful blasts of light on the screen. It was a rerun episode of *Tri-Galactic Trek.*

Petra hadn't been able to stand a single minute more of *Alpha-Dog and Numbers Cat.* That show might be educational, but it creeped Petra out the way that the two characters stared straight at the audience and explained every word they used. The final straw had been when Alpha-Dog said, "Sharing is what dogs do when there isn't enough for everyone to have their own! Do cats share too, Numbers Cat?" and Numbers Cat archly replied, "Sometimes," followed by a laugh track.

Learning about sharing was good. Learning stereotypes about cats was *not.* If that's what the kiddy programs were teaching, then Petra figured her litter was better off watching *Tri-Galactic Trek.* Hell, with how the world was going, space battle strategy might be a far more important lesson than sharing.

Unfortunately, Petra hadn't foreseen that the kittens would want to play along with *Tri-Galactic Trek,* acting out the battle scenes by jumping all over the couch and throwing cushions at each other. After three spilt cups of milk and one broken picture frame, Petra decided that the kittens needed to get out of the house.

What Petra needed would simply have to take a back burner... She had been writing a proposal for requiring all government records to be digitized, but trying to concentrate on writing while the kittens asked for snacks, lost their toys (and needed help finding them), suddenly wanted to know why dogs came in more different sizes than cats, and needed so many other little things was... like trying to do something that Petra couldn't think of because the kittens kept interrupting her.

She'd only been home with the kittens for half a week, and she was already losing her mind. She envied Lucky and Trudith for being at the White House, working with Alistair, talking to *adults*.

It took forty minutes to pack snacks, find her keys (Allison had hidden them in the refrigerator), change the kittens into clean clothes (Pete had dumped milk all over Robin), and get all three of them strapped into the backseat of the car. Sadly, that was pretty good. Getting out of the house with three wild kittens is not easy.

Petra started out driving to the park—but she ended up just driving. The park came, slid past the window, and receded behind them. She couldn't make herself pull over the car. Then she'd have to let the kittens out, and they were contained right now. They were quiet and controlled, strapped in, held still by belts. Sure, they bickered and complaintively mewled, "When will we get there?" occasionally, but it was still quiet compared to the shrieks and screams back home.

So Petra kept driving. She drove in circles. She drove until the kittens finally fell asleep.

Then she heard the sirens behind her. A cop car.

Petra pulled over to get out of the way, but the cop car pulled up and parked behind her. A big dog—some kind of mutt with a scowling, jowly face and a crisply pressed blue uniform—got out of the car and came up to rap his big paw against her window.

Petra rolled the window down. "Is something wrong?" she asked.

The cop leaned over. "Where're ya goin'?"

Petra flattened her ears in consternation. She didn't know where she was going, and she didn't know why this cop wanted to know. "Did I do something wrong?" she asked, a hint of annoyance creeping into her voice.

The cop repeated his words, slowly like he didn't think she'd understood him: "Where ya goin', Miss Kitty?"

His breath was warm; Petra could feel it in her whiskers and ruffling her fur.

"You're leaning too close to the window," she said, ears flatter than ever. "Stop crowding me."

"Answer my question." His voice was menacing. His jowly face looked angry, mean.

In spite of herself, Petra felt a wisp of fear in her stomach. She thought that she was past being afraid of the cops—her brother was president; she wasn't a lowly alley cat anymore. She should be safe.

Still... She thought about telling the truth—*I don't know*—and knew it would sound like a dodge, like she was hiding something. What answer did this dog want? What answer could she give to make him go away?

None.

Nothing had changed.

She was the president's sister, but out here, next to a dog in a police uniform with a gun, she was still just an alley cat.

"Get out of the car," the dog barked. She'd taken too long to answer.

"*Please*," Petra hissed. "*Keep your voice down. I have kittens slee—*"

"DON'T YOU HISS AT ME, CAT!" The dog stepped back from the car and pulled his gun. He lifted the muzzle to point it at Petra, and her vision blacked out in terror. The next thing she knew, his big rough paws were on her, yanking her, clawing her, dragging her out of the car.

The pavement smashed against her face. She felt a foot press down on her back, and her arms twisted around behind her, held tight in the cop's big paws. She heard a quiet, "Mama?" and hoped to high heaven that her kittens couldn't see her right now. She tried to call out reassuring words, but there was so much barking she couldn't hear if she succeeded.

Then she blacked out completely.

Petra came to in a jail cell, face still smashed against concrete. Her first thought was a desperation that filled her body—a primal need to know—and her yowled words echoed off the walls: "My kittens?! Where are my kittens!?"

The response was gentle, soft-spoken, not at all what she expected: "Easy, Pet," Alistair said. "The kittens are with Keith."

Petra lifted herself, shakily from the ground, and looked over to see Alistair in a gray suit on the other side of bars. He looked tired and sad. Petra felt guilty, like it must be her fault, but she wasn't sure how. "What happened?"

"I don't know, Pet. You tell me."

Petra stared at him blankly. His voice had turned judgmental on a dime. And with her face and back still aching from the way that brute police dog had thrown her to the ground, she was in no mood to defend herself.

"They told me you attacked a police officer?"

"*Officer?*" The pitch of Petra's voice rose over the single word into a shriek. "That was no *officer.* That was a bully. A brute. A dog in the worst way. He should be in here! Not me."

"So you did attack him." Alistair didn't even make it a question. He'd already played the part of judge, jury, and executioner in his own mind. She was guilty. Obviously. And he'd punish her with his supercilious coldness.

But Petra had already been punished with fists. Supercilious coldness was nothing to her. She could out-freeze her weakling brother any day. Petra's voice turned icy, and she said, "I want a lawyer."

Alistair laughed. "You are in so much trouble, foolish sister. You have no idea. If the officer booking you hadn't recognized you as my sister, you'd be in a very different place by now. A lawyer won't get you out of this one. I'm not even sure I can." His tail twitched, as if the idea of his sister rotting in prison was a mere irritation.

Seeing her own brother ready to give up on her so completely, Petra's anger—righteous though it might be—drained away, leaving only fear.

"I didn't attack him. I didn't do anything." She babbled at Alistair, telling him everything—how stupid *Alphadog and Numbers Cat* had been, how hard it was to find her keys, how she couldn't get herself to pull the car over, and she had just kept driving and driving. She explained it all, but badly and out of order. She was scared and confused and crying by the time she saw that the look on Alistair's face had morphed into a mask of pure fury.

Terrified to the bone, Petra whispered her fear: "*You don't believe me.*"

"No," Alistair said. "No, I do believe you." His paws balled into fists, but there was nothing good for him to punch. Only iron bars and concrete walls. "I just thought..."

"That it would be different."

"Yeah."

The two orange cats, brother and sister, stood on opposite sides of the iron bars and stared at each other while dogs all over the country believed that only bad cats get arrested. They both knew it wasn't true.

In the end, Alistair didn't promise to get her out, or tell her that he'd take care of it, or that everything would be all right. He didn't even say that he'd do everything he could do. She already knew that without him saying it.

He just said, "Do you want me to have Allison, Pete, and Robin come visit you?"

Petra's heart clenched. She missed her kittens already, but she couldn't stand the idea of them seeing her in here—weak, wronged, unable to stand up for herself. She shook her head, not even able to utter the word, "No."

She did whisper, "Tell them..." *What should she say? Would she be home soon? Be good for Daddy and Trudith?* Her voice caught as she said, "Tell them I love them."

Alistair nodded.

Chapter 12: Kipper

The mysterious machinations of the octopus government in Choir's Deep kept Kipper and the otters on the *Diving Canary* waiting for nearly two days. Kipper did a lot more reading. Trugger found a deck of tarot cards that some previous occupant of the submarine had left behind and invented a card game that was a cross between tarot and poker.

Trugger, Captain Cod, Chauncy, and Pearl took turns laying out cards to tell each other's fortunes, betting on them, trading them, and mixing them up, all while laughing a lot. Kipper declined to play, feeling like she'd already bet too much on her fortune.

When Choir's Deep finally contacted them again, the new message was as short and pithy as the one before: "Prepare for escorts."

Pearl had been the officer on duty in the bridge when the message arrived, so she was the one to relay those words to everyone else, huddled in the barracks around their card game.

"We're going in!" Trugger whooped. "Octopus City, here we come!"

"Either that," Kipper grumbled, setting her data-pad aside, "or they're arresting us."

"Say what?" Pearl asked with her head still poking up from the lower level. Everyone else was too busy singing along with Trugger on his improvised surf song "Octopus City" to have even heard her.

"Nothing," Kipper said. "How should we prepare?"

"SCUBA gear," Trugger said knowingly, cutting his song short. He began gathering together the waxy water-proof tarot cards to put them away.

Unless Kipper was mistaken, SCUBA gear meant more water. At least, it also meant not breathing it.

Captain Cod said, "This is your mission, Kipper, so obviously you've got to be part of the team."

Kipper wished that weren't so obvious.

"I'm the captain, so I'll come along too."

"Me too!" Trugger yelped.

Pearl and Chauncy shot each other a glance that Kipper couldn't read. Then Pearl said, "Chauncy and I should be able to manage the ship on our own." Chauncy nodded eagerly.

Kipper wondered if they were glad to get rid of Trugger. She'd wondered about the fact that she had become so instantly his best friend when she had arrived on the *Jolly Barracuda*. Did he have trouble getting along with other otters?

"That's settled then," Captain Cod said. "The three of us will get our SCUBA gear on and debark from the sub's airlock." He turned to Pearl and added, "Send the octopi a message. Tell them we'll be ready in a matter of minutes."

Pearl saluted and then bobbed back down to the main level. Chauncy followed.

Captain Cod held his webbed paws out, paw pads up. "Let's all join paws," he said, completely creeping Kipper out.

"What? Why?" she objected. But she was a good cat and took hold of one of Captain Cod's paws. Trugger grabbed hold of her other paw.

"We're a team," Captain Cod said.

Kipper nodded respectfully and waited for him to continue onto some some sort of inspirational speech, fabricated anecdote, or tall tale about a bird, but after a few moments, Captain Cod simply squeezed their paws. Then he let go, clapped his own paws together, and said, "Let's go meet some octopi!"

Kipper wouldn't have minded a bit of an inspirational speech.

"Down to the airlock!" Captain Cod practically dove down the hatch to the main level. Once he splashed down, Kipper could hear him muttering to himself about how it was really more of a *"waterlock"* on a submarine, and then pondering whether "waterlock" would be a good word for a warlock with water magic, and wondering if he should invest some money in starting a "waterlock" movie franchise.

Kipper supposed that would have to do for inspiration. She followed Trugger down to the main level. When they got to the outer door of the airlock, Captain Cod handed them each a tangle of SCUBA gear. Like most of the gear Kipper had to deal with around Jolly Barracuders, the SCUBA gear was designed for otters. Fortunately, that didn't make nearly as much difference in a simple face mask as it had in a full body spacesuit. Kipper shuddered at the memory of cramming her ears into the small rounded ear guards designed for an otter, and she cringed at the memory of the useless appendage designed for an otter's rudder-like tail flapping baggily behind her.

Once all three of them—Kipper, Trugger, and Captain Cod—had their face masks firmly affixed and their air tanks strapped on their backs, they stepped into the airlock and sealed it behind them.

The water sloshing around Kipper's waist began to rise. Her heart pounded, preparing her for the moment of panic that always came on the *Jolly Barracuda* when the oxo-agua rose too high, drowning her, and she had to breathe it. But this was not oxo-agua, although it looked eerily the same. It was water, and she was not expected to breathe it.

The tepid water rose past her shoulders, tickled her chin, crept up her face, wetting down her fur, and filled her ears. But Kipper breathed steadily from her face mask, clinging to the stream of air—real air—that the SCUBA gear fed her hungry lungs.

As soon as the water finished filling the small room, Captain Cod signed, "Ready?"

Kipper and Trugger both answered, "Yes," with their paws, and Captain Cod punched the button to open the outer door of the airlock. The door split open, four pieces withdrawing into the walls, leaving a cross of empty space. Outside, the water was devastatingly clear. Except for the water's embrace on her furry arms and the deep, deep blue in the distance, Kipper wouldn't have known it was water.

They stood in the airlock, staring at the crenulated green lobes of Choir's Deep softly lit by the *Diving Canary's* front lights, waiting for the escort they'd been promised. Kipper wasn't even sure what that meant until she saw two giant shapes moving toward them, swimming slowly through the water. Kipper felt her fur fluff, a strange prickly feeling when she was under water. Alarmed, she signed, "Sharks? Should we—"

She was going to suggest closing the airlock and going back inside, but then she saw the octopi clinging to the sharks' speckled backs. Five on one, six on the other, riding them like some kind of giant underwater bus.

"They're too big for sharks," Captain Cod signed.

"Whale sharks," Trugger signed. "They're filter feeders. We have nothing to fear. Nice ride though!"

Nothing to fear. Kipper liked that optimism. Even if it did seem a little blind.

A lifetime of being a common alley cat in a society run by dogs and purebreds had taught Kipper that government officials weren't always on her side. And a government that had chased away Emily, the *Jolly Barracuda's* octopus chef, didn't seem any more likely to be utopian.

As the whale sharks drew closer, the octopi riding them waved their tentacles. Rainbows of different colors flitted over their skin. Kipper felt torn as to whether the sight was cheerful and friendly or disturbing and deeply ominous. Even after all the time Kipper had spent with her friend Emily, octopi were still basically aliens to her.

"This is exciting!" Trugger signed, giving Kipper a big otterly grin.

Captain Cod signed, "A momentous occasion!"

Kipper's stomach churned with nervousness. She waited until the whale sharks pulled up beside the *Diving Canary's* airlock and then signed to the octopi, "Thank you for seeing us. We have important things to... discuss."

The octopi looked at each other, glances exchanged from one pair of golden eyes with rectangular pupils to another. Then their tentacles began to writhe. Kipper couldn't tell if it was an expression of restlessness, a mere emotional gesture, or if they were signing to her—too quickly, too subtly—for her to understand.

"I don't understand," she signed.

Captain Cod put a hand on her arm as if to say, *Don't worry I've got this.* Then he signed to the octopi in big, clear gestures, with no apparent irony, "Take us to your leader."

More writhing. More rainbows. Nothing clear. Nothing Kipper could interpret. Her triangular ears flattened, but her otter compatriots seemed unfazed.

Captain Cod leaned forward and his rudder-like tail undulated, propelling him out into the open water. Rainbowed tentacles reached for him as he approached, grabbed his outstretched arms, and helped him onto the smooth speckled back of one of the whale sharks. He grinned, waved, and signed, "Come on!"

Trugger grabbed Kipper by the paw and pulled her out into the water with him. She was grateful for his help swimming, but she was still wary of what they were swimming toward. When they reached the whale shark, a rainbow of tentacles wound around her, gripping her furry arms with the soft kiss of sucker discs.

Her feline nervous system screamed: *everything that's happening is wrong.* She should not passively let tentacles grab her. She should not be submerged under water. The only small grace was the stream of air that she gulped, trying not to hyperventilate, from her SCUBA mask.

Why did adventures have to be so hard? Here she was, making contact with a civilization one-hundred-years out of touch with her own society, and instead of marveling in awe—she was having a perfectly pedestrian panic attack.

Kipper focused on slowing her breathing until it matched the side-to-side sway of the whale shark's easy swimming. Water flowed past her, ruffling her fur. It was almost relaxing. Except for the tentacles. And the water. And the shark underneath her.

Amazingly, Trugger and Captain Cod seemed completely unaware of Kipper's struggles. They pointed out shining copper fish to each other and signed at the octopi, telling them how excited they were to be here, how great the whale sharks were, and how beautiful it was in the Galapagos. The octopi may have signed back—every now and then, Kipper thought she caught a phrase in the curls and twists of their tentacle tips, increasingly dimly lit by the *Diving Canary's* headlights: *very welcome; like it here; leave soon; dangerous.*

Or was it simply her imagination? Kipper didn't like to ask the otters whether they understood the octopuses' signing in front of the octopi. She didn't want to admit her own lack of fluency. Yet she was unlikely to get a chance to speak with them privately any time soon. She would have to risk revealing her weakness.

"I don't understand," Kipper signed, looking at as many octopi as she could, trying to catch each one by the eye. "Can you sign larger? Slower?"

An octopus with especially pale eyes reached out to Kipper with two arms and embraced her in a hug that Kipper struggled not to find menacing. The octopus' color settled down from the riot of rainbows dancing over its flesh to a simple coral shade. Except for the unusually pale eyes, the octopus looked much like Emily. With all the rest of its tentacles still—eerily still compared to the rainbowy octopuses around it—the pale-eyed octopus held two tentacles up and signed very clearly, "Is this better?"

Kipper's body flooded with relief from her pointed eartips down to her clawed toes. "Thank goodness," she signed. "Thank you. Yes, that's much better." She'd begun to fear that she wouldn't be able to understand these octopi at all. She hadn't realized how much better Captain Cod and Trugger—and all the other otters, she supposed—were at communicating in Swimmer's Sign. In fairness, they had grown up learning it, and Kipper had only taken a crash course a few months ago.

Still, the otters signed slowly and clearly enough for her that she'd begun to think she could actually keep up with them. Apparently, though, it was yet another skill like swimming—no matter how much better she got, she still didn't have webbed paws. And she still hadn't spent her kittenhood bilingual. She might never truly catch up.

The pale-eyed octopus signed slowly and clearly for Kipper again: "You are not used to this language." The way its tentacles curled, the sentence didn't look like a question.

Kipper answered anyway: "No, most cats and dogs don't learn Swimmer's Sign."

The whale shark swam through a round opening in a crevasse of the crenulated green city. Up close, the material the city was made of looked a little like malachite, but paler.

"What is this?" Kipper signed, indicating the walls of the tunnel they were now swimming through. "Is it rock?"

"Coral," the pale-eyed octopus signed. "Genetically modified for building purposes." The octopus's signing grew harder to read as the tunnel darkened, but then light shone through from the other side.

The tunnel opened up into an alcove wide enough for the whale shark to turn around. It did so. Then it settled onto the floor of the chamber. The second whale shark joined it, nestling in beside the first. Once the two speckled behemoths were completely settled, the octopi on their backs leapt and crawled and swam and jetted away. It was a breathtaking spectacle of bumpy, suckery, curling tentacles.

Of course, it was nothing compared to the spectacle awaiting them on the other side of the entrance chamber to Choir's Deep.

Captain Cod swam after the clutch of octopi—an arrow amidst a tangle of string. Trugger grabbed one of Kipper's paws, and the pale-eyed octopus wrapped a tentacle around her other. The two of them pulled her along.

On the inside, Choir's Deep was so large that Kipper wondered for a moment whether they'd somehow ended up out in the open ocean again. She could only barely make out the curve of the malachite colored walls and ceilings in the distance. However, the inside of Choir's Deep was much busier and brighter than the open ocean.

The fish like copper pennies that Kipper had seen outside darted about in schools. Jellyfish floated like serene ballerinas— each ones' ruffled tentacles trailing to a tip under a diaphanous bell like the pointed toe under a tutu. Kelp trees glowed softly green filling the space with a smooth, mellow light. Kipper didn't think that kelp usually glowed and wanted to ask whether this kelp had been genetically modified to serve as a light source, but her paws were both held fast.

Trugger and the pale-eyed octopus continued to pull her along past large floating spheres. Octopi surrounded the spheres, watching much enlarged images within them of octopi signing to each other, embracing each other, working at computer stations. Kipper wasn't sure, but she thought they were video screens, perhaps showing movies or newscasts.

Giant spires jutted out of the ground and ceiling like stalactites and stalagmites, formed from the same malachite-green coral as the rest of Choir's Deep. The stalactite and stalagmite structures were riddled with openings that looked like the mouths of tunnels.

Kipper kicked her hind paws, trying to paddle along as her group turned upwards toward one of the giant stalactites. She didn't want to be entirely deadweight-driftwood dragged on by Trugger and the pale-eyed octopus.

On their way up, they swam past a formation of octopi riding on the disk-shelled backs of giant sea-turtles like they were skateboards or motorbikes. Kipper wondered how the turtles survived down here in Choir's Deep—turtles breathe air like cats, *like her*. Then she saw gills on their wrinkled yellow necks. They must be another example of genetic engineering. How advanced was octopus technology? Kipper began to feel excited about the possibilities. Between the genetic engineering she was seeing in effect here and the force field surrounding Europa, it was possible that octopi were far more advanced than dogs and cats had been giving them credit for.

Perhaps octopi really could make the difference in the impending clash Earth faced against the oncoming raptor fleet.

Ahead of Kipper, the other octopi in her group and Captain Cod disappeared into the mouth of a tunnel at the tip of the stalactite. Trugger and the pale-eyed octopus pulled her after them. On the inside, after a few twists and turns of the tunnel, was an expansive, vaguely round room. The walls of the room were riddled with little nooks that many of the octopi settled into, leaving their tentacle-tips and eyes hanging out like hermit crabs peeking out of their shells. Other octopi had been waiting, already nestled into the nooks. Now dozens of pairs of eyes stared out from the nooks.

The wall spaces between nooks were decorated with glassy surfaces, swirling in glowing color. Kipper couldn't tell if they were electronic screens or some sort of more natural phenomenon. As she watched, their riotous colors faded into a soothing monochromatic scene reminiscent of rolling waves—purely shades of blue. Then greens and browns danced like leaves in the wind. Suddenly, the jumble of clashing colors came back, dancing like jewels in a kaleidoscope.

Dizzying. It was dizzying like something out of a particularly intense catnip trip. Come to think of it, the entire experience of floating in a round room at the bottom of the ocean, surrounded by tentacles, yellow eyes staring at her, and swirling colors felt more like a hazy dream than real life.

There was no clear orientation to the room—no up or down. Since Kipper and the otters didn't fit into the octopuses' nooks, they floated awkwardly over the tunnel they'd entered through.

An octopus entered through an opening on the other side of the room like a spread parachute settling over them all. Seven of its tentacles were normal, fleshy appendages, flushed orange, but the eighth tentacle was silver and shiny. The octopus curled its tentacles inward, making a scalloped shape, and twisted around until its startling blue eyes stared directly at Kipper with rectangular pupils narrowed. None of the other octopi had blue eyes—they were all varying shades of yellow, tan, gold.

"You are the cat," it signed with tentacles that turned a deep cobalt blue, except for the silver tentacle that shone mechanically and pointed at Kipper.

She wanted to hide.

There was nowhere to hide in any part of Choir's Deep she'd seen, unless she could figure out how to fold her body up like an octopus.

Her paws faltered, but she managed to sign, "Yes. My name is Kipper."

All around her, Kipper saw tentacles twitch and twist in tiny, hard to interpret signs. It was a silent whisper, everyone talking, but her unable to understand, left wondering whether they were talking about her. They must be. Right?

It didn't matter. She'd come here for a reason. She steadied her paws and signed on. "There are octopus slaves on Jupiter." No point in being indirect—she'd come all this way; she might as well jump straight to the point. "They're enslaved by a race of raptors. I've seen them—"

"We know," the blue-eyed octopus signed with its mechanical tentacle. "They deserve their fate."

Kipper's paws drifted to a halt while her mind processed the unexpected signs. "They... *deserve*... slavery?" Her paws felt clumsy, fumbling over the hideous idea. *How could anyone deserve the fate she'd seen Ordol living with? His own nervous system repeatedly hijacked to follow the bidding of another's brain? Living in a tank, a mere tool waiting to be picked up and used?*

"Yes." The blue-eyed octopus signed first, but then the sign— *"yes"*—echoed throughout the room, on all the other octopi's tentacles in Kipper's peripheral vision.

"Woah," Trugger signed. "That's cold."

The octopus' blue eyes sparked. Kipper couldn't read all octopus facial expressions, but she recognized that spark of anger.

"You don't know what they did," the blue-eyed octopus signed. "We didn't bring you here to judge us."

"You didn't *bring* us here," Captain Cod signed. "We came of our own accord. We reached out to you, because our planet is facing a threat that affects all of us together."

The blue-eyed octopus continued signing, in complete disregard of Captain Cod's statement. "We brought you here—inside our city—to judge *you*."

Kipper's heart raced. Everything was flipping inside out and backwards. This wasn't how it was supposed to go at all.

"For millions of years," the blue-eyed octopus signed, "we've hidden here under the seas on this tiny planet, exiled from our rightful home in the stars by the foolish, damnable, unutterable crimes of our ancestral siblings inside Jupiter. Until now. Until you revealed us."

"Revealed you?" Kipper signed, wishing she were anywhere on Earth right now other than in the center of this globe of yellow eyes staring at her, judging her.

"To the raptors! They are coming here, because of *you*." The blue-eyed octopus's silver tentacle shone like a dancing scimitar as it signed. "You must pay for that crime."

And like that, Kipper's delicate dream of diplomacy was crushed under the nightmarish weight of a wall of tentacles writhing and twisting into the signs for "pay!" and "crime!" It was as if she'd written the hopes in her heart onto a piece of paper and carefully folded them into an origami octopus—the octopus of her imagination, safe and orderly—only to have a drooling, slime-dripping Cthulhu-monster drop from the sky and squash her, paper octopus in her paw and all.

Chapter 13: Jenny

The red dots on the viewscreen began to converge. Each dot represented a raptor vessel headed straight for them and ready to end their lives. Or worse. Suddenly, the metal hull of *Brighton's Destiny* felt paper thin to Jenny.

Ordol's tentacles, sheathed in their clingy, transparent spacesuit, wrapped tightly around Jenny's shoulders, trembling violently.

"I can't pilot this ship without you!" Jenny signed, between tugging at the tentacles that were now crushing her shoulders in a way that she was sure would strangle her if her neck weren't protected by a rigid space helmet. "And I definitely can't pilot this ship if you crush me with your freakishly strong arms! LET GO!"

Ordol was clearly stronger than Jenny, and her spacesuit gloves felt clumsy against his pure-muscle arms. But her entreaties and yanking must have got through to him, because his tentacles began to loosen and relax.

"Don't let them take me," he signed with quivering, pale tentacle tips.

"I won't," Jenny signed. "Now fire up those engines, and let's get out of here."

The rest of the otters in the strike force chattered over the radio, coordinating their plans as the red dots converged. They planned to flee in formation, rotating positions to give their proton beams a chance to recharge while keeping a nearly continuous volley on any pursuers. But they all had weapons. *Brighton's Destiny* was some sort of science or scout vessel with no weapons as far as Jenny or Ordol could tell. So as far as *Brighton's Destiny* was concerned, the plan boiled down to: hide in the middle of the other vessels, and hope they offered enough defense.

"No disrespect, Admiral Mackerel," Jenny said, "but *Brighton's Destiny* is raptor designed. If we make a break from the team now, before the raptors catch up to us, they won't even know we're with you."

"Understood," Admiral Mackerel said, his voice somber. "I wish we could offer you greater protection."

Jenny wished that too. "We'll see you back on Europa," she said. "Be safe."

Jenny punched the right thruster, and *Brighton's Destiny* spun away from the formation of otter vessels like a whirligig seed falling from a maple tree. This seed had a long way to fall. Jenny looked down at the creamsicle clouds, hoping they'd find some shelter there. Then she looked back at the five ISON vessels like sand dollars and the conical *Riptide*, tiny dark shadows over the stars. Not tiny enough. The red dots on her screen were still heading for them.

And then the raptor vessels were more than dots—giant armored shapes zoomed past *Brighton's Destiny*. Black behemoths blocked the stars on Jupiter's horizon. Ordol's tentacles quivered on Jenny's shoulders. She began to make a reassuring sign— then their little Whirligig Class vessel spun out of control. One of the raptor vessels had flown by too close, unaware of them, and clipped their left wing. Jenny saw the metal wing twisting, brokenly through the side window—still attached, but totally useless. Even if the thruster still worked like that, firing it would simply finish tearing off the broken wing.

They were going down.

"Holy hell," Jenny swore through her whiskers, making sure not to activate the radio. She didn't need to distract the others. Admiral Mackerel was going to have a hard enough time getting the rest of the strike force back to Europa without wasting time on a hopeless rescue mission.

"Well, I promised I'd take us on a suicide dive rather than let them catch us..." Jenny said, still speaking only to herself. For Ordol she signed, "If I find us somewhere to land or maneuver us into a stable orbit, can you fix that wing?"

"No."

Well, that was simple.

They really were going down. And they were going to keep going down. All they could do without the thruster on the broken wing was spin.

Jenny took a deep breath and signed, "Let's find out what the heart of a gas giant looks like. I'll bet you twenty clam chews it's the most beautiful thing we see for the rest of our lives." She leaned into the fall, accelerating *Brighton's Destiny* faster and faster in a downward spiral towards the swirling orange clouds.

As they grew closer, the roiling orange took on depth and texture. An entire alien landscape was rising to meet them in shades and swirls of cinnamon, peach, tangerine, and apricot. Jenny could see pinnacles and valleys, mountains and castles, as if they'd been carved out of ice cream. She could imagine landing their ship—*crashing* their ship—and then getting out to explore.

But those weren't mountains or castles. They were clouds. Immaterial vapor.

And they offered no refuge. Nowhere to land and wait for rescue. The clouds yielded to the falling Whirligig vessel like so much mist. When the atmosphere of hydrogen and helium closed around them in a roar of wind and flames, Jenny shouted, "Yeehaw!" and raised her fisted paws triumphantly.

If they were going down, it might as well be the ride of her life.

Chapter 14: Kipper

Kipper's terror threatened to swallow her whole, but that was all it could do—*threaten*. She steadied her breathing, painfully aware of the limited oxygen in the tank on her back—several hour's worth, but not enough for a lengthy incarceration in an octopus prison.

As she watched the octopi around her through her face mask, Kipper realized that they were scared too. Their tentacles were pale; their golden eyes wide. They were as much afraid of the coming raptor attack as she was. Actually... Much more.

A tabby in SCUBA gear, treading water under the ocean, entirely out of her element, was a much less threatening enemy than a fleet of raptor vessels barreling silently through the night sky. Kipper could hardly blame the octopi for scapegoating her.

Still, their fear was a tool. She needed to use it to turn the situation around on them.

"Would you rather live in fear?" Kipper signed, shifting her gaze about the room to catch as many different pairs of yellow eyes as she could. "Do you want to keep hiding forever?"

The tentacle murmurs of "pay" and "crime" continued around her, but she was done being scared by them.

She signed with strong, clear movements of her paws, shouting them down: "You say the stars are your rightful home? I've been to the stars. These otters—" She gestured at Trugger and Captain Cod, whose expressions she couldn't read through their breathing masks. "—live there in a spaceship called the *Jolly Barracuda*. I've flown with them to Mars, the asteroids, Jupiter, Europa, and back."

After a moment's hesitation, she added, "I... live there with them. Space is our home."

The tentacles around her had quieted and floated eerily still. The octopuses were unified in their stillness, but each one's flesh flushed a different color. All Kipper could think was that they were lost in a riot of different emotions, each reacting differently, individually to her words.

She had broken them apart. That was the first step with any mob. Now she needed to move them.

Kipper squared her sight on the blue-eyed octopus who had accused her. Its silver tentacle curled around it like a question mark. Stilled and waiting.

Kipper signed, "We're not going to hide on Earth, waiting to see what the raptors plan for us. Cats, dogs, and otters are going to fight for our homes—both here and amidst the stars. Join us. *Help* us."

Blue eyes with rectangular pupils narrowed, staring Kipper down. Silence and stillness ruled the room. Then the blue-eyed octopus squeezed its tentacles, including the silver one, tightly together like an intricate Celtic knot. Long moments passed before its tentacles unwound, and the octopus signed, "Brave words, little cat. Do you have the firepower to support them?"

Kipper had been hoping that the octopi had firepower to help her support them. That wasn't sounding likely.

Captain Cod signed, "The Imperial Star-Ocean Navy of the otters stands with us."

"My own country," Kipper signed, "the Uplifted States is drawing its forces together." That much was probably true. Vague but true. Alistair and Petra surely had the cats and dogs of Mericka scrambling to pull whatever defenses they could muster together. Though Mericka's decidedly backward and Earth-bound technology ensured that those forces wouldn't add up to much. "It sounds—" She faltered, realizing it would only reveal weakness to ask whether the octopi had any forces to lend to the cause.

Kipper had come to Choir's Deep envisioning missiles and rockets hidden beneath the waves, amphibious spaceships that would launch straight out of the ocean and fill the sky with defensive lasers. Clearly, those had been kitten dreams. None of that was here. The octopi might have advanced genetic technologies, but there was no hidden space armada.

What they might have, however, was information.

"It sounds like you know about the raptors," Kipper signed. "Give us information to help us fight them more effectively. Share your knowledge with us."

Again the blue-eyed octopus wrapped itself into a Celtic knot, and its tentacles turned an ashen shade of gray. Eventually, its gaze shifted from Kipper to the other octopi behind her. When its tentacles uncoiled, it signed, "Take the cat away."

Kipper shrieked, "Wait!" uselessly into the echo-chamber of her breathing mask, but by the time she pulled her thoughts together enough to remember to talk with her paws, her arms were already restrained by a mass of tentacles from behind, beside, and all around her. The room had become a writhing bowl of tentacles grasping and pulling her. She struggled, but their grips only grew tighter.

Kipper saw that Captain Cod and Trugger had been grabbed by octopi as well. Kipper got one last glaring look at the blue-eyed octopus before they were dragged into a different tunnel than they'd entered by. It was only a flash of a look, but if the octopus understood feline expressions at all, it had to know that Kipper wasn't happy.

In fact, Kipper considered it a miracle of self-restraint that she'd managed to keep her claws sheathed. The octopi might be strong, but their flesh was *soft*. She could have filled that round room with a cloud of blood before they would have—inevitably—pulled off her breathing mask. In truth, a physical fight could never go well for a cat this far under the ocean.

Kipper stopped struggling and let the octopi drag her down the malachite tunnel, waiting to see where they would take her. But only because she hadn't yet given up hope.

Chapter 15: Jenny

Jenny had no hope. Only a fluttery, heart-pounding feeling in her chest that alternated between manic exhilaration and bleakest panic. She didn't want to die panicking. So she clung hard to the feeling of excitement: she was seeing things no otter had ever seen before!

...granted... mostly those things just looked like flat orange mist blocking the window, darkening to a dull brown as her ship fell farther and farther into the crushing atmosphere...

Jenny tried not to think about words like "crushing." Instead, she watched for the brief breaks in the mist when she could see the Jovian cloudscape stretch out before her. Bolts of lightening arced between the clouds.

Jenny felt like she was falling through the levels of hell.

No. It was exciting. Science! Discovery! Death!

Ordol's tentacles squeezed tightly around Jenny's shoulders, and it felt like a hug. Jenny squeezed his tentacles back, hugging her alien companion to her. He'd been a good partner. He wasn't a bad bloke to die with.

Jenny closed her eyes, despair crushing her. There was that word again: *crushing.*

No, no, if she only had minutes left to live—perhaps thirty or so until the ship imploded from the increasing pressure or burst into flame from the soaring temperatures—she couldn't close her eyes.

She opened them again and saw shadows moving among the clouds, shapes that looked almost like balloons or blimps. Were they raptor ships? Lifeforms native to Jupiter's cloudscape? Hallucinations in the mind of a scared otter?

Jenny stared intently at the clouds, and she thought for sure the blimp-shapes had trailing fronds, like they were some form of gigantic Jovian jellyfish. The idea felt soothing. She was falling into an ocean. And it was growing darker and darker as they fell.

Jenny began to think about what would be the most comfortable way to die. It was a subject she'd never thought about before. She hadn't done any research. But she figured that she'd be better off fiddling with her spacesuit's air supply to see if she could put herself to asleep than waiting for the darkness outside to finally— and violently—mangle *Brighton's Destiny* around her.

Though she didn't relish either option.

Before Jenny could bring herself to mess with the very air she was breathing, she realized that the clouds outside were growing light again. At first, she thought it was a trick of the mind—an excuse to avoid taking responsibility for her inevitable death.

But as the minutes passed, the darkness lifted.

It didn't matter. Dark or bright, the end would be violent, horrible.

Jenny was about to turn down her oxygen level, when a burst of tingles, like static electricity, passed through her entire body.

And the clouds cleared.

What had happened? This couldn't be right: Jenny saw a planet before them, silhouetted against a softly glowing, pale yellow sky. For a moment, Jenny thought she was looking at Earth—her home world, flashing before her eyes as she died.

But no, this world was really here inside the heart of Jupiter. A planet within a planet. And they were plummeting toward it.

As Jenny's eyes adjusted to the yellow glow that was above and all around, she could make out clouds spread like white lace across the planet beneath her. A diadem of emerald isles crowned a face of blue under the veil of white lace. It was perfect and beautiful.

And rushing toward *Brighton's Destiny* much too fast.

"We need to slow down," she signed, praying that Ordol was still conscious and had some ideas. "We're going to crash."

Ordol's tentacles stirred. Jenny could feel him shifting his weight on her shoulders, and then he signed in her field of vision, "You want to land? *Down there?*"

"That's the idea," Jenny signed, looking for some sign that *Brighton's Destiny* had an emergency parachute system or something. "You know, so we don't *die.*"

Ordol's tentacles rolled up like fern fronds in tightly furled fiddleheads. He wasn't going to remind Jenny that she'd promised they'd die rather than be captured. He didn't have to. She remembered. But they weren't being pursued, and they had an entire planet laid out before them. There must be somewhere they could land and hide.

And Jenny didn't want to die.

Fortunately, their Whirligig Class vessel agreed with her. It didn't have an emergency parachute system, but it did have an auto-pilot guided landing system powered by micro-thrusters. As soon as the ship's sensors detected their imminent crash landing, the vessel itself took measures to survive. *Brighton's Destiny* shielded itself with a force field, oriented itself for high wind drag and optimal crash positioning, and deployed internal cushioning mechanisms to protect its piloting team.

Bubblegum pink and squishy, a viscous fluid squirted out of nozzles and encased the two pilots like they were airmail packages wrapped up in so much bubble wrap inside the cockpit. Jenny watched their final approach through a filmy pink glaze.

Pink islands expanded, revealing pink mountains, valleys, and even the pink grids and lines of cityscapes, all of them spinning furiously around as the Whirligig class vessel spun downwards. Jenny muttered under her whiskers, pleading with whatever Programmer God had designed her ship's auto-pilot that they not land in the middle of a city. She couldn't keep her promise to Ordol as easily in a city with raptors everywhere.

Her prayers were answered as *Brighton's Destiny* veered away toward a pink coastline. The auto-pilot was probably designed to avoid areas of dense population for the safety of the cities' inhabitants, but Jenny was profoundly grateful to her ship, even if it was trying to spare the lives of her enemies rather than to aid her in avoiding falling into their feathered talons.

The ground rushed upward, spinning, and the thin line of pink beach between the purple ocean and burgundy land widened into a ribbon and finally to an actual tract of land. *Oh starfish.* Jenny squeezed her eyes shut as the reality struck her: the crash was only moments away.

The bouncing, spinning, wobbling wind turbulence of plummeting abruptly broke and was replaced by the rebounding whiplash of...

...blacking out...

When Jenny opened her eyes next, she was still dizzy, and every part of her otter body ached. She didn't know if it had been seconds or minutes. Or longer. But what the hell? Why was everything... pink? Had all the blood vessels in her eyeballs ruptured? Was that a thing? Or... *horrific thought...* had Ordol somehow exploded all over everything?

Jenny tried to reach her paws up to her face, but her spacesuit gloves and helmet got in the way and the viscous cushioning gel dragged on her every move. Oh, that's right. Jenny remembered the nozzles, shooting cushioning gel at her.

The pinkness all around her was probably the only reason she was still alive. Thank the heavens for *pink!*

No matter how much Jenny owed to the pink goo embracing her, she was still glad when *Brighton's Destiny* ka-thunked and the nozzles began sucking the cushioning gel back up with a slurping sound loud enough to hear through her space helmet. *Nice mechanism*, Jenny thought. She had become quite fond of this little ship. She supposed she'd be fond of anything that had just saved her life.

"I sure hope we can fix you," Jenny said, voice raw. Had she been screaming as they crashed? She didn't remember, but her throat sure felt like she had.

The pink goo drained away, restoring the world to its real colors—which no otter had ever seen before. Jenny looked on the heart of Jupiter from inside her mangled little ship, and she felt like she'd fallen into an alternate reality.

The sky was overcast, pale yellow light shining behind streaks and banks of amber clouds. The sand on the beach was gunmetal gray with sparkles of silver, and the ocean was such a deep blue it was nearly green.

How could those amber clouds be the other side of Jupiter's swirling bands of orange? There wasn't supposed to be another side—just noxious gas, thicker and thicker, darker and darker, down, down, down.

Yet, here she was.

The heart of Jupiter. *Cor-Jovis*—that's what she'd call it.

Strange and bizarre as her situation might be, Jenny still had to face practical matters. With the pink goo drained down to mere puddles under her boots, she was able to move again, but when she did, her arms and long back ached. Also, she realized that the side of the ship's cockpit was much too close on the left... and... buckling at a strange angle on her right. She pressed the controls to open the hatch, and it *chucka-chucka-whirred* a few times, managing to open only a crack, before giving up.

She'd have to force the hatch open manually. Ordol was strong and might be a big help with that, but... where had he gone?

Jenny realized with a start that his tentacles were no longer wrapped around her. She remembered back to her insane fear that he'd exploded and flirted with it again. Then she saw the tentacles squished into the corner of the cockpit behind her feet.

Octopi always looked weird and squishy, so Jenny wasn't sure if she should be worried. She reached a gloved paw down, gingerly, to touch him.

No response.

She squeezed one of his tentacles lightly.

He stirred. Briefly. At least, that meant he was alive. It didn't look like he planned on being conscious any time soon. Jenny would need to figure out a way to force the ship's hatch open without him, so she could start assessing the damage.

She leaned out of her seat, twisting her long spine until she could press her paws against the hatch. It was difficult enough to maneuver in such a small space before it had been deformed by the crash. Now she felt like she was performing some exotic new form of acrobatics. Except the extreme version, where her life depended on them.

She did *not* want to die trapped in a broken spaceship, only inches from an alien beach on a planet that no otter had even known existed until she crashed on it. No. *She wanted to explore that beach.*

And repair her spaceship.

And get the hell out of here before any raptors found her and took Ordol back to his life of enslavement that she'd *promised* to keep him safe from.

Scratch, scruffle, skree-each—the sound of talons, scrambling against *Brighton's Destiny's* contorted metal hull. With horror, Jenny realized it was already too late. Raptors had found them. She could feel the hatch rumble and vibrate under her suited paws, and then she saw orange eyes stare through the crack where the hatch had tried to open.

The eyes were round and wide, but they glared from under a severe brow of speckled brown feathers. Their gaze felt heavy, and Jenny's breath caught in her throat, freezing her like a mouse under the appraising, murderous stare of a bird of prey.

The eyes disappeared and were replaced by feathered talons, prying and straining at the hatch. Another pair joined, and then another. There were at least three raptors out there.

Suddenly, Jenny felt like *Brighton's Destiny* was a sardine can, and she was the tasty snack inside that those raptors wanted to spread on crackers.

If she was going to be a snack, then she'd at least give the raptors food poisoning. Jenny reached for the thruster controls. She could see the thruster on the left wing through the ship's windows; it was twisted around so badly that its exhaust was aimed right at the hatch of the ship. Firing it now would blast away the raptors scrabbling to get in.

It would also further damage the ship, and possibly fry Jenny and Ordol as well. Given the contorted shape of the hull, Jenny knew she couldn't assume it would offer its usual protection from sudden, extreme heat.

At least then, Jenny supposed, she would have kept her promise to Ordol, not to let him fall into raptor talons again. She was ready to press the button, when suddenly the scrabbling feathered talons disappeared.

After an eerie moment of silence, Jenny clambered up to stand on her seat so that she could get a higher angle for looking out of the side window. From that angle, she could see the owners of the orange eyes and talons bobbing up the beach, toward the scruffy shrubs at the edge of the sand.

They weren't what she expected.

From Kipper's description, she'd expected jet black shiny feathers on towering beasts, several times her height with angular heads and limbs—not to mention colorful plumes on their elbows and the back of their heads.

These raptors were shaped right, but they looked to be about Jenny's size. Their feathers were neither dark nor colorful. Nothing so striking. They were muted even—soft and speckled, colored in downy shades of brown and white.

Then Jenny realized: she was looking at fledglings. These were raptor children, not fully grown.

As she watched the three fledglings, she found her fear of them receding. They bobbed along the beach, for all the world like any children, searching for shells or driftwood. Of course, when they found long pieces of driftwood and began bobbing back her way,

Jenny saw that their talons, gripping the driftwood looked terribly sharp, and their narrow feathered muzzles housed fearsome teeth.

They might be young, but they had the powerful bodies of birds of prey. Yet, those bodies were not saddled with the electronic collars containing the neuro-tech necessary to hijack Ordol's nervous system. His fear of raptors didn't concern their claws or teeth. These young raptors could kill him, but they couldn't enslave his nervous system to their own, turning his tentacles into *their* tentacles. A fate worse than death. Or so Ordol seemed to believe.

Jenny wouldn't be breaking her promise to keep him safe, as long as she kept him away from adult raptors. Or so she rationalized.

Basically, she'd rather bet on life.

When the young raptors wedged their driftwood levers into the narrow opening of the hatchway, Jenny leaned her weight against them, helping to pry the door open.

Chapter 16: Jenny

The cockpit of *Brighton's Destiny* popped open with a hiss like a tin can of sparkling clam juice. Jenny overbalanced and tumbled out of the hatch, tangling herself in feathered limbs on her way down to plop on the damp silver sand.

The wet sand smeared across the faceplate of Jenny's helmet, obscuring her view of the raptor fledglings as they righted her and began manhandling her spacesuit-clad limbs, moving her around like a poseable doll. Their screeches and chirrups terrified Jenny at first—they sounded like they were screaming at her. But as they jostled her around, examining their new toy from every angle, Jenny pulled herself together enough to remember that the computer in her helmet had some basic sound processing and AI algorithms. Captain Cod had installed them in all the spacesuits, thinking they might be useful for spy activities. They hadn't been. But it might be able to analyze the raptor speech and develop a translation—at least, if it listened to them long enough.

"Computer, record exterior sounds," Jenny said. "Search for patterns; try to parse for language." It was a long shot, but it sure would help to be able to talk to these little birds of prey. Big birds of prey. They might be small compared to the raptors Kipper had described, but they were plenty big enough. Jenny hoped the raptor chicks would want to keep her a secret from any adults. She didn't need any raptors bigger than these around. Especially if Ordol came to.

Jenny was going to need Ordol's help to repair *Brighton's Destiny*, and that meant she couldn't have him dying of fright as soon as he woke up. She needed to get these big baby bird-lizards who were man-handling her under control before he saw them.

Step one: get their talons off of her. That would be easy if she weren't wearing a clunky spacesuit, and the gravity weren't making her feel so damn heavy. Otters are usually quite good at slipping away. Instead, Jenny had to settle for turning on the external speakers on her helmet and saying, "Hey! Put me down you feathered fools!"

The raptor chicks may not have understood, but their orange eyes looked startled. One of them, with feathers colored like tree-bark, took its talons off of Jenny's space-suited arm and stepped away. Its long, feathered tail swished behind it.

The other two watched the first with their talons still gripping Jenny's arm and one of her legs. Emboldened by the first raptor's response, though, Jenny shook herself free. She wobbled to her feet, struggling against the unfamiliar gravity. It was probably similar to Earth's gravity, but lately, she was used to the light gravity on Europa. Finally, she found her footing.

"That's better," Jenny said, backing away from the raptors. With frustration, she realized she was also backing away from the refuge of her spaceship and toward the lapping waves of the green ocean.

The three little raptors screeched and clucked at her, sounding like angry chickens. Jenny didn't know if they *were* angry, or they just *sounded* angry. Either way, it was distressing and disconcerting.

The raptor with feathers like tree-bark stepped toward her. It was wearing simple, green clothing over its torso and legs. The other two raptors had lighter feathers—one of them had a downy white patch on its forehead and wore dark blue clothing; the other was a mottled tawny hue, like Earth sand, and wore shades of gray. Jenny decided to think of them as Tree Bark, White Patch, and Sandy.

Jenny held her space-suited paws up, palms open, trying to gesture for them to give her space. Meanwhile, she continued backing away until she felt her boot splash against the edge of a lapping wave. She couldn't back up much farther. Fortunately, the raptors had stopped following her and instead stood staring at her with orange eyes, heads tilted.

Jenny pointed at the ship and then herself. After a beat, she pointed at the raptors and gestured to her side, away from herself and the ship. They seemed to understand and backed away from both her and *Brighton's Destiny*.

"That's better," Jenny said.

The raptors looked at each other when she spoke. Jenny wondered what her words sounded like to them. Then Tree Bark screeched at her. The computer in her helmet still had no translation. It would take a lot of data for it to get anything. She needed to keep them talking.

So as Jenny approached *Brighton's Destiny* again—carefully keeping her body turned towards the raptors; she didn't feel safe turning her back to them—she told them about everything she was doing, hoping it would inspire them to talk back.

"I'm going to approach my spaceship now. It's broken, and I need to fix it. I need to figure out how bad the break is... whether I can fix it..." Jenny passed the open hatchway and walked along the length of the wing to where the metal was torn and bent, the end of the wing dangling down at a dastardly angle. "It's bad," Jenny said, reaching a paw up toward the break. The ship had settled at such an angle on the beach that the broken metal hovered just above Jenny's head. Where the wing should have risen straight outward, reaching at an even slope toward the sky, it bent downward at a nearly right angle, burying the end of the wingtip, with its thruster, into the sand. "Very bad."

The raptors chirruped and squawked at each other. Either Jenny was getting used to their screechy voices, or they actually sounded less angry. She watched them closely during their interchange, wondering whether her helmet computer would ever be able to tell her what they were saying. Eventually, White Patch bobbed its head, turned, and darted off inland.

If White Patch was going to get their parents, then Jenny didn't have much time.

Maybe she could hide *Brighton's Destiny*...

Jenny looked at the scrub brushes along the shore line—they were like the tops of palm trees, sticking out of the silver sand, all spiky. No shelter there. But maybe, if she could reseal the hatch, it would be possible to push *Brighton's Destiny* into the waves and hide it under the surf.

Of course, that would require distracting Tree Bark and Sandy who were still staring at her quizzically. She'd also need to figure out a way to shove a five-ton spaceship over fifty feet of sand.

Yeah, this was a bad plan.

What she needed was an invisibility shield.

Or to not be deep inside the heart of Jupiter with a broken spaceship and a deathly-scared, unconscious co-pilot who knew way more about their spaceship than she did.

For that matter, these young raptors might know more about a Whirligig Class vessel than Jenny did. At any rate, they knew more about how to drag it across the sand: White Patch returned to the beach astride a long-necked, wrinkle-skinned, camo-colored quadruped, stomping like its legs were tree trunks. It looked like a small brontosaur. Wearing a saddle and bridle. And White Patch was swinging a rope with a hook on the end like some sort of dinosaur cowboy. All White Patch needed to complete the image was a ten-gallon hat on its feathered, avian head.

To hell with her promise—this was far too interesting to do anything other than go along for the ride.

Jenny watched Tree Bark take the end of White Patch's rope and loop it around her spaceship's broken wing. Tree Bark secured one end of the rope with the hook; White Patch secured the other end by tying it to the mini-brontosaur's saddle. Then White Patch pulled the reigns and turned the brontosaur back toward inland.

Brighton's Destiny might have weighed five tons, but the little brontosaur was strong. Dragged behind the prehistoric workhorse, *Brighton's Destiny* scuffed its way across the sand, smashed through the scrubby bushes, and left a skid track of torn grass and scraped dirt all the way across a field.

Jenny watched in awe, following slowly behind. She tried to keep some space between her and Tree Bark and Sandy, but she could tell it was an illusion. The raptors were her size and built for running. And they didn't have cumbersome spacesuits on. The two of them were clearly herding her along with them, unwilling to lose part of the treasure they'd found on the beach.

They had the spaceship; they needed to keep the accessory-spaceman with it.

White Patch and the brontosaur pulled *Brighton's Destiny* all the way through a field where a herd of huge duck-billed, hunch-backed hadrosaurs grazed on spikey grasses. One of the hadrosaurs lifted its head and leaned back into an upright position to watch Jenny pass by. It towered over her, chewing contemplatively as its glassy eyes watched the strange procession through its field.

Were these the dinosaur version of cows? Jenny wondered.

On the far side of the field, White Patch navigated both the brontosaur-steed and spaceship-in-tow through a stand of pine trees. Tiny knee-high protoceratops with horned noses and crested heads scurried about beneath the trees, but they didn't move like wild animals, disappearing at the commotion. No, they scattered, flocked, regrouped, and watched with beady eyes. Several of them followed after White Patch on the brontosaur or approached Tree Bark and Sandy, almost as if they were hoping for treats.

Feeling giddy, Jenny wondered if these were the dinosaur version of chickens. Otters didn't keep cows or chickens, but Jenny knew enough about ancient human and modern canine practices to recognize the similarity to how the hadrosaurs and protoceratops were behaving.

There was an entire pre-historic ecosystem here. Except, it wasn't pre-historic. She hadn't travelled through time. This was all happening right now in the modern space age. On Jupiter. Inside Jupiter.

It was a modern Jovian eco-system. It just happened to involve dinosaurs.

The modern, space-age quality of the current era struck home with the next sight: a structure between the trees that looked like a mechanical giant redwood tree, looming upward from a round base and gleaming of brassy metal, textured like bark, with occasional outstretched branches. It was an impressive, futuristic structure even by otter standards.

As White Patch approached the mechanical redwood, a cavernous sliding door opened at its base. Lights flickered on inside, illuminating a room filled with a disarray of foreign looking tools and equipment. It looked like a very large garage workshop, and it had enough space in the middle for White Patch to ride the brontosaur all the way in, drag *Brighton's Destiny* all the way in as well, and then maneuver around until the brontosaur was back on the side of the room with the door.

White Patch unhooked the rope tied to *Brighton's Destiny*, dismounted the brontosaur, and then offered the lumbering beast a talon-full of blue grasses. The brontosaur huffed happily and arched its long neck down until it could chomp up the grasses.

Next the three raptors screeched at each other for a while, presumably working out their plans for their new treasure. The brontosaur was unfazed by their screeching, but Jenny felt like cowering in a corner, under one of the work tables. If juvenile raptors with downy fuzz and funny fawn-like speckling could be this scary, she could see why Ordol, Kipper, and Trugger all claimed the adults were downright terrifying.

Still, Jenny reminded herself, she was wearing a spacesuit that would give her significant protection if they attacked her.

Suddenly, the screeching stopped. White Patch grabbed a computerized tablet from a work bench and shoved it into Sandy's talons before taking the brontosaur by the reigns and leading it outside. Tree Bark began examining the broken, bent wing of *Brighton's Destiny*, and Jenny felt a well of possessive, protectiveness inside her. Before she could step forward to put herself between the juvenile raptor and her ship—her only way out of this planet and back home—Sandy scribbled something on the computerized tablet and held it out for Jenny to see.

On the glossy tablet screen, Jenny saw a sketchy rendering of *Brighton's Destiny* with its broken wing. Once Sandy saw that Jenny's attention was on the screen, the raptor scribbled another picture next to it—an unbroken Whirligig Class vessel—with an arrow-like symbol between them. Sandy squawked and then gestured with a free talon at Tree Bark and *Brighton's Destiny*.

"You're going to fix my vessel?" Jenny asked. Her own voice sounded small, high-pitched, and reedy next to the raptors' screeches.

Sandy squawked again, and this time, the computer in Jenny's helmet translated the sound, speaking in a melodic but artificial otter voice: "Yes." A moment later, the computer added, "There is an eighty percent chance of inaccuracy. Other possible translations include: no."

Jenny would have laughed, but she didn't think she'd be able to stop. Ever. She would laugh herself to death if she let herself see the humor in her situation. So instead, she set her jaw and did her best Admiral Mackerel impression—it was time to be a very serious otter.

"Yes," she repeated and heard the computer translate through her external speakers into the same squawk Sandy had made a moment ago. At least, whether that squawk meant 'yes' or 'no,'" Jenny was agreeing with the raptor. To make her feelings as clear as possible—which probably wasn't clear at all—Jenny pointed at the picture, Tree Bark, and then *Brighton's Destiny* like Sandy had a moment ago.

Apparently, the sound of a raptor-squawk coming from the spaceman's helmet was *very* interesting, because suddenly Jenny had three raptors staring closely at her with their glaring orange eyes. She had no idea how they'd all surrounded her so fast, but the suddenness of their closeness made her mammal heart race.

"Wait, stop—" Jenny said as the raptors poked and pushed at her. Talons traced along the seams of her suit. Orange eyes stared her down. Jenny's ears filled with a cacophony of voices as the raptors screeched at her, and the helmet computer doubled everything by translating Jenny's own words into more screeching and the raptors' words into confusing, stilted sentences surrounded by computer disclaimers of uncertainty and even more confusing alternate translations like, "Green is now! Five before under. What want fortitude?"

If that was what Jenny was hearing, what nonsense was the computer translating her own words into for the raptors?

In spite of all the confusion—or perhaps because of it—the raptors and Jenny somehow came to a vague understanding: the raptors would back off, giving Jenny more space. In turn, Jenny would get something off of the ship before leaving it for Tree Bark to fix.

The *something* that Jenny needed to get off of the ship was Ordol. She couldn't leave him alone, and—if she understood correctly, which was anyone's guess—White Patch and Sandy planned to take her up to a higher level of the mechanical redwood structure while Tree Bark worked on her broken ship.

Jenny climbed back into *Brighton's Destiny* and gathered up Ordol into her arms. His unconscious mass of space-suited tentacles was unwieldy, like trying to carry a... No, it wasn't *like* trying to carry anything. It *was* carrying an unconscious octopus. And that is quite enough.

With her precious, awkward bundle trying continually to slide out of her arms, Jenny backed out of the spaceship and left it for Tree Bark. She followed White Patch and Sandy out of the cavernous work space. They led her around the outside of the mechanical redwood to the other side where a much smaller door slid open.

The room inside was small, and when the door slid shut behind White Patch, Sandy, and Jenny, it was transparent. It hadn't been transparent from the outside, and Jenny realized it must be the same material Kipper had told her about from the raptor mothership, high up in Jupiter's atmosphere. Opaque on one side; transparent on the other.

Without any sound to warn Jenny, the small room began to rise, quite quickly. The forest floor fell away, and Jenny watched tree branches pass by outside the transparent doorway until they'd risen higher than the treetops.

Then she looked out at the Jovian sky—roiling orange and glowing gold. The raptors on either side of her with their downy feathers and orange eyes that mirrored the orange sky looked like they belonged here. This was their home. Whether or not they'd originally emigrated from Earth millions of years ago, they belonged here now.

Jenny, however, had never felt farther away from home.

Chapter 17: Petra

Petra could have walked home—if it weren't for the locked doors, and the iron bars, and dogs with guns. She might as well have been on Jupiter for all the certainty she felt that she'd be going home again. She knew about cats getting arrested and disappearing. That's something cats did. Disappear. Somehow, whenever a dog went missing, the police always found a way to discover what had happened. That wasn't the case with cats. Sometimes, you just didn't get to know. Sometimes, the case was closed, and the cat never showed up.

Petra told herself that wouldn't happen to her. She was the president's sister. She was high profile. There'd be questions if she disappeared. Questions and riots and violence.

She would get to go home. And hug her kittens without police dogs watching.

Eventually.

Still, Petra felt better when one of the big bearded police dogs dragged in a black-and-white tomcat and dumped him in the cell with her. "You get a room mate, Sissy-Cat." The bearded dog seemed to think she'd be affronted by the idea of sharing her cell, losing her privacy. But Petra didn't have privacy—she had a lack of witnesses if the police dogs decided to do anything to her.

If they were giving her a cellmate, that meant they wouldn't do anything to her that they didn't want anyone to witness. It wasn't much, but it made Petra feel a little safer.

The bearded dog slammed the cell shut behind the tomcat, fixed a withering glare on Petra through the bars, and then sauntered away, tail slowly wagging. *How dare his tail wag.*

Petra and her cellmate eyed each other warily: two cats sizing each other up.

The tomcat was wearing the crispest, blackest, most nicely-tailored suit Petra had ever seen. It screamed, "Expensive!" while perfectly flattering his own tuxedo fur markings. Petra was still wearing the same casual tunic and pants she'd been arrested in—rumpled from two days of wear, sporting milk-stains from the kittens' antics. Petra didn't care much for feeling underdressed while in a jail cell, so she tried to take malicious glee in imagining how uncomfortable the tom's suit would be after he'd been in the cell a few days.

Petra was too tired to feel malicious glee.

She shouldn't be here. She should be in the White House, tracking down the missing money from the budget, doing *something* to help Kipper and Alistair save the world. That money had to lead somewhere. It had been spent on something, and if it was a secret arsenal of weapons, it could make the difference in a fight against the raptors.

"You're the president's sister," the tomcat said. "We should talk about catnip law reform."

Petra rolled her eyes. "I guess I don't have to ask what you're in for. And this is *not* an opportunity for political gain."

The tomcat settled lazily on one of the uncomfortable, spartan benches that jutted out from the cell's walls. The end of his tail swished, and his whiskers twitched like he was trying to hide a smile. "You'd rather be bored? I have forty-eight hours before they have to release me, and there's no telling how long you'll be in for—or how soon you'll get another cellmate to talk to."

Catnip laws were a mess of inconsistencies. The pungent weed was legal in some cities and counties; illegal in others. Worse, some of those cities and counties overlapped, meaning there were huge swathes of the Uplifted States where catnip was both legal and illegal. Usually, that meant cats got arrested for buying, selling, owning, and using—but the charges rarely held, since most cats used catnip at some time or another.

Dealers got used to spending the occasional night in jail. This tomcat was clearly a dealer.

"Fine," Petra sighed. "You can give me your spiel, but it'll be a waste of breath."

The tom skewed an ear. "What? You're some kind of puritan who's never tried catnip?"

Petra snorted. "Hardly. Are there cats who've never tried catnip?"

The tom shrugged. "So I'm told. But if I'm preaching to the choir, what's the deal? We finally have a cat president, so why am I in jail for selling some dried leaves that every poll shows ninety percent of cats agree should be legal?"

"Why am *I* in jail?" Petra shot back scathingly.

Cool as only a tuxedo cat can be, the tom said, "According to the papers, you're in for assaulting a cop."

Petra couldn't even respond. She hadn't touched that dog. And it didn't matter.

Her whiskers turned down, and her ears splayed just a little. In spite of her colorful orange stripes, her face looked as bleak as if all the color had drained from the world.

"Hey, hey," the tom said cajolingly, reassuringly. "I didn't say I believed the papers."

As if it were a confession of guilt—a huge confession—Petra admitted, so quietly the tom could hardly hear her, "I hissed at the cop."

The tom grimaced.

Some dogs didn't seem to be able to tell the difference between a cat clawing them in the face and a cat merely hissing. Cats are supposed to stay calm. Ideally, they should be purring, just to show how calm and content they are. *No trouble here, sir! No, sir, I'm so happy I'm purring!*

Every cat knew that. Petra knew that. But Petra had never been good at purring.

Finally, Petra pulled herself together enough to bring the conversation back to catnip laws—anything was better than talking about her situation. "The first feline president can't waste his power on *catnip*. You must know that. It would make him a joke." Her voice sounded tired, weary to her heart. "It would waste whatever limited power he has."

Mere days ago, Petra had believed her brother had power. She wasn't sure anymore. The weight of momentum in their society was so heavy, it would take more than a single president to shift it.

Well, to hell with it all, maybe the raptors would pulverize them all to dust. Then everyone would be equal.

Except, Petra couldn't really wish that. Not with three kittens at home. Sometimes, she regretted adopting them. She regretted letting herself care deeply enough for anyone to bind herself to this messed up world.

The tomcat must have read Petra's despondency in her posture, because he said, "You can't let those cops get to you like this." The green eyes on either side of his white-splished nose searched Petra's face, as if looking for a sign that she wouldn't suddenly crumble in front of him. "It's only jail."

"It's inequity," she snapped back. "It's injustice. It's everything that's wrong with the world."

"Well, that's not fair," the tom said wryly. "The Blue Sox beat the Yellow Sneakers last season. That's pretty wrong."

Petra's ears splayed at the tom's complete and purposeful non-sequitur. But after several moments of bafflement, she followed his lead out of the dark well of despair she was teetering next to and meekly said, "You follow scramball?"

"Like a religion," the tom said. He held out a paw. It was mostly black until the very tip, as if he'd dipped his paw in milk. "My name's Blaine. Nice to meet you."

Petra didn't reciprocate by offering her name. He already knew it. But she did get up and shake his paw.

Blaine told Petra about the Blue Sox and the Yellow Sneakers for a while. The Blue Sox were mostly boxers and other pug-faced dogs; their best player was a brindle-coated French bulldog, small but powerful. Blaine rooted for the Yellow Sneakers, a team of yellow labs and Golden Retrievers.

"Sometimes, I get a group of cats together to play scramball, you know," Blaine said.

"I have trouble picturing that," Petra said. Though she knew Kipper had played scramball once, most cats didn't seem to care much for the rough-and-tumble physicality of the game.

"We all take a low dose of catnip—enough to loosen everyone up, but not enough to mess up our faculties. Then we launch right in—it's a lot of fun. A couple of Chihuahuas actually started it up. They like playing with cats better, 'cause we're closer in size to them than most pro-scramball players."

"Big dogs," Petra observed.

"Yeah," Blaine agreed. "Though, that brindle-bull on the Blue Sox is how they upset the natural order of things and won last season. Sometimes, a small dog can sneak through where a big dog would be blocked."

Petra's glaze-eyed nod let Blaine know he'd finally lost her.

"I could talk about scramball forever," Blaine said. "But let's hear about you. What's that sister of yours up to?"

Of course, he didn't really want to hear about Petra. He wanted a direct line to the president's ear or the latest gossip on the Hero of Europa. Still... Petra didn't really want to think about herself. It wouldn't be so bad talking about her sister. "Kipper's gone under the ocean to talk to the octopuses..."

Chapter 18: Kipper

Except, Kipper wasn't talking to octopuses. Kipper, Trugger, and Captain Cod had been shut in a small room with several feet of air at the ceiling and a ledge around the edges. Sitting on the ledge felt like sitting at the edge of a public swimming pool, reminding her of cattery days when over-enthusiastic dogs had required all the reluctant kittens to take swimming lessons. Except this was more claustrophobic due to the low ceiling and near walls.

After an hour or so, they'd taken their breathing gear off. The air smelled strongly of salt and felt heavy with humidity in Kipper's lungs. Every sound echoed, and the ceiling would not stop dripping. Moisture clung to the smooth, curved, abalone-like walls, and the movement of the water cast weird, fluttering reflections of the glowing light that came from panels in the ceiling. Kipper hated it.

Trugger and Captain Cod were having the time of their lives.

The octopuses hadn't come back through the sealed hatch in the underwater floor, but occasionally they sent in a dolphin with a puzzle for them. Kipper wondered if the dolphins had been genetically engineered in any way, or even uplifted, but she couldn't tell from their minimal interactions as they delivered the puzzles. Dolphins had always been a naturally smart species anyway. At least, as Kipper understood it. But Kipper had misunderstood a lot of things.

The puzzles ranged widely in style—geometrically locked boxes, computer pads with recurring patterns that looked like abstract video games, a speaker that played whale songs until Trugger and Captain Cod sang along in harmony.

Trugger believed the octopi were thoughtfully providing entertainment for their guests. Captain Cod thought the octopi were testing them, and solving all the puzzles, passing all the tests would prove them worthy; only then would the octopi let them out.

Kipper thought it was all a waste of time. Whatever the octopi were doing, she wanted no part of it. So she sat on the ledge, fur plastered to her body from humidity and the carelessly-splashy dolphins. Her ears flattened yet were unable to block out the echoes.

Chapter 19: Jenny

While Kipper and Petra waited in their prisons—two tabby cats desperate to save Earth yet incarcerated by their own allies—Jenny parleyed with the enemy.

That was generous.

The otter wasn't parleying with the enemy, she was playing games with the enemies' children

Jenny and the two raptor chicks were in a room at the top of the giant mechanical redwood, and the walls were as clear as glass. Jenny had seen the tree from the outside and knew it looked opaque, but from the inside it looked like she was standing on an open platform. She could see out over the jagged green tops of all the real trees. In the distance, more of these mechanical trees stuck out of the forest like towers—much taller and larger around than the real trees. And behind it all, loomed the ruddy agate Jovian sky.

In the back of her mind, Jenny knew she should be looking for information, weaknesses, a way to capture these fledglings and turn them into hostages that would force the entire raptor civilization in Jupiter to leave Earth alone.

Yeah, none of that was going to happen. She'd be lucky if they repaired her spaceship and she was able to escape without being handed over to their parents to be dissected or held hostage herself.

So, Jenny found ways to entertain the fuzzy fledglings, White Patch and Sandy, while their nest-mate, Tree Bark, repaired *Brighton's Destiny*. Jenny assumed they were nest-mates, since they were all about the same size and seemed to live in the same giant mechanical tree.

For a while, Jenny played the point-at-things-and-say-what-they-are game. Her helmet was still uneven with its translations, and she figured the game would help it along. After a while, though, Jenny was sick of wearing her clunky spacesuit, and she knew from its internal sensors that the atmosphere was safe. She decided to take it off.

Jenny unlatched the helmet and removed it. Sandy and White Patch were delighted by the sight of Jenny's fuzzy, brown head with whiskers and round ears. They bobbed their own feathered heads and made a trilling sound that the helmet didn't translate. Jenny thought it might be laughter, but it still set her on edge.

Jenny set down her helmet on a plush ledge next to where she'd arranged the still-unconscious Ordol. She turned the volume up high, so the helmet would work like a speaker and keep translating. Then Jenny stripped off the rest of her spacesuit, leaving her in the tank top and shorts underneath. It was much more comfortable, and it caused another round of high-pitched warbling trills from Sandy and White Patch.

Then, terrifyingly, the raptor fledglings approached her, talons out. Jenny started to back away, but there was nowhere to go. She was in their home at the top of an elevator up a mechanical tree. Jenny closed her eyes, unable to face those terribly sharp talons.

The alien world around Jenny disappeared behind the darkness of her eyelids. If she could have shrunk down the universe to become only the space within her own thick pelt, Jenny would have.

It tickled when the talons traced through her fur.

That's all they did, trace patterns in the fur on Jenny's arms and shoulders.

Jenny wondered if these raptors had ever encountered a mammal before. Their species had probably left Earth before mammals had even evolved.

One of the raptors screeched, and the helmet translated, "Soft bristles! Funny!" Then the computer voice added, "*Possible alternate translations include:* 'Limp needles! Tasty!' *and* 'Broken pinions! Flightless!'"

Jenny was okay with two of those translations. She was indeed flightless, and didn't mind being thought of as funny.

Jenny opened her eyes to find both raptors' staring at her with their fierce orange eyes. They were still stroking her, gently, with their dangerously sharp claws. She felt like a fancy, exotic pet.

Of course, Ordol chose that moment to open his eyes. Jenny didn't notice his eyes open, but she couldn't possibly miss the eight muscular tentacles that began flailing wildly, shoving themselves backwards into the clear window-wall with a series of *smacks*. The spacesuit he wore didn't have the sensitivity and strength of his actual sucker disks contained inside, but it must have employed a related technology, because Ordol managed to clamber several feet up the window.

"They're babies," Jenny signed, knowing it was an exaggeration meant to soothe Ordol. These fledgling raptors might have fuzzy baby feathers, but they'd shown no sign in their behavior of being anything but fully functioning adults. "They haven't done anything to hurt us—they're helping fix *Brighton's Destiny*."

Sandy and White Patch watched Jenny's rapidly moving paws closely. Then the two raptors looked at each other and waved their talons about meaninglessly, wiggling their long claws, as if they were trying to mimic Jenny's carefully articulated signs. It was no surprise to Jenny that they didn't know Swimmer's Sign. To them, it would be a slave language at best. More likely, they knew nothing of it at all.

When the raptor fledglings finished waving their talons, they trilled in laughter, an ear-splitting sound that made Jenny's fur raise, but Ordol didn't react at all, deaf to sound.

Ordol watched the raptors closely.

Letting go of the window with three tentacle tips, Ordol signed, "You promised."

"Would you rather be dead?" Jenny signed back.

"Maybe," Ordol answered, his tentacles flushed as white as death. He tried to scooch higher on the window, but gravity pulled hard against him without water for buoyancy. Hanging against the panorama of orange sky like an eldritch ivory pendant, Ordol did look like he was in his own personal hell.

Jenny said aloud for the raptors, "Stay back; you'll scare him." She hoped the translation came through clearly, and the raptors would obey. Then she stepped toward Ordol and signed, "Come down," as gently as she could before holding her paws out, offering to take him into her arms. "I'll protect you."

Standing between fiercely taloned pre-historic raptors and a creature built of pure wrestling muscle, Jenny hardly felt qualified to offer protection. But she could offer confidence and comfort.

Ordol had few options, clinging to a window on the home world of the raptors. He'd have to take what he could get—even if it was insane optimism from a small golden-brown furred mammal, barely as large as the juvenile raptors eyeing her. So, Ordol reached out and let Jenny draw him down from the window and into her arms. From there, he arranged himself onto her shoulders, returning to the position they used to pilot *Brighton's Destiny*.

In a flail of exasperated tentacles, he signed, "You better know what you're doing." He knew that she didn't. She was improvising like all the otters he'd met seemed to, rolling with the events like she was swimming through a wild white-water current.

But the raptor chicks didn't know that.

And they were awed by the sight of Ordol's tentacles rising out of Jenny's furry shoulders like Lovecraftian wings.

"Warrior," Sandy screeched. The computer offered several alternatives—*hero, leader, captain*—but they all amounted to the same thing: sudden, surprising respect for the otter that had until that moment been a mere pet and plaything.

Sandy and White Patch tilted their long heads down, lowering their orange eyes, and spread their elbows almost as if their feathered arms were wings. They squatted before Jenny in awkward bows of submission.

Jenny knew enough to hold her tongue, but she signed with her paws, "What the hell just happened? They're calling me a warrior?"

Ordol signed back with large, exaggerated movements designed to impress the young raptors shooting furtive glances at him, and still be visible to Jenny underneath him, "They think I'm your slave—that you're controlling me."

Jenny's stomach knotted at the sickening idea of enslaving Ordol's brain and body through a direct neural link to her mind, but if the idea made the raptor fledglings believe she was powerful, it could be useful. She and Ordol could pretend to be joined, but she'd need to start downplaying her paw signals. She signed quickly with small motions, "I can work with that. Follow my lead; stay on my shoulders."

Then speaking aloud, Jenny said, "Up, up. You don't need to bow to me." A truly powerful figure wouldn't need displays of submission, so Jenny didn't want them either. She gestured with her paws for the raptors to rise, in case the screechy helmet translation wasn't clear to them. She could see in her peripheral vision that Ordol mimicked her gesture with his tentacles. That was a nice touch. Good for him. This was going to be weird.

The raptor fledglings' feathers ruffled, and they shot each other questioning glances, but they did rise back out of their awkward bows.

Sandy's orange eyes pierced Jenny as the young raptor screeched a question. Before the helmet finished translating, White Patch screeched another question, then Sandy again, until Jenny couldn't keep track of which raptor the helmet was translating for—it simply poured questions at her in its artificial voice:

"Who are you? What are you? What are you doing here? Where did you come from? What do you want?"

Jenny couldn't keep track of the questions—some were translations, some were alternate translations—but they all circled around the central idea:

"*Who are you?*"

Jenny was tempted to tell them something grandiose or cryptic: I am death the destroyer of worlds. I am the future returned to the past. I am the spirit of the Great Sky River, and your people must change their ways.

Finally, she settled for saying, "I am an otter." She knew the translation of 'otter' wouldn't mean anything to them, but she'd seen another one of those computerized tablets that Sandy had scribbled pictures on earlier lying around. She moved towards it and signed subtly to Ordol, explaining he should pick it up and hand it to her. Once the tablet was in her paws, Jenny said, "Show me how this works, and I'll teach you about otters."

Sandy and White Patch agreed eagerly.

Soon, Jenny and the raptors were lost in their scribbles on the tablet's screen. Jenny tried her best to explain the evolution of mammals through poorly rendered sketches, but she wasn't great at drawing, and there was so little shared culture to start from. The raptor fledglings hadn't even grown up on a world where they could see the stars. Their sky was a blanket of amber, muffling out the sun, let alone the pinpoint of light that was the small blue-green world their species had come from millions of years ago.

Fortunately, Jenny didn't care about educating young raptors. She did care about learning how to use their computer tablet, and Sandy and White Patch were being extremely helpful toward that goal. The more they helped Jenny teach them useless otter pre-history, the more Jenny learned about current raptor computer systems. It was a good trade, and Jenny was almost disappointed when Tree Bark interrupted them.

Chapter 20: Petra

"Hey!" the jowly jailor barked at Petra and Blaine, interrupting their latest conversation about scramball.

Petra was tempted to hiss an answer at the dog, but even with bars between them, it didn't seem like a safe move. Instead, she decided to whither the dog with class. "May I help you?" Her voice practically curdled with almost-purrs.

The cop looked properly and pleasingly unsettled by Petra's unpredictability. "Here," the dog harrumphed, pulling into view a wheeled trolley stacked high with disorderly piles of paper, files, and notebooks. "This is for you." The dog unlocked the cell, shoved the trolley in, and then locked the cell right back up. "Some dog dropped it off for you."

"*Some* dog?" Petra's ears flattened at the uselessness of the description. "A terrier? A black lab? A greyhound?" she prompted.

The jailor just snorted like the questions of a cat were beneath acknowledgement. But Petra found a hand-written note on the top of the papers:

Petra—

I asked those secretary cats for their financial files, and they handed them over no problem. So here they are. I'd have brought them in myself, but we have our paws full dealing with the press response to your arrest out here.

With hugs from the kittens—
Trudith

Petra started to seethe at the idea that those smarmy Siamese secretaries would simply hand all their files to Trudith after giving her such a runaround, but Blaine called her attention to the pages under Trudith's note.

Almost afraid to touch the precious pages, Petra lifted the three brightly-colored crayon drawings, one from each kitten, with shaking paws.

The top picture featured the whole family—Petra, the kittens, Papa Lucky, Uncle Alistair, Aunt Kipper, and even a black blob labelled 'Trwdeeth'—under an expansive rainbow that filled up half the page. It was cheerful, exuberant, and signed 'Allison.'

Pete had drawn a disturbingly good likeness of Petra behind bars, emblazoned with the words, "*Come home soon.*"

And Robin had drawn himself in Petra's arms, two orange figures blurring into each other, with cartoon teardrops all around them. His said, "*Dont be to sad. We miss you.*"

Petra sighed, all the anger knocked out of her. She missed her kittens too much to have room for caring about snubbing secretaries. Besides, those secretaries were nothing compared to corrupt cops who arrested tired mother cats for no reason.

Petra had the files now; she could get to work tracing the missing money, and find out where it had gone. She had something productive she could do with this time in jail, something that might help save the world—and her kittens—from the raptors. That was all that mattered.

Chapter 21: Kipper

Kipper didn't know why the octopi kept sending puzzles to their prisoners, but she wanted Captain Cod and Trugger to stop solving them. Except for the occasional meal of sushi-like rolls and raw fish brought by the dolphins, there was no way to mark the time, but it felt like they'd been held in the dank, watery cell for days. Days of being cut off from the outside world. Days of the raptor ships flying closer and closer to Earth. Days of being wet and useless.

Kipper was restless. Besides, there was something sinister about solving puzzles for captors who never showed themselves. It was time to stop cooperating with their captors. It was time to start planning a way out of this underwater dungeon.

"Has it occurred to you that the octopi could be gathering tactical information about how otters think?" Kipper said to the two otters tinkering with an object that looked like a cross between a tuba and an abacus. "They could be planning to use that information against us."

Captain Cod looked horrified, and Trugger dropped the tuba-abacus like it had suddenly become electrified. It splashed and then floated on the water in the middle of their small room.

"She's right," Trugger said. "We should stop."

Kipper didn't mention that decades worth of daily newscasts from *Deep Sky Anchor*, the otter film industry on Kelp Frond Station, and all other otter media were probably more useful for gathering tactical information about how otters think than the weird puzzles the dolphins kept bringing them. "If you want to work on a puzzle," she said, "let's try to find a way out of here."

Captain Cod chewed his whiskers, like he always did when he was thinking. "The hatch that the dolphins come through is too obvious. I'm sure they have it guarded."

"There must be vents for circulating the air and water," Trugger offered. "Maybe they're large enough to climb through if we find them and pry them open."

Kipper's ears skewed and twisted as she looked around the room, trying to spot the tell-tale sign of a seam in the otherwise smooth abalone walls and ceiling. She got up and ran her paw pads over the walls, which were slick with condensation, feeling for a seam too small to see in the dim light. There was an idea—the glowing patches of light in the ceiling. Could those be removed? Kipper's eyes narrowed to slits as she stared directly into the glow. Before she could decide if the idea was worth pursuing, she heard a ka-thunk, followed by a low-pitched whine, and, oh gods, the water level started rising.

Kipper scrambled for the pile of breathing gear. Trugger helped her get the air tank strapped on her back and the mask over her muzzle. Then Trugger and Captain Cod put their own breathing gear back on. By the time they were all suited-up again, there was only about a foot of air left.

When all the air was gone, the tuba-abacus tumbled, releasing a final bubble to the ceiling, before drifting down to the floor. Kipper watched it fall, so her eyes were on the hatchway in the floor when it opened.

Tentacles rolling in a slow, hypnotic motion and yellow eyes glaring, an octopus ascended into the room. Kipper felt strangely relieved that it wasn't the blue-eyed octopus with the silver tentacle.

"We won't play your games anymore," Kipper signed with shaky paws. She didn't know how dangerous it was to defy these octopuses. She didn't know what could be expected of them— their behavior so far had already shown she couldn't predict them. Not even close.

"Yes, we saw," the octopus signed. Its tentacles moved with the grace and simplicity of calligraphy.

Kipper looked around the room again, trying to see where there might be a camera for observing them, but the room was as smooth as the inside of a shell. It was another puzzle, and Kipper wouldn't waste time solving it. She flattened her ears in irritation and cut to the chase: "If you won't help us," she signed, "let us go. We have raptors to fight."

"You have crimes to pay for," the octopus jailor signed. "But we have decided to release you under restrictions."

Kipper's body flooded with a weird combination of relief and outrage. Before she could make sense of her feelings and decide how to respond, Captain Cod signed, "What restrictions?" Then he ruddered his tail and paddled with his hind paws, pushing himself closer to the octopus. He placed his neotropical otter bulk nearly between Kipper and the octopus jailor, physically signaling that he intended to stand by his subordinate officer. Well, *swim* by her. At least, that's how Kipper interpreted it—she had no idea as to whether the octopus understood.

"You will be released under guard," the octopus jailor signed. "Five guards and the oligarch will escort you and observe your actions. If your actions make a significant difference in protecting the octopi of Earth from the raptors, then that will be taken into consideration when you return for trial."

Kipper nearly jumped, trying to grab Captain Cod's paws to stop him from signing, "What if she doesn't return for trial?" Unfortunately, Kipper still wasn't good at maneuvering underwater, so she performed a useless somersault, and Captain Cod signed the question exactly as she expected him to.

The octopus jailor flushed with red circles and then returned to an impassive peach-gray before signing, "If the cat defeats the raptors, we will be lenient."

Oh great, Kipper thought, all I have to do is defend Earth from a pre-historic alien spaceship invasion force single pawed.

"If the cat does not defeat the raptors—" The octopus jailor's tentacles drifted into stillness.

Each of them took a moment to picture their own personal vision of what would happen if the raptors ravaged Earth— Kipper saw her sister's kittens huddling in a broken down shack, hiding from shiny-feathered monstrosities stalking the streets with blasters ready. Trugger pictured the space elevator broken in half, tearing *Deep Sky Anchor* out of its geosynchronous orbit, and all of it bursting into flame as it fell to Earth. Captain Cod pictured the *Jolly Barracuda* hiding out in the asteroid belt and never getting another fresh shipment of fish.

The octopus pictured itself losing all control of its own limbs and feeling the cold, hard mind of another push it away into subservience, forced to watch its own tentacles do the work of capturing more octopi to join in the living hell of total slavery.

"Got it," Trugger signed. "There may not be a trial to return for if we don't defeat the raptors. But that's okay, because we're going to defeat the raptors."

If skepticism were a living creature, it would have been that octopus, staring down Trugger's unfounded optimism with yellow eyes, and tentacles curled tightly like crossed arms.

Captain Cod signed, "If my ship is to offer hospitality to six octopus guards, then I expect them to return the favor by offering any information that they have on the raptors."

"Do you have any scholars who are experts on the raptors?" Kipper signed. "You should send them."

The octopus jailor's eyes narrowed. "You do not get to pick your contingent of guards, *Cat.*" The sign for cat was distorted and drawn out, as if the octopus were sneering with its tentacles. Kipper had heard the word *cat* spoken that way by many dogs; she knew how it would sound if spoken, the exact tone of voice. She also knew that it meant she was supposed to back down, show proper deference. Now wasn't the time to stand up for herself. She would leave that to Captain Cod. So, she bowed her head and paddled back a few inches, trying to show deference by giving the octopus space.

"My officer is correct," Captain Cod signed. "It's in your own best interest to share any information that you have with us. We all want to defend this planet."

"We will be the judges of that," the octopus signed.

"You will be the judges of many things, apparently," Kipper muttered into her breathing mask, but she kept her paws balled tight and tucked under her arms, staying appropriately silent as Captain Cod negotiated the terms of her release as a paroled war criminal with one of the octopuses that she had come here to help.

Kipper could see why Emily had fled this insane society under the ocean.

By the time the negotiations were done, Kipper was fuming in her breathing gear, ears clasped tightly against her head and claws flexing with tension. She wanted to sink her claws into something—preferably something with tentacles, something squishy and condescending—but instead she let Trugger pull her docilely along when the octopus jailor finally deigned to lead them out of their cell.

Bizarrely, the three of them were not thrown out of Choir's Deep like the week-old trash that Kipper felt like after being locked in a dank cell that smelled of salt and old fish for hours. (Or days?) She had expected to be dumped directly onto the back of another whale shark and immediately exiled—an idea she didn't mind at all. She wanted out of this watery death trap. Yet, now that the octopuses had an arrangement worked out with Captain Cod and her impending trial was properly scheduled, suddenly they were the diplomatic guests they should have been all along.

"While the oligarch and her guards are preparing," the octopus jailor signed to Captain Cod, "I have been authorized to give you a tour. We want you to see the beautiful, peaceful, harmonious way of life that you've put in danger with your reckless behavior, gallivanting about the solar system."

Kipper couldn't see much of Captain Cod's expression behind the breathing mask obscuring his muzzle, but she expected that he looked inappropriately pleased at the idea of himself *gallivanting recklessly*. That was pretty much his aim in life.

The octopus jailor—now tour guide, Kipper supposed—led them all down a twisting malachite-walled tunnel until it opened into a wide room with low ceilings. Several giant sea turtles with broad brown shells, blotchy flippers, and fluttering gills on their necks waited for them there. The octopus drifted lightly, propelled by its jet-like siphon, onto the back of one of the turtles and settled on its shell like a smug fat-cat politician on the only chair in the room.

"These turtles are our ride," the octopus tour guide signed. "Get on." The octopus gripped the smooth surface of the turtle's shell easily with eight tentacles' worth of sucker disks. Kipper could've sworn she saw a glint of cruel glee in the octopus's eye as it added with two tentacle tips, "And hold on."

Kipper dog-paddled to the nearest turtle and clawed uselessly at the hard, sheer surface of its shell. Some sort of saddle or hand-hold would have been really useful, but of course, the octopi had no need to have gengineered those changes into their turtle steeds. They had sucker disks.

Eventually Kipper had to settle for plastering herself awkwardly, belly-down, against the broad, flat surface of the shell and gripping the lip on either side with her paws. It was not elegant. Or comfortable. Yet, somehow, Trugger and Captain Cod managed to make the awkward position look almost cool or fun— like they were surfers about to dive head-long into a crashing blue curl of wave.

Kipper tried to think of it that way as the octopus tour guide signaled to the turtles, and they began flapping their flippers. Kipper felt her turtle steed lift beneath her, pushing its shell against her sprawled body. Then the water around her rushed against her like a thick, slow wind as the turtle swam forward with steady strokes of its flippers. Kipper held on tight and swore to herself about how cats were supposed to ride *inside* vehicles, *not* on top of them.

Even Kipper's cynicism and anger had to fall away though when the dark malachite walls opened up to the brightly colored glory of the cavernous interior of Choir's Deep. The slowly dancing jellyfish, the glowing kelp forests, the penny-bright schools of fish, the strange spherical video displays, and clumps of coral in every color beneath it all—the octopus city remained undeniably beautiful, no matter how its inhabitants had wronged her and denied her freedom.

Kipper loved exploring, but she was tired of doing it on others' terms. She was tired of water in her fur and face (and sometimes lungs); she was tired of modes of travel that didn't fit her.

When all of this was over, Kipper realized, it might be time to move on from the *Jolly Barracuda*—not to go home, but to find a new way to explore. A way that fit her own skin.

A way for cats.

A way without water.

Her path through the water slipped and slooped as her sea turtle surfboard followed the lead of the other three turtles, presumably steered by the octopus tour guide riding on the turtle in the lead. Kipper couldn't see how the tour guide octopus was steering—the turtle wore no reins. Perhaps it was an intelligent steed, and the octopus had explained their route to it before they began.

Or perhaps it was no steed at all—perhaps these turtles were uplifted? And what about those dolphins that had brought those infernal, damnable puzzles to them in their captivity? How many uplifted species lived in this city?

Suddenly, Kipper didn't know who anyone was anymore. Any creature could be uplifted. Jellyfish fluttering like ballerinas? *Maybe they were ballerinas*—maybe they'd spent years training and studying to flutter like that. Except jellyfish didn't live for years. Did they?

Good gods. Kipper was losing her mind. She could see why dogs liked the simple fiction that the only uplifted creatures had been designed—purposefully, meaningfully—by humans, and humans had a plan for them, a plan that was still ticking and turning like clockwork, keeping every dog safely in its place—a beloved, cherished place, waiting for Master to return home.

But Kipper didn't believe the First Race were gods. She'd seen proof first-hand—with gold eyes and obsidian feathers and rayguns in their talons—that humans weren't even the *first* race. Humans may have uplifted cats, dogs, otters, and everyone else in that statue in Cedar Heights, but they'd only been human. Kipper believed they'd been muddling along, useless and confused, as much as any cat or dog.

The four turtles swooped all the way down to the sandy ocean floor of Choir's Deep and stopped at the base of another malachite protrusion, this one a stalagmite jutting up from the floor.

The octopus tour guide disembarked the turtle steed, stepping with coupled tentacles almost like they were legs. It was eerie how much octopi could contort and disguise their bodies. "We're going to start with the most precious part of our entire city," the tour guide signed before gesturing at a dark opening, yawning in the base of the stalagmite. "Follow me."

Chapter 22: Jenny

Jenny would have given up eating clams forever to have a tour guide who simply held out a tentacle—or talon, as the case may be—and pointed to the most precious part of Cor-Jovis. That would have been invaluable tactical information. Instead, she had two eager raptor younglings crouched behind her, calling up video and sound files on their computer pad, seemingly to show her their favorite pop songs.

Raptors danced on the touchpad screen, literally shaking their tail feathers to the rhythmic, stuttering screeches that emanated from the device. Jenny could only assume it was music. Her helmet computer had trouble keeping up with the sound to give her a translation, but most of the words seemed to be about power or love or murder or freedom or slavery or growth or dinner. The helmet computer wasn't sure. Its translations had improved a great deal in certainty over the last few hours, but song lyrics tend to be inscrutable in any language.

Sandy and White Patch had tired of Jenny's clumsy attempts to teach them about otters very quickly, and except for occasional interruptions from Tree Bark taking a break from fixing *Brighton's Destiny*, they'd been playing these "music" videos for hours.

If Jenny didn't fear for her life whenever the young raptors' parents returned, and if the lives of every otter in the system didn't possibly hinge on her finding useful intelligence to bring back to Admiral Mackerel, it all might have been a fascinating cultural exploration. Instead, it was a truly bizarre form of torture.

They were going to die here. Jenny could feel it, the knowledge settling like a cold rock in the pit of her stomach. "I'm sorry," she signed with her paws for the benefit of the octopus crouching on her shoulders. She'd promised to keep him safe, but instead she'd delivered him to the very monsters who had enslaved him before and would almost certainly enslave him again.

As for herself? Jenny would be a lab rat. These reptile-bird-aliens, holdovers from the Cretaceous period, had never seen a creature like her before. Would they keep her alive to experiment on her? Or jump straight to the dissection?

The music stopped. And after a moment of disorientation, Jenny realized her helmet computer was no longer translating cryptic lyrics—White Patch was talking to her: "What is that with your talons? Why do you use your talons that way?" White Patch rotated its own talons in a gibberish imitation of the Swimmer's Sign Jenny had signed to Orodol.

Jenny had no good answer for them and stared in stunned silence until Ordol started waving his tentacles in a way that Jenny could only assume was meant to be menacing. Instead, it drew the young raptors closer with curiosity.

Sandy's long feathered muzzle came close enough for Jenny to feel the young raptor's hot breath in the thick fur on the side of her face. Those orange eyes narrowed, and then Sandy screeched from a mouth filled with terribly pointy teeth. Translation: "*There's no neural connection.*"

Talons reached toward Jenny and she was humiliated to discover that given a choice between fight and flight, she froze.

Sandy's talons grasped Ordol at the base of his tentacles, dimpling the clear fabric of his spacesuit. For a moment, he clung to Jenny's shoulders so tightly, she thought he'd crush her. Then in a burst of blue shades blushing over his tentacles, Ordol fainted. His tentacles fell limply, and Sandy lifted him away from Jenny.

To her even greater shame, Jenny seriously considered darting back to the elevator, scurrying away like a mindless prehistoric shrew from the dawn of the reign of mammals, while the raptors were distracted with examining the unconscious Ordol. But she couldn't abandon her friend. She couldn't betray her partner.

145

Besides, she couldn't pilot *Brighton's Destiny* without him.

Jenny swallowed and found her voice. "Don't hurt him." Could appealing to the raptors' emotions work? Did these reptile-birds even have feelings like her own? Ordol did, and he was physically far more foreign. "He's my friend."

Two sets of orange eyes stared owlishly at Jenny. The raptors' feathered faces fluffed, making them look larger, more intimidating. Then Sandy and White Patch turned to each other and started arguing while Ordol's tentacles draped over Sandy's dark talons as if he were dripping down to the floor. Jenny wished she could melt into a puddle on the floor and evaporate away. But her only true escape was the broken spaceship downstairs, and from the snatches of conversation that her helmet translated, she wasn't so sure that *Brighton's Destiny* would belong to her anymore once it was fixed.

"...not a hero... we could keep... what do you... serious... our own spaceship!"

The helmet couldn't keep up with translating two voices at once, but Jenny was pretty sure that one of the raptors was making a strong argument for keeping *Brighton's Destiny* for themselves. These raptors may have been the younglings while Jenny was an adult otter, but she'd never felt more like a helpless child, hoping the grownups in charge would let her keep her toy. Of course, if the real grownups showed up—the adult raptors with their sleek black feathers and brightly colored crests and plumes—then the toy that Jenny hoped to keep might be her life, not just a broken spaceship.

After a particularly piercing shriek, Sandy dropped Ordol to the floor and began gesticulating wildly, flapping those feathered arms like wings. Any translation of the outburst was completely drowned out by the outburst itself.

Terrified, Jenny knelt down and risked crawling closer until she could gather Ordol's limp, fainted tentacles into her fuzzy arms. His muscular tentacles were heavier without his consciousness holding them up, controlling them, making them lithe. By shifting her weight while backing away, Jenny managed to rearrange Ordol's body so that several of his tentacles draped over each of her shoulders. With his weight spread more evenly, she was able to rise up on her back paws again. She wanted to hide, cower behind one of the structures that was either furniture or an abstract statue... But it was better to stand tall, looking brave and strong.

The raptors continued to argue, screeching, echoed by a helmet that threw disordered words like *want, need,* and *ours to take* into the noisy air. Jenny had to do something—they were going to take her ship away.

"Please," Jenny said. Her otter voice sounded small and mewling, plaintive next to the raptors' caws and cries. But then the helmet mirrored her word with a shriek of its own. "Please," she repeated. "I need that ship to get home."

The helmet's raptor-like cries cut through the actual raptors' argument, and they both turned to look at it. Then White Patch's wide orange eyes turned toward Jenny. The young raptor pointed with a talon at the helmet and shrieked, "Turn. That. Off."

Shaking from head to tail tip, Jenny walked over to the helmet, where it was still resting on the plush couch-like ledge, and turned off the speaker. She dared not defy these taloned beasts.

White Patch pointed next at a stair up to an open hatchway in the ceiling on the far side of the room. Jenny didn't need any translation to understand that she was being exiled. She gathered her helmet and spacesuit into her arms and ascended the stair to the smaller room above.

White Patch sealed the hatchway behind Jenny, and the otter found herself alone in what seemed to be a raptor child's bedroom with an unconscious octopus draped over her shoulders and screeching raptors below. The only way out was back down.

The room below was an entire cross-section of the mechanical tree; this room was a wedge, windowed on one curving side but with opaque walls on the other two sides.

Jenny climbed into the nest-like pile of brightly colored cushions that she assumed was a bed. She set her spacesuit

147

and helmet down on the edge. Then she arranged Ordol gently around herself and rocked back and forth, barely aware that she was humming the *Jolly Barracuda* fight song while she stared at the posters of raptors dressed in bespangled outfits (some of them familiar from the earlier music videos) and shelves of carved figurines (all different shapes of dinosaur) that filled the two opaque walls of the small room.

None of it blocked out the sound of the raptor children screaming. Deciding her fate.

Jenny wondered if she could break the window-wall, smash it with one of the figurines. But then she'd be hundreds of feet in the air. Even if she made it down to ground level, she'd be free on a planet filled with dinosaurs. Even if most of them were harmless herbivores, she didn't relish that idea.

She needed a spaceship to get home.

She needed mercy.

From raptor younglings.

Jenny couldn't imagine that her adrenaline-flooded body had been capable of sleeping, but she must have for the room was suddenly dark, no more light streaming through the floor to ceiling windows. And all was quiet. She felt Ordol's tentacles stir around her. Then yellow light streamed in through the hatchway in the floor as it opened. One of the young raptors—it was hard to tell which, silhouetted like that—entered and pointed urgently with a fearsome talon at her helmet. Jenny groggily turned the translation software and the speakers back on.

As the raptor spoke in quiet caws and chirps, it turned its head and the light caught its feathers—they were the golden hue of an Earth beach. This one was Sandy. "My hatch mates agreed to keep your ship. They've gone to get our brood mother."

Jenny's blood ran cold as if she'd plunged into an icy stream, but Sandy continued to speak.

"They left me to guard you, but I'm afraid of what Brood Mother will do to you."

Slavery? Dissection? Hostage against her own people? None of the options were good. Jenny should have crashed *Brighton's Destiny* into the sea when she had the chance.

"Don't worry, little otter," Sandy said. "I'm going to help you."

Jenny was skeptical. These raptor fledglings had been playing with her like she was a pet since they'd found her. Even when they'd thought she had an octopus slave hooked into her brain stem, they'd treated her more like a playmate than... what? What was Jenny to them? An enemy of their people? A spy? A prisoner of war?

Maybe she didn't want to be treated like anything other than a treasured pet.

"Thank you," Jenny said, hoping to hell and back that Sandy's idea of 'help' didn't mean keeping her and Ordol hidden in a box and bringing them scraps of food.

"Come on," Sandy said, gesturing with a tilt of that feathered head toward the hatchway. Sandy held out a murderous-looking talon, clearly expecting Jenny to take hold of it.

So Jenny did.

Otter paw and raptor talon, hand in hand, they sneaked through the darkened rooms. Ordol was still draped over Jenny's shoulders, and she held her spacesuit and helmet tucked under her other arm.

The raptor didn't lead Jenny back to the spacious elevator that had brought them up. "Brood Mother will come up that way," Sandy explained. Instead, they came to a small chamber on the other side of the building.

Jenny sighed at the sight of a spiraling ladder that stretched as far down as she could see. She couldn't easily climb the rungs with her spacesuit under one arm, so she pulled the suit on and reaffixed the helmet over her head. Then she held her paws out and signed, hoping the limp Ordol was conscious and would see, "We need to climb down this ladder. Can you do that? Or do I need to keep carrying you?"

Ordol's tentacles on Jenny's shoulders writhed in a way that almost felt like octopus laughter. Several tentacle tips twisted into Jenny's view and signed, "How about, I carry you?"

If there was one thing Ordol wanted to do, it was get the hell out of there.

Before Jenny realized what was happening, all the sucker disks draped against her shoulders clamped on, holding her tight. The rest of Ordol's long arms reached for the ladder, swinging Jenny forward and then, down, down, down. She descended the twirling ladder much, much faster than she could have under the power of her own paws. It felt more like a controlled fall than climbing.

At the bottom, Sandy opened a door out to the darkened forest. *Why was there night here?* Jenny wondered. The daylight had to have been artificial; there was no way that true sunlight had filtered through so many layers of soupy noxious Jovian atmosphere. The raptors must have designed an artificial day/night cycle for their world.

With her paws back on the ground, Jenny felt Ordol settle his weight back onto her shoulders, tentacles wrapped around her like an ornate organic shawl. When she stepped outside, Jenny heard the sounds of night time animals—croaking and trilling, the strange calls of alien dinosaurs. She looked up to see the starless Cor-Jovis sky peaking between the towering trees. The darkness above was textured like storm clouds, and there was just enough light for her eyes to adjust. At least she wouldn't trip and stumble in the alien gloom.

"This way," Sandy cawed.

Jenny followed the young raptor around the curve of the tree-like building, back to the garage where *Brighton's Destiny* stood in all its hopeful glory.

The ship's maple-seed wings stretched out proudly again, all fixed, and the cockpit called to Jenny. She wanted to scurry into it, strap herself in, power up the engine, and get out of here. She also didn't want to make any sudden movements in front of a prehistoric alien with talons as long as her whole paw. She still couldn't quite believe the young raptor was helping them.

"Thank you," she said, wishing she had a small token to give the raptor. "Wait a second..." Her spacesuit wasn't pressurized yet, so she unsealed the side of the torso segment and reached underneath. She unpinned the little ornament that all of the *Jolly Barracuda* crew wore at their collar as part of their uniform—a tiny gold sailing ship.

Jenny held the little gold ornament out to the raptor on the palm of her spacesuit glove. Talons delicately plucked it up, and Sandy examined the ornament closely before tucking it into a pocket. "Thank you," the raptor squawked.

Jenny resealed her spacesuit and began pressurizing it as she walked to *Brighton's Destiny* with slow, measured steps, but before she could climb into the ship's cockpit, Sandy called out, "Take me with you."

Jenny turned and stared at the raptor in surprise, but Ordol was in no mood to wait another second. He was within reach of the cockpit, so he stretched out his arms, grabbed on, and began pulling the spacesuit-clad otter in with him. His strong arms strapped her into her seat while she tried to explain to the raptor, "I can't do that... There isn't room in this ship, and you don't belong with my people. Your brood mother—she'd think I'd kidnapped you."

For an instant, Jenny wondered if a hostage would be valuable... but, no, a single raptor child would have no military intelligence or value to offer. It would only be a liability. "This is your home," Jenny said. "And we're not coming back. One-way trip."

Sandy maneuvered into the hatchway to the cockpit, spread its talons to block the door from closing, in spite of Ordol mashing the door-close button with his tentacles.

"I want to see all the little mammals," Sandy squawked. "The cats and dogs and other otters."

Jenny raised her paws for Ordol to see and firmly signed, "*Stop.*" When he didn't stop, she cupped her paws over the door-close button, blocking his tentacles, so that the cockpit door would stop bouncing off of the raptor child's head.

Ordol signed a couple of choice swear words in front of Jenny's faceplate, but then he slumped on her shoulders, tentacles knotted up with the tips twitching, like a petulant teenager with his arms crossed and foot tapping impatiently.

Jenny tried to ignore the muscular ball of unhappy octopus on her shoulders and focus on the overly earnest raptor. "I wish I could bring you to meet my people," Jenny said. "That would be wonderful—if we could visit each other's worlds and simply learn about each other. But that's not possible right now."

Sandy's feathered arms were still stretched out, blocking the cockpit door. As Jenny spoke though, the young raptor's plumage that had puffed up with excitement began to smooth down, and disappointment entered those owlish orange eyes.

Jenny wanted to tell the truth and say, *"Our people are at war. Your people have been killing mine. Raptors murdering otters."* But it was too dangerous. She didn't know how much the raptor civilians knew, let alone a raptor youngling, and she couldn't risk Sandy re-thinking the choice to let them go. So, Jenny simply said, "Maybe someday."

Sandy's feathered arms dropped and folded up like wings. The raptor's feathered head bobbed, sadly acknowledging that Jenny wouldn't be taking a passenger.

As a final thought before lifting her cupped paws from the door-close button, Jenny said, "Tell your brood mother about me and the other otters. Tell her... tell her that we're your friends."

Sandy looked up, and a glint of hope entered those orange eyes. Jenny wished that she could feel that hope, but she didn't expect her message of friendship to start a worldwide revolution on this raptor planet. There were still raptor vessels headed towards Earth. There were still octopuses—how many hundreds of thousands of them?—enslaved on the raptor vessels.

The cockpit sealed, closing away the strange, fascinating world of Corjovis. Jenny wouldn't be seeing Sandy again. Or the other young raptors. Or anything else of this planetary time capsule. The hope in Sandy's heart—that raptors and otters would visit each other peacefully—was foolish.

Jenny didn't feel hope, but she did feel lucky. Her comrades would have assumed she was dead by now, and by all rights she should be. Instead, she'd been very, very lucky.

Ordol revved the engine, and *Brighton's Destiny* rose gently from the ground. Ever so carefully, the octopus and otter piloted the two-man vessel out of the garage shop where it had been fixed and between the sparse trees at the edge of the forest. As soon as the wide wingspan cleared the forest and *Brighton's Destiny* was flying over the wide meadow, Ordol rammed the throttle. The Whirligig vessel careened upward, leaving a wake of startled brontosaur-like creatures scattering through the meadow in its wake.

Flying straight up into the thickly clouded Jovian sky, Jenny did allow herself a small glimmer of hope: *maybe, just maybe, if their luck held a little longer, they'd actually make it home.*

Chapter 23: Petra

Every piece of paper in front of Petra told a story. The rows of numbers; the columns of... *pointless, stupid text that meant nothing to her.* The story the papers told was one of frustration and boredom. She wanted the papers to tell a story of corruption and secret societies, money being funneled into an underground military complex—an army that would rise up from their massively expensive hidden bunkers to save Earth from the raptors—*all because Petra found the number trail leading to them in these papers.*

But for that to happen, Petra would have to see more than dry charts and records. She growled, flattened her ears, and lowered her head to the pile of papers, laying her muzzle against their cool, smooth, unhelpful surface. The wheeled trolley under the papers wobbled unsettlingly.

"Giving up?" Blaine asked from the other side of their cell.

Petra groaned, a deep unhappy rumble in her throat. She turned her head, still pressed into the papers, until she could see Blaine. The tuxedo cat was stretched out on the bench on the far side of the cell, casually examining his claws.

"I could take a look at them," he said. "If you'd like."

Blaine's offer sounded casual, but Petra still thought he was trying to find some way to get political gain from sharing a cell with her. Either that or she'd simply become physically incapable of trusting anyone.

"What the hell," she said, clawing the papers out from under her weary face. She sat up and shoved the trolley so it rolled toward Blaine. Once the trolley was out of her way, she curled up on the uncomfortable cell bench and wrapped her orange-striped arms over her head. She squeezed tight, imagining that she was back in the cattery she'd grown up in.

The cattery had been a dreary place, but when she was there, she'd liked to imagine that the mother she'd never known was holding her tight. Petra, Alistair, and Kipper had pretended their mother was named Theresa B. Goodkitty and had only left them at the cattery while she went to fetch her hidden fortune. Somehow, remembering the phantom of her imaginary mother could still comfort Petra at times.

"You're not an accountant, are you?" Blaine said, his voice nearly breaking into a purr.

Petra's left ear twitched and turned towards Blaine. "Why do you sound happy?" She lifted her head from her arms to see Blaine staring at the papers, eyes darting back and forth as if he were watching tiny fish flitting about under the surface of a pond. His white-tipped black paws traced over the papers as if he were about to pounce and catch himself a goldfish. "You found something," she said. "What did you find?"

"There's money missing." Blaine looked so pleased with himself—he thought he'd caught the fish. But he hadn't.

"*I know that*," Petra growled bleakly. "Where did it go? Who took it? Those are things I don't know."

The glow in Blaine's eyes didn't diminish. "Look," he said, pointing at the papers.

Grudgingly, Petra came over, but all she saw under his pointed claw were the same useless numbers that she'd been wrestling with before. Blaine traced the sharp tip of his claw across the papers, zigging and zagging like he was following a path on a map. He chanted mumbo jumbo about calendar years versus fiscal years, amortization, and itemized reports. Petra had done enough accounting during her years working as a temp to keep up. Barely. Finally, Blaine's claw came to rest on a name Petra recognized but hadn't noticed in the sea of documentation before: it was a receipt for an order form to Luna Tech

Industries, signed in swooping, calligraphic letters by Sahalie Silbernagel.

Petra hissed the name, "Sahalie. She tried to have my sister killed when we uncovered that she'd been embezzling."

Blaine eyed Petra. He was keeping something from her. She could tell. "Say it," she hissed. "What am I missing?"

"I'm guessing that wasn't just about embezzling." Blaine pulled his paw back from the papers and straightened his tie nervously. Anything that could make a cat as smooth as him nervous couldn't be good. "Look, what I'm seeing here is a lot of money, disappearing really slowly, over the course of years—but it's not the amount that's scary. It's where it's been going."

"What's so scary about Luna Tech?" Petra snapped impatiently. "They were sending purebred cats to Mars. So what?"

"It's not just Luna Tech," Blaine said. "It's an array of industries—chemical companies, manufacturers, research engineers. Luna Tech was only the tip of the iceberg. According to what I see here..." Blaine swept his white-tipped paws over the mess of papers. "There's been a wide-spread government conspiracy going on for years, and they've been smuggling nuclear missiles, piece by piece, to Mars."

"You mean..." Petra said numbly, feeling the pieces fall together in her head. "Siamhalla has the nuclear missiles that the Uplifted States spent the last few decades dismantling."

When Kipper had chased Violet the Luna Tech employee all the way to Mars, that cat hadn't simply been emigrating to the isolationist purebred cat colony there—that cat had been smuggling pieces of nuclear weaponry. So, Siamhalla wasn't merely a radical splinter sect of society; it was one with really sharp claws.

Blaine might not have uncovered a bunker of secret armed forces ready to rise up from the Earth, but if he was right, the missing money *did* add up to weaponry in allies' paws. Compared to cold-blooded raptors, even crazy pure-bred-fetishist cats were allies.

"This could actually be good news," Petra hazarded. "If Siamhalla can be convinced to use their missiles on the raptor fleet, they might be able to stop or at least damage the fleet before it gets to Earth." A terrible thought struck her. "Wait—is Mars between Earth and Jupiter right now?" Those nuclear missiles would do them no good if they were on the far side of the sun, but Petra knew next to nothing about Solar geography as a function of time. She'd never needed to before.

Blaine shrugged, and Petra looked around the jail cell frantically for a moment, as if a computer or helpful guard would pop up and show her orbital charts of the planets. Of course, none did.

"Dammit," she said. Kipper would know. More than that, Kipper had a contact on Siamhalla. "I need to call my sister."

The tuxedo cat shot her a bewildered look. "Shouldn't you bring this to your brother? The *president?*"

"Yeah, he should know too," Petra conceded. Though, she had less and less faith in the efficacy of his office, and as little as she liked to admit it, Kipper had become a force to reckon with in this solar system. She had connections, and she got things done. "For dealing with Siamhalla, though, Kipper's the expert. Now, how do I get the attention of those guard dogs and convince them to let me make a call?"

Blaine looked at her sadly. "You are new to this, aren't you?" He raised his paws to gesture at the concrete wall to one side of them and the iron bars to the other. "You wait. The guards will come when they feel like it—nothing you do will speed that up."

"What if I was sick?" Petra asked. "What if I was crying out in pain?"

Blaine shook his head.

That made Petra angry. She pressed harder, "*What if I was dying?*"

At first Blaine didn't answer. He just looked away, green eyes staring at the concrete around them. He looked like he was remembering something he'd seen during one of his other incarcerations, something horrible, too horrible to tell her about.

"What? They'd let me die?" Petra didn't believe that. Did she? She didn't want to.

Finally Blaine said, "I don't know. Maybe they'd treat you differently, because you're the president's sister. You're famous, and there's a lot of news about your arrest. But they'll check on us eventually anyway, without you doing anything that could be seen as causing trouble. If I were you, I'd just wait." It sounded like he was pleading with her. Though he couldn't look her in the eye. "And when the guards do come, *ask nicely.*"

Petra felt cold inside. She had military intelligence that could change the course of a war, and she was still at the mercy of a few low-paid copper dogs who didn't like her.

Was the world ever going to change? Had all the change so far been nothing more than veneer? An illusion of equality, over a plunging chasm of inequity?

Chapter 24: Kipper

The giant malachite stalagmite towered in front of Kipper like an underwater skyscraper. The octopus tour guide led her, Trugger, and Captain Cod into an opening at the base that turned into a dark, narrow, winding tunnel. After several sharp twists and turns, the tunnel opened into a conical chamber that must have filled nearly the entire stalagmite.

The octopus city outside the stalagmite had been a heady visual opera of colors and motions. The inside was literally dizzying. Kipper had to turn her head down and close her eyes, shutting the visual noise out for a moment before she was ready to face it again.

In every direction, videos played of octopuses signing, text streaming, colors flashing. The entire conical chamber seemed to be lined with video screens, seamlessly forming the walls, and more of the spherical video-playing bubbles floated... everywhere. In the middle of the chamber, another much smaller spire rose from the floor. It was dark, pockmarked stone, and its surface was riddled with small caves. Kipper stared at it, trying to block out the visual clutter of all the videos everywhere else. She saw that most of the small caves' ceilings hung with clumps and clusters of white grapes. Almost like strings of pearls. Octopi crouched in some of the caves, tending the clusters lovingly.

"This is our nursery," the tour guide octopus signed.

The clusters were eggs. The octopi tending them were the mothers who had come here to die. This is what Emily had told Kipper about—why she had fled octopus society. After a mother octopus laid her eggs, she was expected to tend to them, starving and wasting away, until she died. Emily had lived, and there was no place for her in octopus society as a female who had already laid her eggs, so she'd come to live with the otters. Now she was the chef on the *Jolly Barracuda*.

Kipper didn't understand octopi. In fact, right now, thinking about how they were treating her and how they'd treated Emily, she didn't like them at all. Still, she was here. She should learn. So, she focused on reading the octopus tour guide's signing tentacles.

"We all come from here," the octopus signed. "This is our birthplace, hatchery, nursery school..." The octopus's yellow eyes gazed into the mid-distance, and Kipper realized the water throughout the giant chamber was filled with tiny, floating, nearly-translucent baby octopi, swirling through the blue water like dust motes in a sunbeam. "Only a miniscule fraction of those who hatch survive to adulthood, but those who do are entirely prepared for their adult lives by the time they leave this chamber."

"Is that what the videos are?" Captain Cod signed. "Education?"

"Of course," the tour guide signed.

"Why do so few survive?" Trugger signed.

"We are so small when we hatch..." The tour guide's signing tentacles moved with such grace, they barely disturbed the water at all. "Some eat. Some are eaten."

"They eat each other?" Trugger's paws didn't show his feelings, and his expression was hidden behind his breathing mask. So he didn't have to hide that he was horrified—it was already hidden for him.

"No," the tour guide signed. "Larval crab, shrimp... we compete with our own food to survive."

Kipper wanted to pay attention to the tour guide, but it was hard to concentrate on the signing of a single set of life-sized tentacles when so many larger-than-life tentacles loomed on the screens around her. She couldn't keep up with their rapid signs. They were much faster than the tour guide's, so she couldn't tell much of what they were signing about. It didn't seem much like the neon kiddie programs that Robin, Pete, and Allison watched. More like tech talks or lectures on advanced mathematics.

Kipper wondered who chose what kind of videos were shown in this chamber. Was it a political branch? Were the choices highly contested? They would be if dogs and cats were trying to agree on one set of videos to show all the kittens and puppies in the country.

Before Kipper could ask, the octopus tour guide startled her by jetting through the water over to the pockmarked stalagmite in the center of the chamber. The tour guide floated beside one of the caves that was empty now and signed, "This is where I laid my own eggs, many years ago, when I was young enough to be a mother." She laid her tentacles delicately, fondly, even sentimentally over the curve of the cave's mouth. "Thousands and thousands of beautiful, perfect eggs. I often wonder if any survived."

Kipper was stunned. This octopus was *female?* And had laid eggs *years ago?*

If Kipper hadn't been wearing breathing gear, she would have stuttered stupidly, making a fool of herself to this octopus like she'd made a fool of herself to the squirrel in Tree Town. Instead, she had time to gather her thoughts and try to sign something coherent. Her paws moved mechanically through the words, "We have an octopus on our spaceship. She told me that she came to space because there's no room in octopus society for females after they've laid their eggs." Even with a chance to gather her thoughts before speaking, Kipper still felt like a fool. *How little could a cat know about her own world?* At least she was getting used to feeling ignorant. "She said they always die."

The tour guide stared at Kipper for a long time before signing, "There are religious sects who believe that. Hundreds of years ago it was a common belief. Not anymore."

Maybe Kipper wasn't the only one who was ignorant. Or maybe Emily hadn't told her the whole story of her culture. She didn't know.

Kipper tried to imagine growing up in a cavernous chamber, raised by videos, and surrounded by millions of strangers and siblings, all mixed together. No family. More than that, *family* would be a meaningless word. Cohorts, perhaps. But mostly, society would exist on two levels—the individual and then *everyone*. At least, that was her guess, but her guesses had been proving to be way off.

Kipper held out a paw, and the water swirled around her motion. She cupped her paw and held it still until one of the tiny octopuses, with a mantle barely larger than a single one of her paw pads, came into view. She placed her paw behind the octopus, blocking the noisy colors of the chamber, so she could see its delicate, jelly-like body in contrast to the plain gray skin of her paw pad.

The octopus baby squirmed and squiggled. Its tentacles writhed and wriggled. Its skin was translucent white with tiny black speckles, and its mantle was much larger relative to its tiny tentacles than on a grown octopus, making it look cute and babyish. Kipper wondered if it could change its colors yet. She wondered how old it was, and how old it would have to be before it was guaranteed to be one of the octopi that survived to adulthood. Perversely, Kipper wished she could tuck the tiny tentacled baby in a pocket and smuggle it out of here to raise it with a family. She and Emily could keep it and raise it together. That would be a nice family.

Does it count as kidnapping if the child is fated to die? Of course, it wasn't *fated* to die—it had the same chances as any other octopus baby here. Very, very slim.

Kipper dropped her paw to her side, and the currents in the water whisked the baby octopus away, tentacles flitting and flailing. It became one of a million, all mixed together, tiny specks of life swimming through this chamber.

The rest of the octopus tour guide's words, signed with deft tentacles, passed in front of Kipper's eyes but never translated into language in her brain. She couldn't stop thinking about her own family—her niece and nephews especially, but also Petra, Alistair, Trudith, and even the crew of the *Jolly Barracuda* who she'd come to think of as family. All of them were whirling through space, flitting and flailing, just hoping they'd be among the ones to survive—that their whole world would survive.

Kipper couldn't save a baby octopus, and she didn't feel like she could save the world.

By the time the octopus tour guide led them back out of the nursery stalagmite, Kipper's mood was morose. Fortunately, she wasn't called to do more than follow along, docile and polite, as their octopus retinue—five guards and the oligarch, who turned out to be the creepy blue-eyed octopus with the silver tentacle—was assembled and prepared to leave Choir's Deep.

Each of the five octopus guards wore a backpack strapped around its waist—below the eyes, above the tentacles, with the bulk of the pack hanging down beneath the mantle. The effect looked strange to Kipper, as she'd come to think of the span of skin between the eyes and where the front tentacles divided as an octopus's face, and the backpack straps covered that span like a gag or blind fold.

Of course, it wasn't a face. Octopuses don't have faces in the same sense as cats and otters. What Kipper thought of as a face was merely a blank span of skin that could take on expressive qualities depending on an octopus's posture. Nonetheless, the black straps holding on their backpacks made the retinue of octopus guards look like ninjas to Kipper—an effect that might have been cool if she'd felt like they were on her side. She liked the idea of octopus ninjas fighting back against the raptors. She didn't so much like the idea of octopus ninjas assigned to guard her so that she would return and pay for her supposed crimes.

Though, the idea that she was a powerful and scary enough cat to require *five octopus ninjas* to guard her... Kipper supposed that was kind of cool.

The whole crew of them—six octopuses, Kipper, Trugger, and Captain Cod—rode two whale sharks back to the *Diving Canary*. Once they were back onboard an otter vessel, Kipper took a savage pleasure in climbing up to the sleeping quarters on the upper level where it was *dry*. Sure, her octopus guards could have followed her.

They had brought breathing gear in their packs that would let them function out of water—Kipper had asked—and octopi are freakishly strong, in spite of developing in a liquid atmosphere. But they didn't follow her. They swam around on the lowest levels, under the water, like weird tentacle monsters hiding under everyone's feet, and Kipper got to enjoy a small modicum of rebellion and privacy.

For two days, Kipper read the history books on her data-chip from Cedar Heights and pretended that a fleet of killer raptors wasn't flying towards Earth. She didn't have a choice—deep under the ocean, the *Diving Canary* was out of touch with the news above sea level. When they finally surfaced, a few hours out from the docks at Guayaquil, the news from the previous week hit Kipper—and all the otters onboard—in a rush.

The Europa base attack had successfully shut down the energy beams from Jupiter to the raptor fleet. For six hours. Then the energy beams were back online, and the raptor fleet began accelerating toward Earth again. Jenny was gone. So was Ordol. Riots had begun all over the Uplifted States. Cats wanted Petra freed. Dogs wanted a president who would "protect" them—in other words, another dog. The International Star-Ocean Navy was assembling a brigade to fight the raptors, but by the time they'd be ready, the raptor fleet would be nearly to Earth. No one liked Earth's prospects.

But there was one good piece of news. A short video call from Petra. Two police dogs stood behind the orange tabby, at the back of a drab room. Petra's clothes were wrinkled and stained, and her fur looked greasy and unwashed. Her ears twisted back, clearly listening to the police dogs behind her who were both staring away, at least pretending not to listen. Petra whisper-hissed into the camera, voice very low, "Kipper, I know where the missing money went—Siamhalla has nukes. Nuclear missiles. They're armed to the teeth. You know what to do." The picture fizzed out. That was it. But it was *good* news.

And Kipper did know what to do. She was elated that she might not have to rely on the crazy octopuses that she'd fished up from the bottom of the ocean to save the world—just crazy isolationist pure-bred cats. She routed a call immediately through *Deep Sky Anchor* to Mars. According to the data in the corner of the vid-call window on the tablet computer, the charges for the call would be exorbitant, but the time-delay was low—only about five minutes, because Mars and Earth were close together this year. Though, the time-delay didn't matter—Kipper didn't need to hear anything back; she simply had something to say.

"Josh," Kipper said, as soon as the vid-call window showed that it was transmitting. She could see her own green-eyed, tab-by-striped face on the screen, just as it would be transmitted, but she pictured the handsome blue-eyed Siamese who would receive this message. He wouldn't like it. But he had to hear it. She drew a deep breath and started:

"I know that Siamhalla has teeth. My sister traced the money. The news will come out eventually—the question that you and everyone else on Siamhalla need to ask yourselves is whether you want the news to be that Siamhalla was responsible for embezzling and smuggling... or that Siamhalla was responsible for embezzling, smuggling, and standing by while their fellow cats on Earth *died*." Kipper paused a moment to let those words sink in.

"You have teeth. Use them. Bite hard. Bite with every tooth you've got. Or else I will personally see to it that if we survive the raptor assault, the Uplifted States of Mericka reclaims every piece of property you stole and drags every last one of your sorry tails back to Earth where you can rot in jail for treason."

Kipper's ears flicked back uncomfortably at the sight of her own green eyes flashing with anger. It was strange watching herself trying to intimidate someone. "Look," she said, softening a little. "You have a chance to be heroes. *Be heroes.* Kipper out."

Kipper swiped a paw pad across the screen, ending the transmission. The crisp, bright video image of herself disappeared and was replaced by her ghostly reflection on the blank black screen. She stared at it for a while wondering what Josh would think. They'd been pen-pals since she'd visited Siamhalla, and she believed he was a good guy. But more importantly, he seemed smart. Too smart to let this warning pass by. He would do the right thing. Siamhalla would do the right thing. Kipper had to believe that. They might restrict their own residency to purebred cats, but that didn't mean they would stand by and watch other cats die.

Besides, there were still purebred cats on Earth. It was insane that their empathy for the cats on Earth might depend on their pedigree...

Trugger popped his head up from the lower level of the submarine. "We're docked. Pack your stuff. It's time to get this travelling circus back to the *Jolly Barracuda* and kick some raptor tail." He said the words with bravado, but then his expression wavered—whiskers almost drooping. Kipper could see the fear in his eyes. He was the only otter who'd been with her to see the raptors first-hand. He knew what they were up against.

Kipper stowed the borrowed tablet computer in her beat-up purple duffel bag. It was starting to feel like that purple bag was her real home. Wherever she went, her purple duffel came with her. She almost wanted to see if she were small enough to crawl inside it and turn the universe inside-out so that all that was left was the inside of that small purple bag. She'd be shielded from the raptor's talons and pinecone-like bludgeoning warships by a thin layer of purple fabric.

Siamhalla would come through. They had to. They would use their nuclear missiles to shoot down the raptor vessels, and Kipper wouldn't have to face the raptors again. She knew they would, because if they didn't, she would *destroy* them.

Chapter 25: Jenny

Jenny and Ordol landed *Brighton's Destiny* lightly atop the Europa base. It touched down like a lonely whirligig maple seed that had spun its way improbably down through an arctic sky to the surface of an iceberg, a small stretch of cold land, floating on Europa's choppy gray ocean.

Wind whipped through the hatch when Jenny broke the seal. The door swung aside, and Jenny climbed out of the ship. Ordol followed her, clambering over the flat ground like a basket of snakes slithering together in a complicated knot. The sky above them was clear and bright with stars. Jupiter hung low on the horizon, where it should be—far away, rather than under Jenny's paws.

The atmo-dome loomed ahead of Jenny like a giant soap bubble on the surface of this iceberg. It was built from a filmy, plastic material, and its airlock jutted out of it like the entrance to an igloo. It only took a few moments for the airlock to cycle, and Jenny was relieved to be able to pull off her space helmet. She could see through the filmy plastic that everyone on the base was gathered around the airlock waiting for her and Ordol. She signed for her octopus co-pilot, "See? I kept my promise. I got you home."

Ordol's eyes stared up at her enigmatically, slightly magnified by the bulbs of glass-like spacesuit around them, but he raised a few tentacle tips and made a very small sign—literally, it meant, "Yes, you did." To Jenny, it felt like the equivalent of a curt nod of acknowledgement.

They'd been through enemy lands together. They were partners.

The inner door of the airlock opened to reveal a surprising scene: streamers and colorful lights hung from the curved ceiling of the atmo-dome, strung in decorative, scalloped patterns; barrels and crates were set out like tables, sporting intricate spreads of snacks and appetizers; and all the otters, cats, and dogs on the base crowded around, smiling and grinning unabashedly.

They were in the middle of a war—a war they might be losing—but one of their own had come home. A friend who they'd thought they'd lost—a hero and a leader—had come home.

"Welcome back, Base Commander." Admiral Mackerel held out a paw, but instead of waiting for Jenny to shake it, he seemed to change his mind and pulled her into a tight embrace. "We thought we'd lost you." Then he stepped back and said grimly, "The raptors repaired their satellites in a matter of hours. It was a good try, but it didn't take."

Jenny translated the admiral's words into signs for Ordol. She felt like the admiral expected her to say something in response, but she had no words—only a ball of bitter disappointment roiling deep in her belly. After all that danger, all that risk... nothing. She'd assumed the streamers and lights, the party atmosphere, had been a celebration of their success. But it was only a celebration of her own return.

Admiral Mackerel said, "The empress wanted to cancel the party, but I think we need it even more now." He leaned close and whispered, "You did right, ordering them to prepare it. In the darkness, we need a little light."

After that, Jenny was passed from one hug to the next until all of her fellow Barracuders, a couple of the navy otters, and even one of the Howard dogs had given her a welcome home embrace. One by one, the otters knelt down to sign their thanks and welcomes to Ordol as well. Though, as soon as the octopus could, he slithered his way through the crowd to the elevator platform and descended into the watery depths of the base. Jenny couldn't blame him. He'd been away from his natural atmosphere, stuck inside that clingy spacesuit for far too long.

Even so, she was sorry that he was missing the welcome home party. The Persian empress and the Howard dogs had done an excellent job of following her orders while she was gone—the snacks were clever concoctions of canned tuna, dehydrated milk, and other goods that must have been stored securely enough to survive the Persian colony's submersion under the rising Europa oceans. They'd even rigged up some sort of stereo system, and bouncy, fun music vibrated in the air.

It felt surreal to listen to a puppy band howling out inane lyrics about sunsets and California beaches inside an atmo-dome under the watchful face of Jupiter. But the Howard dogs danced like they'd never heard the word shame, shaking their hips, wagging their tails, and bobbing their heads until their ears flopped. They looked hilarious—most of them had clearly never danced on a moon before. Their rhythmic shakes and shimmies threw them too high due to the low gravity, and they fell too slowly to match the beat of the music. Their dancing was exuberant, but wildly out of sync.

Otters aren't usually slow to join a party, but most of the otters here were navy officers, on deployment and still in their starched, stiff uniforms. Even so, they began swaying and swinging their rudder tails too. Several of the otters clearly had experience dancing in low gravity—Destry and Amoreena were especially deft-footed, flipping themselves into complicated somersaults and double-steps with their flipper feet.

The Persian cats—ex-empress and members of her cabinet—sat around the edges, watching the merriment with their perpetual snub-nosed frowns. Somehow, they looked happy anyway. How could anyone be unhappy in the face of such canine buffoonery and lutrine skill?

Jenny stripped off the rest of her spacesuit and stowed it behind one of the improvised crate tables. It would be easier to dance without a bulky spacesuit on, and she could feel the wiggles and jiggles working through her long spine in response to the music. It had been a hard mission, and she hadn't been at all sure

169

she would survive. She was ready to *dance*. But before she could join the mass of jumping, jiving furry bodies—one of the navy otters had even wrapped his short arms around the Howard dachshund's long waist and launched into a breath-taking and incongruous slo-mo waltz!—Felix grabbed her paws. She thought he was going to dance with her, but instead he pulled her away from the dancing crowd.

Felix led Jenny to the edge of the party but not entirely away from it. He turned his back squarely away from everyone and started signing with his paws, holding them close to his chest so only she could see. "We have to make a decision. I haven't told the Admiral, because I don't..." His paws faltered, and he started the phrase again. "I don't trust him with something this... big."

"What is it?" Jenny asked aloud, figuring the question was bland on its own, and her voice was unlikely to carry over the pulsing noise of the party. Whatever Felix had to say, he must be awfully worried about being overheard if he wouldn't risk speaking it aloud even amidst all this chaos, chatter, and music.

"I can stop the raptor fleet," he signed.

For a moment, Jenny was elated, but Felix wouldn't be acting so secretive and scared if there weren't a catch. "...but?"

Felix's face showed all the emotion, all the torment that would have been in his tone of voice if he were speaking. His paws hurried on in a rush, signing, "Everything started working when we flooded the base—all the controls came online, and I've been studying them, but I don't understand them. I don't know what this base is supposed to do, but it's powerful. Very powerful. I can't use it the way it's supposed to be used—not yet—I don't even know what that way is. But... I know I can cause it to start building up energy in the core of Jupiter. It would take weeks... all the time we have left. The fleet would be nearly to Earth. But..."

"What would take weeks?" Jenny signed, keeping her paws close, feeling too afraid herself now to commit her own thoughts to voice.

"We could destroy Jupiter. The whole planet."

170

The gravity of his statement took a moment to sink in. Then the world did a somersault in Jenny's mind. "Are you serious?" her paws flung wide with the signs, carefulness falling to the wayside. She could hardly understand how she and Felix were having this conversation. They were Jolly Barracuders—otters who flirted with piracy and chased down every chance for fun in the Solar System. They weren't warriors deciding whether to commit genocide.

And yet, Jenny and Ordol had been fighting for their lives. Otter ships had been destroyed by raptor vessels—no chance for mercy, no bargaining, no diplomacy. Otter lives lost. And cats. The Persian colony had been attacked mercilessly. Jenny didn't know how many Persians had been lost before the *Jolly Barracuda* had saved the survivors.

"This is too big to trust to the navy," Felix signed. "I needed to bring it to you."

Jenny looked up at the sky. Jupiter's marbled face was hazy through the plastic atmo-dome ceiling. It was big. Bigger than Earth. Destroying it was more than genocide—it was restructuring the solar system. "Would it be safe?" Jenny signed. "For Earth. Would it throw off Earth's orbit or... I don't know... Would it hurt Earth?"

"No," Felix signed. "I've run the numbers over and over again. "Jupiter would crumple in on itself. It would start out slow, but the effect would cascade. Earth would barely notice."

"We could threaten the raptors," Jenny signed. "Not do it; just threaten to."

"We could," Felix signed. "But that would give them a chance to stop us, and they might succeed." He frowned, whiskers downturned and dark eyes serious. "If we want to do this, we need to start now."

Jenny put a paw to her collar and felt the empty place where her *Jolly Barracuda* sailing pin used to be. All she could think about was that stupid gold ornament in the talons of a baby raptor. Not a baby. A child who was old enough to make a choice, and who

171

had chosen to save Jenny and Ordol. Jenny had made a promise to that raptor. She had said, *"Maybe someday."*

Way, way down beneath the quagmire of toxic gases that looked like cheerful creamsicle clouds, there was at least one raptor who believed raptors and otters could be friends, that *maybe someday* they could visit each other peacefully.

"We can't destroy Jupiter," Jenny signed.

Felix looked relieved.

For a moment, Jenny was relieved too. The decision was made and over. But then the true weight of it came crashing down on her: she had a chance here to stop the raptors once and for all, and she was passing it up. Any animal they killed from here on out would be blood on her paws, because she could have stopped them. At an astronomical cost perhaps, but still—stopped them.

She needed a better alternative, and she needed it weeks ago. "Felix," she signed, not feeling up to fighting the blare of the music with her voice. "I need you to walk me through everything you've learned about this base." She looked around at the party, feeling sad that she was about to join Ordol in skipping it. But there would be other parties. At least, there would be other parties if she could find a way to use this base to protect Earth and all otter-kind from the raptors. "And I need you to do it now."

Jenny strode straight to the elevator platform without a single look back at the merriment, and Felix followed her. The two otters strapped on breathing masks and descended into the depths of the ancient octopus base, hoping to learn the secrets of the ancient octopuses.

Chapter 26: Kipper

Octopuses keep their secrets.

But cats can keep secrets too.

Kipper kept and coveted the secret of Siamhalla's missile armament, coddling it close to her heart, hoping it would be the salvation she needed. Of course, the octopus brigade that escorted her and all her otters back to the *Jolly Barracuda* might not give her credit for saving Earth from the raptors if Siamhalla did it. They might want to drag her back to their cartoon court and convict her of war crimes.

If so, she didn't like their odds of extraditing her.

Six octopuses might be an intimidating force under the ocean. They might even be an intimidating force in the *Jolly Barracuda's* travelling atmosphere of oxo-agua, but Kipper had no doubt that she could give them the slip in the crowds of otters on *Deep Sky Anchor*. She'd given a pair of police dogs the slip in those crowds before.

So, as the occupants of the *Diving Canary* travelled by ferry to the base of the space elevator, rode the elevator up to *Deep Sky Anchor*, and then found their way to the *Jolly Barracuda's* berth in the docking section, Kipper watched closely for where her best chances at escape on the trip back would be. She would be prepared. Choir's Deep had been a fantastical place to visit, but she had no intention of returning there to live out her life as a prisoner.

Aboard the *Jolly Barracuda*, Kipper returned to her old habits and hid away in the kitchen with Emily, the ship's octopus chef. Usually, she hid there because she had joined the *Jolly Barracuda* crew as a passenger originally and wasn't much help on the bridge or in the engine room. She didn't know a lot about running a spaceship, and she could be more useful—and out of the way—in the kitchen.

Now she hid in the kitchen because the entourage of octopus guards from Choir's Deep seemed to want to avoid Emily. The octo-ninjas gave Kipper a wider berth and thus more privacy when Emily was near. So she chopped fish and rolled it in seaweed, helping Emily make the daily meals for the *Jolly Barracuda* crew. On their previous trips, Kipper had helped less, leaving her paws free to sign and chat. With her eight arms, Emily could cook and sign all at once, but Kipper had to concentrate on either activity— she'd been using Swimmer's Sign for less than year, and she had to be very careful trying to maneuver knives and ingredients in an atmosphere that allowed small objects to float away with the slightest current caused by a careless motion. Strange swirly atmosphere.

Besides, Kipper didn't want to chat. She was still troubled that everything she'd learned from Emily about octopus society had matched so poorly with what she'd actually observed. She would feel betrayed or lied to... Except that she apparently didn't understand her own society all that well. She wasn't sure that she trusted second-hand observations anymore. If she were free to travel wherever she wanted, Kipper decided that she'd like to meet the mice in Mousfordshire. Perhaps spend a few months in Cedar Heights. There had clearly been a lot to learn there. Of course, she would only get that chance if the raptor fleet could be defeated.

Yet as the days passed and the raptor ships approached Earth, Kipper grew more and more certain that the Siamhalla missiles would stop them. She followed the news from Earth—the riots were worse; cats were marching for Petra's freedom; catteries were burned down and the dogs responsible were released on parole while Petra stayed in jail. But Kipper knew it would all get better when Siamhalla saved Earth by stopping the raptors.

She was half right.

Siamhalla launched their missiles—more than a dozen nuclear missiles, their entire armament—along with a recording of Josh and several other members of their ruling council stating their support for Earth and all the animals living. They released the missiles and the message at dawn on the East coast of the Uplifted States of Mericka. It was the middle of the night for Kipper on the arbitrary sleep cycle aboard the *Jolly Barracuda*, but Chauncy and Pearl who were on the night shift woke everyone else up.

Everyone crowded onto the bridge to watch the news roll in. The main viewscreen showed a live video streamed from a telescope observatory on the moon: Siamhalla's missiles showed up as a white streak, like a cluster of shooting stars, headed towards a bumpy mass of red and orange spots that were only visible due to an infrared enhancement. The missiles' course looked true. Kipper held her oxo-agua breath, knowing that in only a few minutes time this whole war could be over.

The otters and octopi around her signed to each other in a flurry of webbed paws and tentacular arms while close-captioned videos of newscasters—mostly otters, but also a Golden Retriever—filled the smaller screens around the bridge with further speculation and commentary. The video of Josh and other Siamhalla cats played over and over again, moving from one screen to the next, as every newscaster took a turn dissecting it.

"*Every puppy and kitten will remember where they were on this day,*" scrolled the words under the Golden Retriever. She seemed to assume that the missiles would be successful and waxed philosophical about what it meant for a nation of felines to save Earth. The otter newscasters were by and large more circumspect, speculating as to the exact force that the missiles might deliver and how deadly of an explosion the raptor fleet could probably withstand.

As the missiles drew closer to the raptor fleet, the flurry of signing paws and tentacles on the *Jolly Barracuda's* bridge settled down. Even the newscasters' eager analysis slowed to the occasional inane observation—"*They sure are getting close now!*"—as every eye focused on that shiny streak of missiles.

Siamhalla's teeth.

Would their bite be fatal?

Captain Cod looked away from the screen and stared directly at Kipper. "Did you know about this?" he signed. "Is this your doing?"

He was giving her a chance to take credit in front of the octopus guards. Their colors flushed through a variety of patterns. Except for the oligarch with the metal tentacle whose natural skin stayed deep, deep red and spiky.

Kipper signed, "I knew about it."

Captain Cod nodded and turned back to the main viewscreen, but the oligarch signed, "It matters not. Whether or not you knew, this is not your doing."

Kipper felt the soft, probing of a tentacle wrap around her shoulder and the many kiss-like touches as another coiled around one of her paws. She looked over to see Emily's yellow eyes staring at her with hope and worry. No one understood Kipper's fears better than Emily—trapped between the raptor fleet and the octopus guards from Choir's Deep. Emily signed to her, "If this works, and the guards still drag you back for a trial, I'll go with you. I'll advocate for you and defend you." They were in this together. Except that Kipper had every intention of fleeing incarceration.

Siamhalla's teeth met the raptor fleet, and the bumpy mass of red and orange shone bright, bright white. The *Jolly Barracuda's* pilot—Boris, a sea otter with rows of golden hoops piercing both of his little round ears—signed, "Well, that's that."

A shade of blue rippled along the octopus guards, each of them reacting to Boris' statement with the same hue. Kipper guessed it meant skepticism, but none of them signed anything that could have elucidated their true emotions.

The Golden Retriever newscaster barked ecstatically, and the caption read, "*What a sight! What an explosion! What a day! Victory for all of us!*" The various otter newscaster gave more measured responses: "*It does seem to have been a direct hit,*" said a river otter.

A sea otter on a different channel offered, "*It's hard to imagine that anyone on those vessels survived a nuclear attack like that.*"

The bright white spot on the screen dimmed back to red and orange splotches. The raptor fleet looked unchanged, although the trajectories of the individual vessels had been altered. They were no longer travelling in formation, but slowly drifting away from each other.

"*What the hell is going on?*" the Golden Retriever barked. "*Are reptiles un-killable?*" The sea otter offered, "*Of course, just because the vessels survived, that doesn't mean there's anyone alive onboard...*"

Then the vessels began, one by one, to change direction. Minor course corrections altered their trajectories until they were travelling in formation again.

Emily's tentacle wrapped tighter around Kipper's wrist and arm. She was scared. Kipper was scared too. Suddenly, facing a jury of octopuses trying her for war crimes didn't sound so bad. She had truly believed that Siamhalla would stop the raptors, and she would escape from the octopus guards when they returned to *Deep Sky Anchor*. But she would have gladly gone back to Choir's Deep with them and faced the prospect of a few years in a dank octopus jail cell if it meant those red and orange blobs had been obliterated from the screen.

The river otter newscaster said, "*The course corrections that we're seeing could be part of an auto-pilot system.*" The words were comforting, but the newscaster's glum expression was not.

They all knew the truth. The raptors were still coming.

Chapter 27: Petra

What does it look like when the world changes? Does it have to be hundreds of cats, marching together, holding up banners that read, "Free Petra!" and singing folk songs?

Or is it just one dog? Afraid to meet a cat's eyes and mumbling, "The charges have been dropped, and the officer who assaulted you has had his badge taken. He's not a police officer anymore. We're sorry."

Maybe the world was changing. If a police dog could be punished for assaulting a cat—if his fellow officers would even admit that he'd committed assault—maybe the world could get better. Petra wasn't sure. She was sure that those police dogs had cost her dearly. Whether the world had changed or not, Petra had changed. She was more afraid. And her own home had continued changing daily—as a home with small kittens does—while she'd been gone. And she'd missed it.

The kittens looked lankier, like someone had stretched out their arms and legs. They also acted differently. Pete started babbling a mile a minute the moment he saw her, trying to catch his mother up on everything she'd missed—though his tales of kittenish escapades were jumbles of nonsense to someone who hadn't been there to watch them. Allison had turned sulky and morose, seemingly unable to communicate except by twitching the tip of her gray-striped tail. Robin, who had always been clingy, a true mama's kitten, was polite but distant which broke Petra's heart.

It was hard to believe her kittens could have changed so much in only a few weeks. Precious minutes and hours that a police dog bully and his friends who believed him had stolen from her.

Then there was the house itself. Lucky had tried and failed to build bunk beds for the kittens, so the boys' bedroom was filled with lumber, nailed together at weird angles; the living room had been rearranged into a permanent fort with one couch upturned to stand on its end and the other couch pushed up against it; blankets were draped over everything, filling the room with ad hoc tents.

Bizarrely, the kitchen was sparklingly clean. Without Petra around, Lucky had been finally able to let his tenacious terrier tendencies scare the piles of dirty dishes and mostly-but-not-quite empty cartons and jars into submission. It was the one room in the house where everything was in its place, perfectly arranged. Everywhere else was chaos.

Petra let the chaos wash over her.

Lucky had planned a big celebratory dinner to welcome Petra home—fish-burgers and milkshakes with Alistair, Trudith, and Keith. They all kept the conversation conspicuously away from politics. They stayed to safe topics—which school the kittens would go to, which parks had new playground structures, what kind of books the kittens were reading.

Petra played along, but it made her feel small and trapped. She understood what they were doing—no one wanted to talk about anything big. If her family which included the president of the country had found itself helpless in the face of its own justice system ("justice"—what a joke), how much more helpless were they in the face of a raptor fleet from Jupiter? They didn't want to talk about it, because there was nothing left any of them could do. They were all waiting.

Waiting to see if they'd survive whatever attack the raptors had planned.

Waiting to see if there would be a future.

It didn't make sense to plan for a future that might not happen.

But Petra had spent weeks in a tiny cell. She needed the world to be big and expansive. She needed to make plans in spite of what that cop dog had done to her. In spite of the raptors.

After dinner, the kittens dragged Trudith and Keith into their epic blanket fort to play a game they called *Golympics!* It seemed to mostly involve climbing all over Trudith, pulling her floppy black ears and stepping on her shoulders, while arguing over which of them had won the gold medal, which was actually just a shiny brass lid from a jar of sardine salsa. Keith played the role of arbiter and made sure each kitten got a turn gloating over the brass lid.

"I never get tired of watching that," Alistair said.

"What?" Lucky asked. The terrier's sleeves were pushed up high, and his paws were filled with dishes to take to the kitchen. Somehow, that made him look extra-scruffy. "The kittens playing?"

The two adult orange tabbies—Petra and Alistair—looked at each other. Petra knew what Alistair meant. But of course, a terrier mutt who'd grown up in a family with his own parents didn't. "Playing with an adult dog who loves them," Petra said.

Lucky's bearded muzzle twisted into a lopsided smile. "They have lots of those. In fact, my brothers have been talking about moving closer, then they'd have some aunt and uncle dogs around. Also puppy cousins."

Lucky disappeared into the kitchen with his pile of dirty dishes while Petra reeled at the idea of a whole family of terriers moving to be closer to them. She wished it made her feel safer. It didn't. But it might make her kittens feel safe. Someday, the puppies they played with would grow up to be dogs who weren't afraid of an unarmed cat who happened to hiss. Maybe.

Alistair leaned in close and whispered, "Who'd have thought that you'd be the big family cat, huh?"

Petra foresaw a lot of family dinners and backyard barbecues in her future with kittens and puppies running rampant. But those weren't the sort of plans she wanted to make. "We need a space program," she said.

"What?" Alistair's green eyes looked startled, and his orange ears twisted about as if he were listening for reporters waiting to pounce on The President's any word. He lowered his voice to the quietest of whispers and said, "*There's no way to build a space program that fast."* Even in the privacy of Petra's home with secret service dogs posted outside and the covering noise of kittens mewling about pretend gold medals, he didn't mention the raptor fleet.

Petra didn't either. That wasn't what this was about. If she was having trouble visualizing a better future on Earth, maybe what the world needed was to become larger. "I don't mean for protection," she said. "Exploration. Expansion. Colonization. I don't know. What the otters are doing—we need to do that too. It shouldn't just be purebred cats—"

Alistair interrupted to say, "And Kipper."

"—and Kipper up there. It needs to be all kinds of cats and dogs. It needs to be the Uplifted States of Mericka too. We need a space program. We need hope." She needed hope.

Alistair started to object, but suddenly the kittens were on them like a whirlwind—laughing and mewing, scrabbling over their mother and uncle in the pursuit of yet another imaginary medal. Next, all three kittens fell to the floor and began somersaulting about the room like orange- and gray-striped tumbleweeds.

Before Alistair could catch his breath, Petra pressed her point further: "We need something to look forward to. I can't just hold my breath, waiting to see if there will be a tomorrow—if my kittens will get to start school next year. I need to assume they will. We need to assume that there is a tomorrow worth building. Everyone does."

Alistair frowned grimly and echoed Petra's words, "We need a space program." The way he said it, it wasn't entirely clear if he was mocking her or agreeing with her. But he sighed deeply and added, "Put together a budget. Find the money, and I don't know. I'll see what I can make happen."

Petra wasn't sure if he was humoring her because they were siblings or if this was how he treated all policy requests—tolerant, tired, noncommittal. She also wasn't sure that she believed in his ability to get anything done anymore. That one dog cop had shaken her faith in most of the world. No matter. She would take it. She would work out a budget and a plan.

When Trudith and Keith had said goodbye and Alistair had departed in a swarm of secret service dogs who'd been waiting conspicuously outside, Lucky put the kittens to bed. Petra watched from the doorway for a while as the terrier helped with pajamas, brushed sharp kitten fangs, and read picture books about otters dancing in the sky. She'd already had her goodnight hugs—although with Robin, she'd had to settle for a goodnight handshake, which was hilariously adorable but also sad. Apparently, he didn't do hugs these days.

Petra felt a pang of guilt stepping away from the door—shouldn't she be the one inside the sanctuary of the kittens' room, performing the rites and rituals of the bedtime sacrament, surrounded by scattered and forgotten toys and games? Shouldn't she want to be? She had missed so much, shouldn't she be making up for it? But she could never make up for it... An extra ten minutes now wouldn't give her back the days she had lost.

She'd had her goodnight hugs, and now she wanted to call Blaine.

The Jellicle cat had give her his number before he'd gone home, leaving her alone in that jail cell. There'd been nothing to write it down with—in spite of all the papers Trudith had brought for them to analyze, they'd been given nothing to write with—but she remembered it.

Petra sat down at the computer in the corner of the chaotic living room and waited for Blaine to answer her vid-call.

When his image appeared, the Jellicle cat was as impeccably dressed as he'd been before—black and white splotched fur perfectly complemented by a pin-striped suit. He looked amused, and Petra realized he must be reacting to the half-knocked-over blanket forts behind her. "What happened there?" Blaine asked.

"Kittens," Petra answered matter-of-factly.

A moment later Lucky came into the room and said, "The kittens are in bed now. Oh, I didn't see you had a call. Hi." Lucky waved at the screen for Blaine to see. Then he came over and squeezed one of Petra's paws. "Don't stay up too late trying to save the world." He brushed his bearded muzzle against the top of her head, leaving a kiss between her pointed ears before going.

"Save the world?" Blaine asked when Lucky was gone.

"It's a joke," Petra said. "Lucky thinks I'm always trying to save the world. But tonight, I'm just hoping to change it."

"Okay," the Jellicle said with an intrigued smile under his whiskers. "How? And why call me?"

Petra explained that she wanted help putting together a budget for a space program, and Blaine looked pensive. His ears skewed, and he finally said, "Aren't you the cat who thought catnip laws were too big to tackle?"

"What do catnip laws have to do with a space program?" Petra saw one of her kittens—orange-furred, so one of the boys— peering out of the hallway into the living room. She gestured to him that he could come over, and moments later Robin crawled into her lap and nestled his head against her chest, right under her chin. It was awkward balancing his weight against her own in the desk chair, but it was also the most peaceful feeling she could imagine—holding her little boy in her arms, with his soft fur ruffled against her own. His breathing was so steady. Petra closed her eyes for a beat, just to enjoy the feeling, while listening to Blaine answer her question.

"Are you kidding?" Blaine said. "Catnip isn't even mentioned in the Book of the First Race. Whereas space travel is *specifically* prohibited. There are whole poems—*whole books of psalms*—that basically amount to the holy humans holding their hands out and saying, 'STAY!' to all of dog-kind before they left Earth. The entirety of dog religion is founded on the idea that dogs—and by extension cats—" Blaine rolled his eyes dramatically at the idea that cats were only an afterthought. "—are meant to stay put, paws firmly on the ground."

"First Racers can't take that seriously," Petra said, trying not to disturb the kitten who was now purring against her. She stroked his pajama-clad back.

"They do," Blaine said, green eyes blazing. "If they didn't we'd already have a space program. And a lot of other technology for that matter. You should really read the Book of the First Race. It determines more of our lives than most cats realize. Did you know that some First Racers believe we're not even meant to have networked computers? Or cell phones?"

Petra's ears skewed. She'd battled dogs and their beliefs before. And won. "Look, I just need you to help me with the budget. Will you do that?"

"It's a waste of time..." Blaine argued, but Petra could see that he wanted to be won over. Hope is better than despair and futility. She was offering hope.

"Let me worry about that," Petra said. "I'll figure something out." With Robin sleeping and purring in her arms, Petra felt powerful. She would change the world for her kittens. If Robin believed in her, she could do anything.

Chapter 28: Kipper

Kipper was trying really hard to believe she could do anything. More specifically, she was trying really hard to believe that she could swing a magnetic grappling hook across empty space, snare a passing raptor vessel, and successfully board it as the *Jolly Barracuda* passed it by. Trugger had explained how it would work to her a hundred times. She'd had weeks to get used to the idea— numb to it even—but now that she was wearing her spacesuit, standing in an open airlock and staring that empty space directly in the eye, she couldn't believe she'd let herself get into this situation.

The otters standing in their spacesuits on either side of her seemed confident. Grimly confident. Like they were facing a suicide mission. Except they expected their suicides to come at the talons of raptors inside the approaching vessel, not by spinning out into empty space and dying a slow death of asphyxiation due to messing up with their grappling hooks and never making it to the approaching vessel in the first place. Which was definitely what Kipper expected.

A robotic voice spoke in Kipper's helmet: "We're nearing the moment of closest approach. Be ready." It was the computer's text-to-speech voice, used by Boris the pilot since the *Jolly Barracuda* was still filled with its oxo-agua atmosphere. He was the only otter who'd stayed onboard. All the rest of them were lined up in the airlock, packed closely side-by-side like sardines (a comparison Trugger had made several times, possibly because he was hungry), waiting for Boris's order.

"And... go!"

Half a dozen otters and, a moment later, Kipper fired their grappling guns into the darkness of space that yawned in front of the open airlock. The magnetic grapples shot straight out, leaving their ropes behind like vector lines. Kipper felt the rope snap taut just as her eyes made out the shadowy bulk of the raptor vessel, sailing silently through the vacuum like an eerie space whale. Her grip on the grappling gun held, and she felt herself pulled out of the airlock, bumping against the otters beside her.

Kipper squeezed hard on the grappling gun and it began to reel her in, recoiling its rope and pulling her toward the raptor ship. The otters around her sailed toward the vessel on their own grappling lines.

"I really feel like a pirate!" Trugger's voice came over the helmet speakers, sounding thin. "Boarding an enemy vessel!"

Captain Cod's voice followed, uncharacteristically serious: "Stay focused. The *Jolly Barracuda* will take several hours to finish decelerating and swinging around to join us. We're on our own until then."

Kipper kicked her hind paws up in front of her, and her space boots thunked solidly onto the side of the raptor vessel. The boots were magnetic too.

"Whaddaya know?" Trugger said. "Cats land on their feet in space too, without a single planet in sight."

One of the otter-shaped spacesuits pointed into the sky, and then Pearl's voice came over the helmet speakers, "That one's a planet... and that one..."

"*Focus*," Captain Cod hissed. Kipper hadn't known otters *could* hiss. "We need to find an airlock or some other hatchway."

The otters dispersed, crawling over the raptor ship's hull like barnacles with a purpose. Or like... otters... trying to break into the biggest clam they'd ever seen? A flock of seagulls fighting over a coconut? Could Kipper go home now? Could Kipper go home ever?

She needed to pull herself together. This was a suicide mission, but maybe it was a suicide mission that they could win. If Kipper

186

could save her family on Earth—if she could protect Earth for all the kittens and puppies before she died—then surely that was worth the paralyzing fear she felt standing on the outside of a warship hurtling toward her homeworld through the vacuum of space.

Nonetheless, Kipper couldn't bring herself to move a single paw until she heard Chauncey over the radio say, "I found a seam in the hull... yeah... definitely, this is an airlock hatch."

Captain Cod barked, "Everyone to Chauncey!" and Kipper found her paws drawing her inexorably across the dark metal hull towards the congregation of space-suited otters. One of the otter figures knelt down and traced the edges of a panel beside the airlock hatch with the nozzle of an oilcan-shaped tool. Kipper wasn't sure if the nozzle was applying heat or chemicals, but the metal corroded away like it was being burned through by acid.

"Gather close," Captain Cod said, and Kipper realized he was the one holding the oilcan. He stood up and hooked the oilcan tool onto the back of his spacesuit along with the other tools there—including a two-handled sword that the otters called a lobster-sabre. Kipper had only seen them in movies before and had thought Trugger was joking when he'd insisted she'd need to learn how to handle one for this mission.

The four double-edged blades of a lobster-sabre curved towards each other in pairs, pointed outwards in opposite directions from the double handhold in the middle. Kind of like a pair of lobster claws, except made from shining metal blades. In the movies, they were deadly. In real life... Well, Kipper didn't doubt a lobster-sabre could still be deadly in her own paws—she just hoped it wouldn't be deadly to *her*.

Once all the spacesuit-clad otters were crowded close, Captain Cod knelt down again and removed the metal panel that he'd burned free beside the airlock. Underneath the panel, wires wrestled in a tangle. "When I hotwire this emergency lock," the captain said, "the raptors will know we're here for sure. So, as soon as the hatch opens, I want everyone inside the airlock as fast as...

187

as fast as..." He faltered for a metaphor. The stress was clearly getting to him.

But Trugger was quick with a save: "As fast as a swallow-tailed swift with a rocket pack and a strong tailwind!"

There was a long pause during which many of the otters tried to picture such a tiny bird wearing a rocket pack, and Kipper found herself praying to First Race gods she didn't believe in.

"Thanks," Captain Cod said. "When we get through the inner hatch, everyone fan out. Damage anything you can. That includes raptors themselves—this is a time to be heartless." The captain's voice broke a little on the word 'heartless.' Even if the raptors were a dire threat to his own people, he was not an otter who could order murder lightly. "Look for the bridge. Look for the engines. If we're going to take down the other vessels in this fleet, we need to capture this one. That means taking control of the bridge or engineering. Everyone got that?"

A chorus of otter voices yipped, "Aye aye!"

Captain Cod turned his head, taking a moment to look each of his officers in the eye. When he reached Kipper, the curving reflection of her own spacesuit on his faceplate obscured his expression. Then he tilted his head, and the reflection disappeared. Instead, she could see framed inside the helmet: downturned whiskers, a grim mouth, and dark eyes glinting like obsidian, sharp and hard. He wasn't the Captain Cod that Kipper knew and loved. He was a planetary hero.

A martyr.

No.

Kipper couldn't think that way. She couldn't afford to. She was going to get inside this enemy vessel and fight her hardest—for all the kittens back home.

Captain Cod worked his magic on the exposed wires, and the airlock hatch slid open. Kipper felt the rumble of its motors in the hull under her feet.

"Go go go!!" the captain shouted, and all the space-suited otters squeezed inside the airlock. Kipper squeezed in last.

Opening and closing the airlock hatches from inside the airlock was much simpler—Captain Cod only had to punch the single large button in the wall with his gloved fist. The outer hatch closed; air rushed in from vents in the walls; and then, breathless moments later, the inner hatch slid wide.

One after another, the otters emerged from the airlock and drew their lobster-sabres. Kipper felt her heartbeat echoing and pounding in her pointed ears as she reached behind her back and drew her own lobster-sabre. The curved sword settled heavily in her gloved paws. She did not want to swing it. She didn't want to be holding it.

"The bridge will be in the nose of the ship," Captain Cod said. "This way."

Kipper couldn't see Captain Cod's gesture from behind all the other otters, but the group of them began to move to her left, many of them releasing the magnetic hold on their boots so they could float freely in the zero gee. As they cleared away, Kipper could see the ship they'd entered better: the airlock opened into the middle of a wide tubular corridor; fern-like plants grew in four evenly spaced stripes along the corridor—ceiling, either wall, and floor—except that those terms had no meaning in a radially symmetrical tubular corridor with no gravity.

Kipper felt a pang of homesickness for the *Jolly Barracuda's* tacky fake-wood paneling and iron grated floors. With its decor like a cheap seafood restaurant, the *Jolly Barracuda* hadn't been her original idea of a spaceship, but it sure was a whole lot friendlier than this gleaming tube with its hydroponic ferns.

Or maybe that was just because Kipper felt sure she would die here. In this death tube.

And there stood death—with ruffled feathers, iridescent black, full of the swirling colors of an oil pool. Two raptors floated at the end of the corridor with their wing-like arms outstretched as if they were flying. They looked startled, if Kipper could read raptor expressions at all. They hadn't expected an unscheduled airlock cycle to mean they would find their corridor filled with space-suited otters wielding curved swords. Who would have?

In the lead of the otters, Captain Cod kicked off of the floor and sailed through the middle of the corridor, lobster-sabre swinging. The sharp blade grazed one of the raptor's wings and a cloud of feathers and blood exploded into the air to hover mesmerizingly in the zero gee. A gory cloud of black feathers and red droplets.

Captain Cod's momentum carried him between the raptors, narrowly escaping a sharp-clawed kick from one of them. He hit the corridor wall on the far side and tumbled through the ferns. After that, Kipper lost track. Lobster-sabres gleamed; otters tumbled, and their spacesuits tore under the sharp claws and teeth of the two raptors. Even without weapons, the raptors—easily three times the size of a cat and twice the size of a big otter—were formidable: angry tornadoes of feathers and muscle, ripping and slashing with their hooked toe-claws.

Kipper's feline body shook with terror and adrenaline, but her fight-or-flight response did not say fight. Every fiber of her body screamed for her to flee, and the sword in her paws didn't spring to life, fighting for her people. It hung dully in the zero gee. At best, a shield.

"Look out from behind!" a breathless otter voice shouted over the comm. It sounded like Chauncy. "They're coming from both directions now!"

Kipper spun around, still anchored to the side of the corridor with her magnetic boots, and saw three more raptors winging toward her. Tentacles rose from their shoulder blades and wielded rod-like weapons that crackled with electricity at their tips. Kipper had no intention of staying around for that.

The terrified tabby dove for cover in the nearest stripe of ferns. Under their green fronds, shame filled Kipper to the tip of her brushed out tail. She pressed her faceplate against the clear hydroponic plating that the fern stems grew through and watched the water rushing by around their roots underneath. Otters shouted warnings and orders to each other in her ears, but she couldn't muster the willpower to raise her sword and join them. If she was going to die, did it matter if she died fighting?

The rushing water under the clear plating reminded Kipper of the rivers on *Deep Sky Anchor*. Rivers in space. Rushing water... Where was it rushing to?

Wherever it was rushing to had to be better than here. Kipper raised herself up, held her lobster-sabre high, and then with all her strength, brought the curved weapon down on the hydroponic plating.

The transparent sheet shattered.

Water bubbled and spurted, spraying into the zero gee corridor, and Kipper dove through the hole in the broken plating. The jagged edges scraped against her spacesuit, but it didn't tear. No water seeped in.

Kipper dragged the lobster-sabre in one paw and swam for her life. The channel of water was barely wider than herself. The raptors wouldn't fit in it. This was truly an escape route. "Captain Cod," she said, pulling herself back together, "there are channels of water under the ferns!" There was no response, and she kept swimming, half dog-paddling and half kicking off the walls of the narrow channel, all the while trying not to panic at the sensation of being trapped in a tiny tube of rushing water. "Captain Cod?" He must be too busy fighting... They were all too busy. "Anybody?"

"Right behind you," Trugger answered. "It's a mess out there." It was comforting to hear his voice over the helmet speakers.

"I've no idea where this leads," Kipper admitted, fearing that she'd led one of the soldiers from the fray for nothing.

"Doesn't matter," Trugger replied. "At the very least, these channels have to tie into some sort of pump, moving the water throughout the ship. We wreck that, and we'll cause some real chaos and confusion."

Just what we need more of, Kipper thought. Although, truly, chaos and confusion were the friends of a small and losing battalion. This was not how Kipper wanted to die. She pawed her way through a particularly thick knot of fern roots and found that

191

the channel split on the other side. She steered away from the clear plating along the corridor and into the new channel, slightly wider and metal all around. After a few strokes, the new channel opened into a wide tank. Kipper paused in the entrance to the tank and myriad pairs of yellow eyes with rectangular pupils stared at her. Tentacles roiled in a pastiche of pastel colors all around.

This was where the raptors kept their octopus slaves.

Chapter 29: Kipper

Blackness. Beautiful, soothing blackness. Not the infinitely deep blackness of space, nor the red-green blackness behind closed eyes, but a swirling fractal cloud of blackness. Watery blackness. Ink. Enough ink to be from a dozen octopuses.

When the water cleared, all the octopuses were gone. Kipper doubted for a moment that she'd seen their yellow eyes at all. Then she saw subtle crinkly curves in the gray metal walls. It was like an optical illusion—if she focused her eyes just right, all the walls were covered with clinging camouflaged octopi. If she let her eyes unfocus even a little, all she saw was plain metal walls.

A yellow eye cracked open among the tentacles, and Kipper didn't hesitate to drop her sword and start signing. "Help us," she signed. "We want—" The yellow eye shut again. Looking at her deadly four-pointed sword floating beside her, Kipper could hardly the blame the octopuses for hiding.

"We need their help," Kipper said for Trugger to hear. "They know this ship, and we don't. They'd double our forces."

"They don't look like they want to help," Trugger said. He paddled up beside Kipper. "We can't make them revolt."

Kipper burned with frustration. And terror. And adrenaline. "We can't even *ask* if they won't look at us."

Kipper wanted to shout at the octopi and *make* them hear her out, but she couldn't do that in Swimmer's Sign. All she could do was lay her paws on them and hope they'd look at her. So, she dog-paddled her way over to the one that had peeked at her with its yellow eye and lay one gloved paw, as gently as she could, on the bulbous curve of its mantle. She couldn't feel the delicate flesh through her clumsy glove, but the octopus's skin flushed and fluttered with pinks and orange in response to her touch. Its eyes opened again. Both of them this time.

Kipper withdrew her paw and signed more slowly this time: "We're fighting the raptors. Not you. If we win, we can take you with us—all of you. There are whole cities of free octopuses where we come from. Help us, and we can free you."

"Those are big promises," Trugger said to her.

"Shut up," Kipper snapped.

"Also big ideas," Trugger said, ignoring the temper in Kipper's tone. "Ordol wasn't very good with Swimmer's Sign to begin with... Even the octopus half is pretty different from his dialect, and you're signing in the otter half."

"I know," Kipper said through gritted teeth. "But we haven't got anything better..." She trailed off as the octopus in front of her started to move.

The octopus's color shifted and sharpened into a bright cherry red, and its tentacles moved in a flurry of sign language—expressive, deeply meaningful, and far too fast for Kipper to decipher.

"Are you getting any of that?" Kipper asked Trugger, hoping she wouldn't have to sign to the octopus asking it to slow down.

"Not much," he said. "Like I said, the Jovian octopi don't use Swimmer's Sign. I think it's a dialect of a more ancient language that Swimmer's Sign was originally based on. Oh wait... That sign—" The octopus twisted two of its tentacle tips together. "That's the sign for friendship, isn't it?" Trugger made the corresponding sign with his gloved paws.

Kipper signed too: "Friend. Help." Over and over again, she signed those two words until her paws fell into a rhythm with the octopus's tentacles. They signed the words together in a silent chant.

The octopus's color faded and flushed, finally settling on a mottled pinky-gray. Then it floated toward Kipper and reached out for her lobster-sabre. She grabbed the curved sword from where it floated and handed it over more than willingly. The octopus wrapped its tentacles around the handholds and hefted the blade, maneuvering the lobster-sabre through the water, measuring its heft and momentum.

"Is it a good idea to hand over your sword to a stranger?" Trugger asked. "The enemy of our enemy isn't necessarily our ally. No matter what this octopus seemed to be signing."

The octopus flipped the sword deftly in its tentacles and proffered it back to Kipper. The tabby took it back more reluctantly. She'd kind of liked the idea of the octopus doing her fighting for her.

Maybe, Kipper thought, she didn't have to give up on the idea so easily...

The octopus jetted away from her and Trugger, back to the deceptively plain metal wall. It touched its tentacles to the disguised metal-gray tentacles of its fellows, moving across the wall, caressing one after the other. And one after another, pairs of yellow eyes opened, stared skeptically at Kipper or Trugger, and then turned querulously to Kipper's new ally.

Kipper started to get excited, and her paws moved to sign, "Join us! Fight with us! Fight for your freedom!" But in the time that it took her to sign those simple words, her octopus ally's tentacles danced and twisted and wriggled more words than Kipper could follow. She imagined an entire eloquent speech, beseeching the octopi to rise up and fight the raptors... But she was only guessing. Her excitement betrayed her, and she breathed the words, "We'll free these octopi, and then someday we'll free them all." She only meant the words for herself, but her helmet radio was transmitting.

"What do you think is happening here?" Trugger asked.

"Revolution," she whispered. "An uprising." She could picture these octopi leading her and Trugger to victory.

"These octopi have been enslaved by the raptors for *generations*. Probably longer than either of our species have been uplifted. Possibly *millions* of years. You think because a cat shows up with a sword and says, 'fight with me,' that you're suddenly going to start a revolution?"

As if Trugger's words were a dark wind, the yellow lights of all the octopi eyes in the room began to extinguish. One by one, they shifted their tentacles, signed a single word that Kipper could easily recognize, and closed their eyes, disappearing again into the smooth metal wall.

The word they signed was *no*.

Kipper's ears bumped uncomfortably inside her helmet as they tried to flatten with shame, but they couldn't shut out the echo of Trugger's words. His question twisted and mocked her: "What do you think? You're going to start a revolution?"

That was exactly what she'd thought, but she meowed, "*No,*" defensively anyway. "I had to try. We have to try everything that could stop these ships."

Captain Cod's voice crackled to life over the radio, and Kipper's body flooded with relief. She hadn't realized how scared she was that he'd already died. She'd thought for sure—after their prolonged silence—that the others were long gone. All of them. Instead, she realized with guilt that they'd simply been too busy fighting to speak.

"It's a good idea, Kipper," the captain said. "But we need all paws on deck now. So, if the tentacles aren't with you—" The captain's spacesuit rushed through the water, right past Kipper and Trugger. He swam like a torpedo in a hurry. "—then it's time to move on." A dozen more space-suited otters barreled startlingly through the watery room, following the captain. They didn't stop to consort with octopi. They swam straight through and continued towards the nose of the ship. "Thanks for the shortcut though."

Kipper looked at the octopuses all around. Their subtle curves blended into the walls in a complete denial of Kipper's plea. These octopuses knew the layout of the ship. They knew where the bridge was, and they might even know how to work the controls. But only one of them would even look at Kipper now, and the soft crinkles in the skin around its eyes didn't give the tabby any hope.

The octopus had watched the brigade of otters pass through the chamber with a piercing, judging intelligence. When it turned its yellow gaze back toward Kipper, its tentacles began to roil and twist in motions so fluid that Kipper barely recognized them as signs. She was used to Emily's signing, and Emily's signs were more punctuated—a motion, then a pause, then a motion. Was Emily always talking slowly for her? Like the octopi in Choir's Deep had had to?

The words in this octopus's roiling tentacles weren't clear to Kipper; something like *before, too early, sorry,* and maybe *good luck.* The octopus's tentacles slowed, and it drifted back towards the wall of the chamber to rejoin the others.

Whatever it had said, the octopus was done with her. They were all done with her. As Kipper watched the octopus disappear against the smooth metal wall, she signed, "Thanks anyway," only moments before it closed its yellow eyes, winking out entirely.

Then she felt Trugger's gloved paw on her shoulder. "Come on," he said. He swam past her in his spacesuit—a torpedo reluctantly moseying along, none-too-eager to reach the battle ahead but grimly determined to play his part. "The others need us."

Kipper hefted her sword and kicked her back feet, propelling herself awkwardly through the water after the otters. "For Earth," she said, and she was answered by a chorus of otter voices, echoing her words: "*For Earth!*" It wasn't an army of octopi who knew secrets about the ship they were on, but it was an army. A small one. Kipper was not alone. She wouldn't die alone.

Kipper followed Trugger through the narrowing passageway, swimming faster as the current picked up. When the passage got narrow enough, she kicked against the walls, half-crawling and half-swimming. Fern roots tangled with her paws, and half of the panels lining the passageway were see-through. Through the water and transparent panels, Kipper saw a wavery view of the raptor ship.

They were swimming in the walls of a busy room. Raptors flapped about the room like giant black condors, moving from one station of gleaming screens and buttons to the next. Behind them was a star-scape. No wait, a giant viewscreen. Oh god, this was the bridge. They'd made it to the bridge.

197

"Here's our stop!" the captain announced cheerfully. The metal walls of the watery passageway vibrated as Captain Cod smashed his lobster-sabre through a transparent panel. The other otters followed suit, and even Kipper finally swung her curved double-sword. The transparent panel shattered under the lobster-sabre's points, and Kipper spun in a splash of water into the raptors bridge, carried by her sword's momentum.

Kipper tumbled head over tail, trying to regain control of her sword in the zero gee, surrounded by total chaos. Lobster-sabres flashed; feathers flew; water spurted from the broken panels; and the star-scape on the viewscreen flickered out as Captain Cod shattered it with his lobster-sabre.

Static.

Sparks.

And suddenly a searing pain in Kipper's right hind paw. She swung her sword and grazed a raptor's wing more by luck than design. Her blade came away bloodied, and Kipper's stomach churned. She could hardly see who she was fighting, but she clung to the double handholds of her lobster-sabre for dear life. She swung the bloodied blade madly, throwing any momentum she could gather from a stray kick against a wall or ceiling into her swings. She swung at raptors. She tried to avoid otters... which was getting easier as the raptors took them down.

Kipper landed a blow on the wing of a raptor who'd already lost its brightly colored feather plumes, but before she could pull the sword away, the raptor gripped one of the pincer-blades with its talons. Blood floated away from the raptor's claws, but it held tight, wrenched the weapon out of Kipper's grip, and left the tabby floating helpless and unarmed.

"Help!" she cried, but as she looked around the bridge, she saw her compatriots cornered, disarmed, being torn out of their spacesuits. Not one of them still held a sword.

Tearing. Kipper felt the sensation as if her spacesuit were a second, numbed skin. Muggy warmth flooded through the rents in her spacesuit, and Kipper felt herself turned until a raptor face stared directly at her through the thin faceplate of her helmet. Its teeth were too close. Too sharp. It fogged the faceplate with its breath, and then it continued tearing her spacesuit open with its claws—peeling her as if she were a fruit for it to eat.

"Don't hurt me," Kipper whimpered. She didn't expect the raptor to hear or understand her, but the words spilled out of her anyway. Then she felt the strangest vibration rising up from her throat. It was a truly perverse sensation. But she found herself... purring.

She was so scared that she started purring.

This is the way the world ends, she thought. *Not with a yowl, but with a purr.*

Chapter 30: Emily

Emily's world had ended before.

A prismatic kaleidoscope of lives had hung around her. Strings of seed pearls; each pearl an entire life waiting to unfold; an entire life she had created.

Before Emily had laid her eggs, she'd been a chef like she was now. That was her first life. And she'd shed it entirely, like a snake's old skin, when she'd felt the urge to lay her eggs. She'd retreated to a nursery cave—like the ones in Choir's Deep, except Emily had lived in a much smaller octopus city, much deeper in the ocean. Their ways were different. More ceremonial, less metropolitan. More bound by tradition, but it was a tradition Choir's Deep octopi scorned.

When Emily had felt the urge to lay her eggs, she'd quit her job, abandoned her home and belongings, and said goodbye to all the friends she had. It was the end of her life, and she'd gladly accepted it.

Emily tended her eggs, lovingly watching as the tiny fetal octopi developed inside their translucent orbs. Each one different. Each one perfect. Each one an entire life ready to unfold. She'd felt her heart expand to love every one of their thousands, and she'd felt her soul spread and prepare to disperse, carried away into their multitudinous, branching lives. She would lose herself and become many.

Instead, the pearls broke open, and Emily had watched her babies drift away into their own lives.

She stayed inside the Emily-skin she'd been ready to leave behind. A lonely octopus alone in a cave filled with strings of broken eggs, abandoned and confused.

She had waited, but she didn't die. She didn't ascend. She grew bored... And she tried to go back to her old life, but the friends she'd said goodbye to treated her like a ghost. Her home and belongings had been claimed by another.

Eventually, Emily travelled to a larger octopus city—one where the octopi were horrified at the idea of mothers dying with their eggs' hatching. But Emily was horrified by them. She didn't feel less like a ghost, she simply felt like the city was crawling with ghosts—women who should have died. She should have died, and they should have too. That's what Emily had been raised to believe, and it was a belief too deep inside her to die when she hadn't.

Where does a ghost go? Emily had drifted, until she found herself among the otters. She didn't feel like a ghost among otters. They treated her like a bizarre, exotic alien creature, so she became one for them. She went back to being a chef and learned to cook clam chowder.

Sometimes Emily wondered about those tiny sparks of life that had left her behind. How many of her children had survived their arduous childhoods? Who were the octopuses they had become? Kipper would believe that Emily should care about them. Emily knew that from watching Kipper sign about her niece and nephews—kittens that weren't even related to her.

But Emily had never expected to know her many thousands of children. She had expected to become them, her soul escaping from her own limited body and multiplying thousands fold.

Those tiny, perfect octopi had denied her. Rejected her. Instead, the funny, fuzzy brown mammals of the *Jolly Barracuda* had accepted her, taken her in, and given her an entirely different life than she'd ever expected.

And now they were on a raptor vessel—fighting for their lives or possibly dead. The only fuzzy brown mammal left on the *Jolly Barracuda* was Boris the pilot, and he was on the bridge with the octopus entourage. It felt morbid to Emily, the way the octopi from Choir's Deep had been watching Kipper, judging her, and now they were on the bridge waiting to see Kipper and the otters fail. Emily wanted no part of it.

Well... That wasn't entirely true.

Emily felt an intense sadness in her middle-left arms, a sadness that desperately missed Kipper and wanted nothing more than to wait on the bridge for any drop of news. Her right arms, though, were restless and needed to be in the kitchen where they could stir and chop, whipping up salmon and tuna confections, keeping too busy to worry about Kipper and the other fuzzies. Though her left arms kept worrying: *who would eat these confections if the fuzzies never came back?*

Emily's hindmost-left arm kept curling and uncurling, completely uncooperative with her cooking and only interested in counting out a beat to the moments that Kipper was gone. It was driving the rest of her arms crazy.

Emily had never felt so divided before. Half of her had accepted that her life on the *Jolly Barracuda* was all but over; half of her was ready to move on and wanted to get this horrible transition over with. Her other half... It was afflicted with hope. Torturous, horrible, awful hope.

The oxo-agua in the kitchen shifted around Emily; she recognized the feeling—it meant the doors to the galley had opened. The galley was a large, long room filled with rows of tables; it appended Emily's small kitchen, separated only by hanging cupboards and the long countertop she used as a bar for serving her food. Unless the *Jolly Barracuda* was docked and drained, then the kitchen could be separated by transparent walls, turning it into Emily's personal aquarium.

Emily put down her pot of yellowfin, placed three knives on the magnetic knife-block, and turned to see what had caused the disturbance. Boris's bushy face looked in through the door of the galley, and when he saw Emily looking at him, he started signing. His paws moved in a rush; they looked like they were shaking. "The raptors are boarding our ship. I'm sorry. Hide if you can."

Emily's brittle reality shattered. The others had lost, and the end was coming. It was shaped like a nightmare with feathers.

Boris continued signing, "I'm heading to engineering to try to blow the engine, destroy the ship. I don't think I'll succeed, but wish me luck if you don't want to be taken by the raptors." He disappeared out the galley doors in a streak of brown fur.

Emily wasn't sure whether she should wish him luck. If he succeeded, and the ship exploded, she would die. It was hard to wish for that, no matter the alternative.

Seven of her eight arms went numb; the eighth stretched out to flip the switch that raised the aquarium walls around her kitchen. She wasn't sure how strong the walls were, but they had to be strong enough to hold in the liquid atmosphere when the rest of the ship was filled with a thin gas.

Whether they were strong or not, they made Emily feel safe.

From behind her transparent walls, Emily watched shadows pass by the open door to the galley. She could no longer feel their movements, cut off from the rest of the ship inside her aquarium. So it didn't feel real when she saw a pair of feathered raptors look through the door, tentacles rising from their shoulders. If they were real, she should have been able to feel them in the motion of the water.

But her kitchen stayed perfectly still.

They didn't see her; or they didn't care about her. Either way, the raptors moved on, and Emily sank down to the smooth surface of her chopping counter. Her tentacles glued her tightly on, and her skin wrinkled and flushed, instinctively matching the diamond-and-squares tessellation pattern. If the raptors came back, they'd have to look really closely to see an octopus in the kitchen at all.

For better and much, much worse, the next raptor to come by wasn't looking for hidden octopuses—it was chasing the silver-armed octopus oligarch.

The oligarch jetted into the galley like a tornado of tentacles, whirling and changing direction, feinting to get away from the awkwardly swimming—flying?—raptor. The raptor's black feathered arms waved out of rhythm with the water, dragging against it instead of propelling the raptor forward.

The liquid atmosphere clearly gave the oligarch a huge advantage over the raptor, but the raptor had friends. Three more raptors with tentacles rising from their shoulders swam purposefully into the galley. They didn't seem to be wielding weapons, but they all had sharp teeth and claws.

Emily closed her eyes, telling herself that it was to make herself less visible—with her skin camouflaged, her yellow eyes were her most visible part—but it was really to shut out the vision of the next few moments.

With her eyes closed and the aquarium walls shielding her, Emily couldn't sense the raptors and their senseless, bloody murder at all. She could have been anywhere. She could have been back on Earth in the cave with her strand-of-pearl eggs by the thousands, still waiting for them to hatch and carry her soul away with them into myriad thousands of lives.

Emily opened her eyes; she couldn't keep them closed forever. The water in the galley was murky with blue and black. Blood and ink. Blue octopus blood. But the raptors were gone.

Emily knew she should stay put. If the raptors didn't know about her, she could wait them out. They'd abandon the ship eventually, and she could fly the whole thing away. She'd flown the *Jolly Barracuda* before during disasters. Maybe that was the new life coming for her: Captain Emily of the *Jolly Barracuda*.

It sounded lonely. She would miss her brown fuzzies.

While Emily's left arms worried about the future, her right arms took action. None of Emily's arms had any love for the octopus oligarch, but she had to know if the oligarch had survived anyway. So, Emily lowered the aquarium glass and jetted into the muddy cloud; it tasted sour and tangy on her sucker discs.

At the darkest part of the cloud of ink and blood, Emily found the oligarch, still twitching and still bleeding blue, clinging to a tabletop. Two of her tentacles had been ripped off entirely, and a third was torn down the middle, splitting it hideously in half. The oligarch wouldn't last long, but her uncannily blue eyes opened and fixed on Emily.

With her remaining tentacles, the oligarch shakily signed, "I can't die. You have to carry on for me." Then her shining silver tentacle cracked down the middle, revealing a normal tentacle inside, laced with thin wires. The wires withdrew from the oligarch's flesh and floated eerily as if searching for a new tentacle to burrow into.

Emily's tentacles—all of them—backed away, recoiling from the hideous sight of a maimed and dying octopus trying to give her its cyborg arm. But the oligarch lifted the empty mechanical sleeve and held it toward her; its blue eyes pleaded with infinite sadness.

One of Emily's mid-most left arms reached out and allowed the oligarch to press it into the silver sleeve. Wires burrowed into Emily's flesh as the sleeve closed around her arm, but she was too busy to feel the prickly pins and needles sensation.

Memories flooded Emily's nerves, bouncing between her arms, telling her that she was hundreds of different octopuses—no, thousands. *She had lived for millions of years. She had come to Earth on a spaceship escaping the Jovian raptors before fuzzy mammals had even evolved. Before that... she had uplifted the raptors.*

Octopi came first.

Octopi were the first race.

Octopi hadn't even come from Earth; they'd travelled from another galaxy—possibly a parallel universe—and had found the pre-uplift raptors on Earth, thought they'd be useful, and uplifted them. Enslaved them. Then the raptors had rebelled.

Octopi had fallen from interstellar travelers to slaves of their own creations on Jupiter and exiled, forgotten refugees on Earth. They'd rebuilt, so slowly. The metal arm had been passed down from one oligarch to another; this was the first time it had returned to space in sixty-five million years.

All these memories came to Emily first-hand, stored in the mechanical tentacle. It was an older form of life than anything she had ever known and its memories overwhelmed her. She fell into them like a hall of mirrors, reflecting different lives and selves who had all become one through bonding with the silver tentacle.

Emily remembered the first time she'd ever looked down on Earth from space, when the primordial planet had crawled with dinosaurs. The raptors had been far and away the smartest dinosaurs, easily the best choice for uplift.

Emily remembered training her first ever raptor steed; she'd been so proud and fond of him. His strong bipedal legs had let her stride across dry land; she'd known right then it was the beginning of a Golden Era for her species.

An era that had cracked and twisted when the raptors had found a way to reverse the control modules in their saddles, letting them perversely control the arms of their own makers like possessed marionette puppets taking control of the puppeteer.

Emily remembered her own raptor turning on her, fitting her as she struggled into the saddle that had once let her control him.

She remembered lying catatonic, too stunned to move, the taste of blood and ink in the water, as a stranger raptor lifted her again.

Wait...

No...

She didn't remember that; it was happening now.

Emily reached through the millennia of memories, trying to fill out her own tentacles, shake them back into motion and consciousness, but seven of her arms were too stunned by the parade of memories, passively watching as lifetimes lived themselves in shadow, partial and regurgitated, too vivid to tell them apart from the now, from the reality. Only her silver tentacle struggled as the raptor fitted Emily into the electronic seat between its shoulders.

Chapter 31: the Oligarch and the Raptor

Enzz'rr'kk was a junior officer whose pin-feathers had barely come in. Only a few months before, he'd been covered in downy speckling instead of regal raven black with bursts of purple on his elbows and cranium. Now he was a full-fledged warrior, complete with the tools of his trade—pliant octopus tentacles to extend his reach and capabilities.

Unfortunately, his octopus had been injured while fighting the fuzzy brown creature on the spaceship his squadron had been sent to secure. It had lost several tentacles, and the pain the octopus felt was distracting. So when Enzz'rr'kk saw the two octopuses on the galley table—one mangled beyond use but the other in perfect condition—he decided to trade for an upgrade.

He didn't worry about the difference between Earth octopi and Jovian ones, though he should have. His superior officers would have, but Enzz'rr'kk was young and foolish raptor. He didn't think to worry about the silver tentacle either. He simply lifted the silver-tentacled octopus into the harness on his shoulders, and plugged her brain into his, like he'd done with dozens of octopi before.

Such small choices are the hinges the universe turns on.

Enzz'rr'kk had felt the minds of the octopuses he used for their tentacles bleed into his own before, but their lives were small and manageable, easy to forget, easy to ignore. Raised in aquariums, kept as slaves, their lives were a quiet noise that he'd learned to shut out. Also, although he didn't know it, the Jovian octopi, trained in their servitude, had practice hiding their thoughts from the raptors who enslaved them.

Emily had no practice shielding her mind from raptors.

Emily had no practice managing the whirlpool of memories pulling herself down.

Enzz'rr'kk was totally unprepared to be pulled down into millennia's worth of octopus lives with her.

Drowning in memories together, Enzz'rr'kk and Emily sensed each other—each of them infinitely young in comparison to the silver tentacle—and clung to one another, trying not to lose their individual selves entirely to the tentacle's wealth of being.

Wave after wave of memories hit them—love affairs, rivalries, great discoveries, and the minutia of day-to-day life that wouldn't be worth remembering except for how it howled out in contrast— each inheritor of the silver tentacle looking backward and being startled by how the previous generations had lived, the technologies they didn't have and the ones they did, the customs and beliefs that seemed immutable and yet gave way in time to new inviolable laws.

Through it all, a story became clear: the silver tentacle had enslaved raptors, run from them, and hidden on Earth, deep in the oceans. It spoke for octopi. It led octopi. It was octopi—it had been so many of them, and now it was Emily, and she was scared.

Enzz'rr'kk was scared too, and through the molasses of time, he found his own feathered body again and reached with his taloned arms to remove the whirlpool of memories inside the tentacles sprouting from his shoulders like wings. He threw the ball of tentacles away from him, and in the thick watery atmosphere of this strange alien ship, the octopus who he now knew as *Emily* floated there, still lost in the memories of the tentacle, and stared back at him with yellow eyes that during the eons of memories they'd shared had become the eyes of his friend.

Enzz'rr'kk reached out to Emily with talons that could have shredded her soft flesh to tatters and gathered her tentacles delicately, tenderly against his feathered breast. He rocked her like a new hatchling, knowing nothing else he could do to save her from the memories that roiled and bubbled inside her.

For her, there was no escape; the silver tentacle was part of Emily now, and she was part of it. She'd live forever, but she'd never entirely be herself again. Enzz'rr'kk knew all of that from the time he'd spent in the whirlpool of memories with her. The only comfort he could imagine for her was returning her to the small fuzzy creatures she loved—the gray striped one and the bushy brown ones. They'd been taken captive, but they were safe. The raptors weren't interested in killing mammals; they hardly registered, and certainly didn't seem threatening, as they'd been nothing more than scurrying feral mice and shrews when raptors last lived on Earth.

It was the octopi they'd been afraid of; their gods who had uplifted and enslaved them.

But apparently, the raptors had nothing to fear.

The octopi of Earth had retreated and become small. The vessels that had begun to sprout outward from the raptors' old homeworld belonged to the harmless little mammals, not the tentacled intergalactic travelers of old. No eldritch horrors needed to be razed from the oceans. Earth could be left in peace.

Now if only Enzz'rr'kk could convince his commanding officers...

Chapter 32: Kipper

Kipper couldn't convince Captain Cod to stop singing. The captain led his merry band of imprisoned otters in one round of sailing ditties after another, insisting it was the only otterly way to face certain death.

Kipper wasn't sure she liked it any better than she'd liked facing death with a lobster-sabre in her paws. She thought that perhaps the best way to face death might be with a strong dose of catnip, a rich mug of cream, and quiet contemplation, though she wasn't sure. All the boisterous singing around her made it too noisy for her to properly contemplate it.

How could they sing so cheerfully, plastered on the floor of a high-gee raptor jail cell, with their arms and legs immobilized by little electrical cuffs that the raptors had strapped onto their ankles and wrists? Bitterly, Kipper wished the raptors would hurry up and do whatever they had planned, so she wouldn't have to listen to chirpy otter voices sing sea shanties while her stomach twisted itself in knots anymore. Then she immediately regretted her curmudgeonly wish when a dark shadow fell over her.

Kipper twisted around awkwardly on the floor by wiggling her hips and shoulders, dragging her arms and legs like useless lumps, until she could see the three black-feathered raptors that rose over her and the otters like dark angels of judgement day. Demonic executors of doom. The foremost raptor's skull and forearms were crested with royal amethyst plumes of feathers, and enslaved tentacles stretched out thin and pale from its shoulders like skeletal wings. The two raptors behind it bore golden orange and yellow feathers; the tentacles on their shoulders draped list-lessly like shawls of souls.

All three of the raptors seemed undisturbed by the crushingly high gravity; they were apparently freakishly strong.

The foremost raptor's skeletal wings shivered, a slight flutter, and then they started signing. The bone-pale tentacles twisted haltingly into the words: "Does work? You understand? Speak if understand."

"Yes!" Kipper yowled, rocking her body madly against the high gee, trying to wake up her electronically-numbed limbs. She couldn't sign back without her arms.

The otters around her chorused her answer and began speculating: "Have the octopi taken over?"; "Are we going to be freed?"; "Let us go!"

The foremost raptor's eyes glinted at the floor full of moaning, squirming mammals, and it looked over its shoulder at the raptor with yellow crest feathers, screeched and cawed as if conferring with its compatriot, and then the second raptor came forward and removed the electronic cuffs from Kipper's forepaws.

Kipper tried to shake some feeling back into her tingling paws, and then she looked up at the purple-crested raptor looming above her to sign, "Thank you." She didn't know if she was signing to an octopus controlling a raptor or to a raptor controlling an octopus, but either way, it seemed safest to be polite.

The foremost raptor's head bobbed in a seeming expression of surprise, and then its tentacles signed, "Understood that. You're welcome."

The raptors screeched at each other for a while, and the longer they did, the more convinced Kipper became that the raptors were still in charge. The octopi had not overthrown them while Kipper and the others lay in this cell. That had been too much to hope for.

Eventually, the foremost raptor's enslaved tentacles began wiggling again; it signed, "Never talk like this before. Not expect work. Simple words please. Need to know: octopi hurt you?"

Kipper's brain scrambled in confusion. Was she being offered a way out? If she gave the right answer, was there any chance the raptors would let them live? *Let them go?* She had to game this question... But she had no idea what the raptors were looking for, and all the otters around her were shouting different answers at her, along with complex, confusing metaphors: "Tell them 'not a hair off a halibut's head!'"; "Two sardines don't make a salmon!"; "An algae's a better friend than an urchin!"

And finally, "As your commanding officer, I order you to tell them 'Never a bass, always a bassoon!'"

"*I don't think confusing them will help,*" Kipper hissed.

"It might," Trugger countered, almost reasonably.

Kipper couldn't think clearly enough to figure out what the raptors wanted to hear, but she knew that even in Choir's Deep the octopi had never actually hurt her. She signed, "No. Never."

The two raptors standing behind the foremost one made a coughing sound that could have been laughter until the foremost raptor cut them off with a screech.

"Octopi dangerous," the raptor signed with totally subdued and submissive octopus tentacles. "Must control octopi. Don't control you?"

"No one controls me," Kipper signed. She heard Captain Cod harrumph and mutter something about bassoonists behind her. Kipper kept signing: "I'm in charge." If the raptors were giving her a chance to negotiate, she would take it and take complete responsibility. This wasn't simply a *Jolly Barracuda* matter. Right now, Kipper spoke for all the cats and dogs on Earth. Even the squirrels and mice, and anyone else she didn't know about yet.

The three raptors looked at each other and then cawed to each other in quieter tones. Eventually, the orange-crested one left the chamber and returned a few moments later with a smaller, midnight blue-crested raptor clutching an octopus to its feathered breast. The octopus had a silver tentacle like the oligarch, but when it opened its eyes—

"Emily?" Kipper said and signed.

"Know this octopus?" the foremost raptor signed. Suddenly, in comparison to Emily's self-animated tentacles, the raptor's neurologically-controlled tentacles looked especially creepy.

"Yes," Kipper signed. She wanted to elaborate. She wanted to say Emily was her friend and beg them not to hurt her, but she dared not risk it. If she said too much, she might say something they didn't like. She didn't know what they'd like.

"Octopus say stay under oceans," the raptor signed. "Not spaceships. Not hunt raptors. Not enslave little fuzzies."

"Right," Kipper agreed. "Octopi harmless."

The raptor pointed at Kipper with its own feathered talon while signing with the octopus tentacles: "*You* in charge?"

"Yes," Kipper affirmed while Captain Cod grumbled about insufferably independent cats in the background.

The raptor shifted its weight from one strong feathered leg to the other, drawing attention to the sharp hooked claw on its largest toe. That hooked claw was distressingly close to Kipper as she lay under the crushingly high gravity, still mostly immobilized, on the floor.

The octopus tentacles rising out of the raptor's shoulders began signing again: "Why little fuzzies attack raptors?"

This was it. This was the moment of truth. Kipper couldn't help but notice that suddenly her chorus of otter hecklers had grown eerily silent. They had no offers of help for her now.

Kipper signed, moving her small striped paws very carefully, "Protect home." She waited a few moments, and then she turned the question back at the raptor: "Why raptors attack little fuzzies?"

The raptor's fore-talons lifted and stretched out, almost as if the raptor wanted to sign with its own hands instead of the enslaved octopus' tentacles. Then the tentacles twisted into the signs to say, "Not know little fuzzies. Only mean attack octopuses. Raptors go home now."

Kipper was floored. Well, she was already lying on the floor, but now she was floored both literally and figuratively. She couldn't believe it was over. Somehow, they'd saved the Earth from the raptors.

"What about us?" Captain Cod called out, knowing the raptors couldn't understand him but that Kipper would know she should translate.

"What about us?" Kipper signed and then gestured around at the crew of the *Jolly Barracuda* ingloriously sprawled on the cell floor with their limbs electronically paralyzed.

"If give ship back, will leave raptors alone?"

"Yes," Kipper signed.

"Then give ship back." The purple-crested raptor pointed at Emily, jumbled in the smaller raptor's arms. "Want octopuses? Found seven on ship. Three still alive. Want them? Or kill them?"

"Want them!" Kipper signed in a rush, three times fast, to be sure.

"Valuable?" The foremost raptor looked at Emily as if appraising her. Then his feathered wing-like arms flopped in a gesture very nearly like a shrug. "Want replace dead ones? Have extras here."

Kipper faltered over how to answer that—she'd be rescuing them, right? Or would she be ripping them from their families? The lives they knew?

"Want?" the raptor repeated.

"Yes," Kipper signed, taking a risk.

After a round of screeching and cawing, the orange-crested raptor went around releasing the otters from their electronic cuffs, and the yellow-crested raptor left the room, presumably to turn off the high gravity, since the newly freed otters were once again able to float off of the floor. Kipper suddenly found her stomach churning much less; apparently, some of her distress had come from the jail cell spinning to pin them down with artificial gravity, not merely from the gravity of the situation.

The small blue-crested raptor approached Kipper and held Emily out to her, a slippery mass of ropy sucker disc-covered arms. Most of Emily tumbled eagerly into Kipper's furry embrace, but

214

one of her tentacles stayed stretched out, all the way to its limit, twisting its wire-thin tip around the blue-crested raptor's talon. The small raptor and the octopus looked at each other, separated now by a gulf of species and cultures but still joined by the bond they'd formed through the silver tentacle.

The silver tentacle itself curled around Kipper's neck and shoulders, looping around and around, embracing the little cat with all the tenderness an octopus could ever feel for a cat.

Finally, Emily let go of the raptor, and the rag-tag crew of the *Jolly Barracuda*, all the little fuzzies, were escorted through the zero-gee hallways of the raptor ship to where the *Jolly Barracuda*—a much smaller vessel—had been taken onboard.

The Barracuders' debarkation was a strangely ceremonial event, markedly different from the sloppy heist they'd pulled in getting onboard the raptor vessel. Two rows of raptors stood, creating a narrow passage that the otters and Kipper had to float through to get to the airlock of the *Jolly Barracuda*. At the entrance, they were handed three unconscious octopi like some sort of diplomatic offering, and suddenly all the raptors dipped their heads. Kipper wasn't sure what the gesture meant from them, but it felt like they were bowing to her, and she wondered if she should bow back. She tried, but between the zero-gravity and the octopus wrapped around her neck like a very afraid and affectionate scarf, Kipper wasn't sure that her attempted bow would be noticeable even if the raptors were familiar with the custom.

Once the *Jolly Barracuda's* airlock closed behind them, Kipper felt like she ought to whoop and hurrah that they'd won and escaped with their lives. Or at least turn to her fellow otters and start picking apart every detail of what they'd seen on the raptor vessel and everything that had happened to them.

The otters certainly whooped and hurrahed, but Kipper didn't join them.

Instead, she stared numbly at her paws while oxo-agua flooded the airlock chamber. She'd never acquiesced to breathing the damnable liquid so easily before. But after losing everything and then getting it all back—totally unexpectedly—Kipper didn't have the energy left in her to care about minutiae like what kind of substance filled her lungs.

All Kipper cared about was swimming through the familiar halls of Captain Cod's ship to Emily's kitchen where she crammed herself into one of the cupboards to hide. She wasn't sure what she was hiding from anymore. The raptors were back there—still on their own vessel and soon to fly away, back towards Jupiter. But Kipper needed to hide anyway, and Emily seemed to understand. Emily seeped into the cracks around Kipper where she didn't fit the rectangular shape of the cupboard and filled it up with her squishy, amorphous body.

The two of them stayed there, octopus and cat, hiding from nothing and everything, safely alone together for many, many heartbeats. When Trugger finally came looking for them, he signed through the cracked open cupboard door, "I thought I'd find Emily here. I didn't expect Kipper as well." He pulled the cupboard door open wider.

"Remember when I first met you?" Kipper signed with cramped paws inside the cupboad. "You had purple spikes tattooed in your fur."

Trugger looked down at his plain brown body. His red tiger stripes had completely grown out. "Hasn't been much time for stuff like that lately, has there?"

"I liked the blue swirls, when you did those," Kipper signed. "They made you look like an ocean."

"How should I have it dyed next? When we get back to *Deep Sky Anchor*... You can pick."

"Have you ever done polka dots?" Kipper signed.

Trugger grinned. "I look good in polka dots." He held out his short brown-furred arms and stared intently at them, as if picturing the polka dots that had apparently been there at least once before. "Purple again?" he asked.

"How about green?" Kipper signed.

"Your call," Trugger signed back. "Now, is it time to get out of the cupboard?"

"Tabby stripes," Emily signed. "Make him get tabby stripes to match you."

"But green ones."

"Yeah." It was a simple sign, needing only one tentacle, but the tentacle Emily used was her new silver one from the oligarch.

All three of them—cat, river otter, and cyborg octopus—stared at the tentacle for a long time after it spoke. Finally, Kipper asked, "Does this make you the new oligarch?"

Emily signed again, this time with a different, wholly organic tentacle, "Yeah. There are eight oligarchs. I'm one of them."

"Do I still have to go back to Choir's Deep and face trial?"

"No," Emily signed. "I pardon you."

Kipper almost asked, "You can do that?", but decided it was better not to press the point and settled for, "Thanks." Then she asked Trugger, "How are the octopi that the raptors... gave us."

"Clearly drugged," Trugger signed. "Very groggy. They were signing something about going to Earth, though. It didn't quite make sense, but it's the right direction. They're with the two remaining octopi from Choir's Deep now."

Kipper was glad that they weren't obviously distressed about being taken from the raptors. She still wasn't sure if she'd made the right choice in accepting them. "What do we do now?" Kipper asked.

"Besides get out of the cupboard?" Trugger offered one of his paws to the tangle of Kipper and Emily, like he thought they were stuck and wanted to help pull them out. When neither cat nor octopus took it, he signed, "The war's over. Things go back to normal."

Kipper was a cat who'd spent most of the last year breathing a liquid, and Emily was an octopus with memories that spanned more than centuries. Neither of them could picture normal. They couldn't go back to normal. Each of them needed to invent something new.

"I don't think that's an option," Kipper signed, but before she could sign anything else, Emily stirred all around her. Her tentacles flexed and pulled and she floated out of the cupboard.

Emily's soft skin stretched, the webbing between the broad bases of her tentacles expanding almost like an umbrella opening. She became very large, and her skin flushed pink, all of it except the new silver tentacle. "I'm an oligarch," Emily signed. Her silver tentacle flashed, and she looked regal. "I have to go back to my people."

"Day-blind owls!" Trugger swore. "We'll have to get a new chef. Don't go!"

The skin around Emily's eyes crinkled with fondness. An octopus smile. But when she turned her yellow-eyed gaze to Kipper, there was no tractability in it. She was leaving the *Jolly Barracuda*.

And Kipper realized that she needed to do that too. She couldn't be a cat underwater anymore. She needed to breathe again.

She just wasn't sure where she would go.

Chapter 33: Jenny

"Are you sure?" Jenny signed to Felix and Ordol.

The otter physicist and octopus translator were at one of the workstations inside the flooded Europa base, and cryptic iconography scrolled hectically over the ancient-yet-insanely-advanced computer screen in front of them. The octopus and otter shared a look—enigmatic on both ends due to Ordol's lack of a mammalian face and the breathing apparatus obscuring Felix's nose and mouth—and then Felix shrugged. "Pretty sure," he signed.

"With technology like that..." Jenny's paws drifted to a halt. She'd been managing the complicated feelings and jurisdictions of navy otters, corporate dogs, and cat royalty for months, keeping them off of Felix and Ordol's backs, promising that her team would find a way to stop the raptor fleet... And they had totally failed.

Instead, her scientists brought her a treasure trove of ancient octopus technology. She could hardly believe the technologies they claimed to have discovered blueprints for—faster-than-light engines and instantaneous communication relays—none of which would make a whit of difference in stopping the raptor fleet.

Jenny wanted to scream at them, but in the Europa water that filled the base, the best she could do was sign angrily. And that wouldn't do. So she turned her rudder-tail on them and swam away.

Jenny swam up through the giant chamber, following the poles that laced through the watery space. She wondered whether a faster-than-light spaceship could be used to... well... No, even if blueprints were the same thing as an operational prototype, a prototype could dance around the raptor fleet, hopping ahead of it and behind it. It could take you... anywhere. But it wouldn't stop them.

And instant long-distance communication...

Well, it would have let Jenny know that the raptor fleet had already turned around. But she didn't know that yet, and instantaneous communication felt like the most useless technology imaginable. It would, what? Let the otters orbiting Jupiter talk faster to their friends and family back on Earth while they were bombarded from the sky with lasers or torpedoes or whatever weapons the raptors preferred.

No help. No help at all.

Jenny swam into the narrow tube-like corridor that led to the elevator pad and rode the wide elevator up to the surface of the Europa base. When the elevator pad emerged from the column of water, she ripped the breathing apparatus off of her muzzle and stomped, dripping, toward Admiral Mackerel's tent. It was time to report yet another failure to him. Yet another failure he could report back to the International Star-Ocean Navy command offices on Kelp Frond station. But, hey, if he included the blueprints for that instantaneous communications relay, then the next time he relayed a failure back to the ISON offices, it could be FASTER.

Unusual movement in the sky caught Jenny's eye, and she looked up at the atmo-bubble that gently distorted Jupiter's golden face. Stars streaked across the far horizon like a meteor shower—dozens and dozens of brightly burning stars. *Raptor vessels.* An entire fleet of raptor vessels must be orbiting Europa.

Jenny's heart went cold.

The flap on Admiral Mackerel's tent whipped back, and one of the navy otters looked out. "Base Commander Jenny!" the officer cried. "Get in here!"

Inside the admiral's tent, a whole slew of navy otters and several of her own officers were crowded around a small console with a vid-screen showing a broadcast of a fluffy sea otter news anchor.

"That's right, folks," the news anchor said into her mic. "The raptor fleet has changed course. Calculations show that their new course will take them back to Jupiter where they came from and not to Earth." The sea otter's chirpy voice effervesced with relief and excitement. The video cut to a telescope view of the pine-cone-shaped raptor vessels, looking exactly the same as they had before.

Until one of them blew up in a fiery flash, like the ship was a grenade and someone had pulled out the pin. Shrapnel flew through space. Then another explosion. And another.

"What the hell?" one of the navy otters in Admiral Mackerel's tent cried, and the sentiment was soon echoed by all the other otters crowded into the tent, and then by the previously happy news anchor on the screen.

"I... I don't know what this development means..." the news otter stammered.

Jenny broke through the noise in the tent to say, "We have a more pressing concern than raptor ships halfway to Earth." She held back the tent flap and pointed at the star-streaked horizon. "We have raptor ships right here."

Until now, the ancient octopus base's shield had protected Europa from any raptor vessels, but Jenny had never seen a fleet like this one. If they were coming in force like that, they must have a plan.

"We're receiving a signal," one of the navy otters said from a second console crammed into the crowded tent.

"Patch it through to this screen," Admiral Mackerel responded, and moments later, an octopus face appeared on the screen where the news otter had been.

The octopus was ash gray and splotchy. Its tentacles signed, over and over again, "*Seek asylum. Please help. Lower shield.*"

The navy otter said, "There's a text file accompanying the video feed." She was looking at it on the smaller computer screen on the

221

second console. "It seems to be a roster of ships and certificate of assurance that they're all octopus controlled now."

"Let me see," Jenny said, pushing her way through the other otters until she could lean over the secondary console. It was a long list of ships. No wonder there were so many new stars. "Can you send a message back to them?"

"Sure," the navy otter said. "There's a vid-feed in this console. Ready?"

"Ready," Jenny said. Then she stared straight at the console and signed as clearly as she could, "More information, please. Are there raptors with you? What is the state of your homeworld? Should we expect more ships to follow you?" She had so many questions, and she wasn't sure that she was asking the right ones. So, she added one more simple one: "What happened?" She dropped her paws and said to the navy otter, "Send it on repeat."

The navy otter sent the file, and after a few moments said, "There's a response already."

Once again, the splotchy ash gray octopus appeared on the larger vidscreen. The octopus's color brightened a little, more pink around the sucker disks, and it started signing, "*Revolution. Long time plan. Escape. Many octopus wanting... go to Earth. First stop Europa. Please help. Raptors confused. Military decimated. Will take time to recover. We use time to regroup. Finish escape. Maybe rescue more.*" The octopus's color rose, growing pinker and stronger as it signed. Finally, its tentacles trailed off, and it ended with, "*Please help,*" before the video began to repeat.

"Can we trust them?" the navy otter working the secondary console asked.

"They're refugees of a civil war," Jenny said. She worked her way back through the crowded tent until she could look through the tent flap at the sky again. Shooting stars continued to streak across the horizon. So many of them. So many escaped octopi. Slaves who had freed themselves. "This isn't about trust. It's about compassion. Compare the roster we received to the vessels we can detect with our own sensors. If they match up..." Jenny could feel her role as Base Commander coming to an end. By all rights, this base belonged to those octopi. Their ancestors had built it. "...drop the shield and let them in. This is their base after all."

The navy otter cut off the video of the ash gray octopus refugee, and the sea otter news anchor returned to the screen. "...*half of the vessels have exploded. We have no idea what this means. Stay tuned for more information as it comes in.*"

"Hell's pelicans," Destry said. "It's a coordinated effort. That raptor fleet was never going to make it to Earth after all."

"I hope some of them do," Jenny said, thinking of the octopi that must be rebelling on them. She took the admiral by his uniformed arm and pulled him out of the tent. Once outside, she said, "Our role here is about to change drastically."

Admiral Mackerel frowned and nodded in agreement. "We should prepare to withdraw our forces. The octopi may need a while to sort themselves out, and unless we're wanted, we'll just be in the way."

"But we can aid in the transition of giving the base back to them," Jenny said. "I'm going to check in with those Howard Industries dogs and the Persian empress. If they want to look up everything they can about octopus anatomy, maybe they can set up a temporary medical station, in case there are injured octopi. Otherwise, they need to get out of here."

"Good idea," Admiral Mackerel said.

"As for you," Jenny said, "my team in the base has found some information..." She hesitated, remembering her frustration with the blueprints Ordol and Felix had found only a few minutes ago. Now she realized that the technology they'd found would be life changing. They were lucky to have found it before handing the base back over to its rightful owners. Jenny made the biggest understatement of her life: "...some information that may be useful. I need your officers to see if they can build something, and we need to send the blueprints back to Earth too."

Then after that, Jenny could go tell Ordol that his people were coming.

Chapter 34: Kipper

Alistair's orange striped tabby face appeared on the *Jolly Barracuda* main viewscreen. The entire crew had gathered on the bridge to watch his message. Alistair was wearing a navy blue suit that contrasted his fiery fur nicely, and two secret service greyhounds wearing sunglasses and wires stood coolly behind him. He looked very presidential, but to Kipper, he just looked like her brother.

"Congratulations and our sincerest thanks from all of us here on Earth to the brave officers on the *Jolly Barracuda*!" Alistair's mouth moved, and Kipper wished she could hear his voice, but she had to settle for reading the captions beneath him.

The *Jolly Barracuda* was still filled with its oxo-agua atmosphere so it could fly back to Earth at full speed, escorting half of the remaining fleet of raptor vessels, now controlled and filled solely by octopi. The other half of the fleet that had survived the octopus uprising was on its way back to Jupiter, filled with the surviving raptors. They were not wanted on Earth, and by the sounds of it, they were sorely needed on their own homeworld. While octopus slaves had primarily been used in the raptor military, their mass exodus had left an entire strata of raptor society completely in shambles. The war had been swift and final. From what the octopi who'd been gifted to the *Jolly Barracuda* had explained, their uprising had been a long time in the making. All the octopi had wanted was to leave. Emily would be very busy, now that she was an oligarch, integrating all of the Jovian octopus refugees into Earth octopus society.

Perhaps, when the raptors finished clearing up the wreckage of their military and coming to terms with the mass escape of the octopi they'd enslaved for so long, they would find a way to reach out to Earth peacefully. Kipper didn't plan to hold her breath waiting for it.

"Obviously, we are deeply grateful to all the otters and octopi who risked—or lost—their lives in this operation," Alistair continued. "But today, I'm reaching out to you with a message for your one feline officer."

The movement was too fast for Kipper to be sure, but it looked like Alistair winked at her.

"The Uplifted States of Mericka has recently approved a modest budget for beginning our own space program, and I can think of no one more qualified to lead the project than your own Kipper Brighton."

Otter faces turned to Kipper, wide with grins, and otters all over the bridge swam in tight corkscrews, looping about with excitement.

"Congratulations, Kipper!" Captain Cod signed. "Of course, we'll be sorry to lose you..."

There was only one sad face on the bridge. At least, Kipper was pretty sure that Trugger's face looked sad. It was hard to be sure, since he'd turned away and wouldn't look at her. He knew her too well to think she'd turn down this opportunity.

"Of course," Captain Cod added, "this doesn't have to mean that you stop being a *Jolly Barracuda* officer. I mean, if the Earth cats and dogs are putting together a space program... Well, it couldn't hurt to have a spy involved, keeping me updated on it."

Kipper held up her paws, signaling for Captain Cod to stop. "I'm sorry," she signed. "I can't be Ship's Spy and also the leader of my country's space program. I'm not a double agent. Though..." She looked over at Trugger. "I could probably use an otter consultant, and once I'm no longer a member of the *Jolly Barracuda* crew, I wouldn't necessarily know who you handed my title off to..."

Captain Cod beamed and swam over to Trugger. "How about it, Trugger?" he signed. "I think our little tabby's offering you a job as consultant in her new space program."

Trugger started to object, signing something about how the *Jolly Barracuda* was the greatest vessel ever built and Captain Cod the greatest captain. But Captain Cod looked over his shoulder at Kipper and then conspiratorially turned his back so that she could no longer see his signing paws. The two otters signed furiously at each other for a few minutes while Kipper politely looked away, pretending not to know that Trugger was being handed the baton of her old job.

Finally, Trugger came swimming to her, gave her a big hug, and signed, "I gladly accept your offer. Let's go make a space program!"

"Now," Captain Cod signed. "If you'd like to call your brother back, we can try out this new doohickey that Jenny and Felix had us build."

"I'd like that," Kipper signed. It was going to be weird communicating with Earth without a time delay, but it would let her get started on making plans. The future was full of new possibilities for a tabby cat with a space program to run.

About the Author

Mary E. Lowd lives in Oregon with her husband, daughter, son, a variety of cats and dogs, the occasional fish, and zero otters. She spends the majority of her time pretending animals can talk and writing stories about them.

Mary started her first novel at the age of eleven; it bore a striking resemblance to Brian Jacques' Redwall, replete with little woodland animals eating feasts and battling each other with swords. Her next abandoned novel had more in common with The Pride of Chanur by C.J. Cherryh, featuring first contact with a race of space-faring feline aliens. Her first finished novel was Otters In Space. The Otters In Space series (and its spin-off In a Dog's World) are the inevitable culmination of a childhood spent watching Star Trek: The Next Generation and Lady and the Tramp.

In addition to her novels, more than eighty of Mary's short stories have been published. Her short fiction has won an Ursa Major Award and two Cóyotl Awards.

Learn more at www.marylowd.com.

About the Publisher

FurPlanet Productions is a small press publisher serving the niche market that is furry fiction. We sell furry-themed books and comics published by us and most major publishers in the community. If you can't get to a furry convention where we are selling in the dealers room, visit www.FurPlanet.com to shop online.

CPSIA information can be obtained
at www.ICGtesting.com
Printed in the USA
FFOW03n2015310518
46941801-49196FF